Praise for *The Glenwood Treasure:*

"*The Glenwood Treasure* has suggestions of the late Timothy Findley and more than a hint of the old Nancy Drew mysteries. But, given the strength of this book, it seems more fitting to drop the comparisons and allow Moritsugu her own place on the literary landscape."
~ *The Globe and Mail*

"Kim Moritsugu is a witty social observer and the book deftly blends a comedy of manners into the mystery."
~ *Toronto Star*

"A cozy read ... Moritsugu is a good writer with an appealing central character that will awaken the inner girl in all of us."
~ *National Post*

Praise for *Old Flames:*

"Delightful ... it sings ... the first person narrative creates an intimacy between the reader and the characters, who lift off the page and become old friends."
~ *The Globe and Mail*

"Like her protagonists, Moritsugu's writing style is neighbourly and clever ... a breezy enjoyable read ... a poignant reflection of the choices we make."
~ *Montreal Gazette*

THE RESTORATION OF
Emily

- a novel -

Kim Moritsugu

SIMON & PIERRE FICTION
A MEMBER OF THE DUNDURN GROUP
TORONTO

Editor: Barry Jowett
Copy-editor: Jennifer Gallant
Design: Jennifer Scott
Printer: Webcom

Library and Archives Canada Cataloguing in Publication

Moritsugu, Kim, 1954–
    The restoration of Emily / Kim Moritsugu.

ISBN 10: 1-55002-606-2
ISBN 13: 978-1-55002-606-1

    I. Title.

PS8576.O72R48 2006   C813'.54   C2006-900528-1

1   2   3   4   5   10   09   08   07   06

We acknowledge the support of the **Canada Council for the Arts** and the **Ontario Arts Council** for our publishing program. We also acknowledge the financial support of the **Government of Canada** through the **Book Publishing Industry Development Program** and **The Association for the Export of Canadian Books**, and the **Government of Ontario** through the **Ontario Book Publishers Tax Credit program**, and the **Ontario Media Development Corporation**.

Printed and bound in Canada.
Printed on recycled paper.

www.dundurn.com

Dundurn Press
3 Church Street, Suite 500
Toronto, Ontario, Canada
M5E 1M2

Gazelle Book Services Limited
White Cross Mills
High Town, Lancaster, England
LA1 4XS

Dundurn Press
2250 Military Road
Tonawanda, NY
U.S.A. 14150

"If you can't say anything good about someone, sit here right by me."

— *Alice Roosevelt Longworth,*
1884–1980

~ CHAPTER ONE ~

My first fun appointment of the fun-filled day ahead is at 9:30 a.m., to see a specialist about some sharp pains I've had for months in my right arm. When my GP diagnosed the problem as an ordinary affliction with the prosaic name "frozen shoulder," I was tempted to go on ignoring the jabs of hurt, avoid using the arm for anything strenuous, and wait for time's healing power (and/or my body's ever more glacially paced self-healing capabilities) to make the problem go away. But the pain has become worse instead of better, has begun to wake me at night, and is making me crankier than my normal, pain-free, non-sleep-deprived cranky self. Hence the visit to the rheumatologist, about whose curative abilities I am skeptical, since, in my experience, competence is rare.

My suspicions are not allayed when the doctor turns out to be markedly younger than I am. In her late thirties, I'd guess, from the bags under her eyes, the faded bloom of youth on her skin. She addresses me by my first name, Emily (better that than the sort of formality I've disliked since childhood), introduces herself as Joan rather than as Dr. Anything, and takes my history.

She expresses no surprise upon hearing my birth year, does not exclaim that I look younger than my age, a line I have become accustomed to and, I'm afraid, quite fond of, from my regular doctor, a wrinkled woman in her sixties who I fear is losing her memory and mind, because I am, have been since I turned forty. Though how funny is it (not) that I never think my GP feeble when she declares my blood pressure that of a young woman or tells me I'm lucky I inherited the skin gene from my father's side and not my mother's, because fair complexions go old so fast, look at hers.

Dr. Joan asks my occupation, and when I tell her, says, "An architect? Have you designed anything famous?"

I have an urge to lay claim to a set of Mies van der Rohe skyscrapers downtown, or to a Frank Lloyd Wright house in Michigan, or to the Red House in Kent. My anti-authoritarian impulse — because she didn't say I looked young? Sheesh — is to jolt her, to disturb her calm the way the occasional obstreperous client does mine. But I hold back, and when her polite smile seems to invite more detail, I say, "I restore old houses."

She shares that she lives in a loft-style condo in the meat packing district, an area filled with arty boutiques and funky restaurants built within smelling range of abattoirs. She has no affinity for old houses, in other words. Good. We are both relieved to return to the matter at hand. At arm. She says, "You've had pain in your shoulder how long?"

"Six months."

"Show me where."

I point to the outside of my bicep.

She frowns. "Have you taken any anti-inflammatory drugs? What about physiotherapy?"

I tell her that the drugs didn't work and that I did physio for three months but saw little improvement. Which is why I'm here. That and because my fourteen-year-old son, Jesse, has started to do a maddening but accurate imitation of me clutching my arm and wincing whenever I ask him to help me execute a routine action I can no longer accomplish painlessly, like opening a door or reaching a bowl down from a shelf.

In the examining room, I don a tasteful but still humiliating blue striped hospital gown so that Dr. Joan can run a knitting needle up the sole of my foot (my foot curls like a snail), and tap me hard on each knee with a hammer. My legs jerk out in turn and I suppress curses at this treatment, at the indignity of my body's involuntary responses. "Reflexes seem fine," she says, and holds her hands up in front of her, palms facing me. "Push on my hands with yours. Now pull. Hard."

She barks out more instructions to move my arms up, down, to the side, this way, that way, behind my head, behind my back. She speaks fast, moves fast, shows impatience if I don't understand or fail to obey immediately. I wonder if she treats all her patients so brusquely, and if the elderly man with the cane whom I saw in the waiting room will be subjected to this attitude. Why is she like this? What has annoyed her? Isn't she too young to be burned out by the frustrations of treating recalcitrant patients? Hell, at her age, I still worked in a big architectural firm and dealt with office politics on top of a slate of difficult clients. I also developed a twitch in my eye and sleeping problems. Maybe she isn't too young to be fed up.

When she sees how little mobility I have in my right arm, she says, "That's a frozen shoulder, all right. Common in perimenopausal women. Are you doing stretching exercises for this at home?"

I have been stretching, though not as often as I should. When I admit this, Dr. Joan says, "You must do the exercises. I'll give you a cortisone shot today, but you're not going to get better unless you aggressively exercise that arm. Do that and your shoulder might be fully functional in a year. Don't, and you won't be able to unhook your bra with your right hand for two years. Got it?"

What I've got is a need to tell her to fuck off and drop the condescending tone. But I say, "I'll sure try!" in the tone of a character from a Mickey Rooney–Judy Garland musical. Sure that Dr. Joan won't recognize the reference or the sarcasm.

She prepares the needle, inserts the syringe into the vial of cortisone. "This may increase the pain over the next few days, but an over-the-counter pain reliever will help you manage as needed."

If my life were a movie, Dr. Joan would prescribe me prescription painkillers that I would become addicted to over the next year until I screwed up the drawings for a project and caused the accidental death of a labourer on a contractor's renovation crew. I would then be led off to rehab, if not also to jail for criminal negligence. With my career and life in ruins, my custody of Jesse would be handed over to my ex-husband, Henry, who would make him come live in New York, where Jesse would get lost in the big-city shuffle and not realize his promise as, as, well, as whatever it is he will become. All signs currently point to unemployed disc jockey, but if he lived with Henry, he wouldn't even become that.

Dr. Joan swabs my shoulder, I look away, she pricks me with the needle. I grimace, not at the sting of the needle's penetration, but at the drag when she pushes down on the syringe, when the tip stays under my skin and too slowly deposits its load. I want to bat the needle away, pull it out, make it leave. I want to expel it like I used to — in the dim past, when I was still having sex — want to expel a penis that had ejaculated inside me and lay there afterwards, heavy and still and unwanted. Or like a tampon. Out, out, damned anything and everything.

~ ★ ~

When I arrive home after the cortisone shot, my across-the-street neighbour, Vera, is in her front garden in full gardening garb, rubber clogs, wide-brimmed hat, and all, kneeling on a garden mat. Like all the lots in our downtown neighbourhood, on our narrow street, hers is on the small side, but over the five decades she has lived here, she has transformed the fenced-in plot into a lovely English garden, a profusion of colourful flowers.

Since Vera's husband died five years ago, she's forged on alone, filled her days gardening, walking, doing volunteer work at a hospital, and hosting family get-togethers on holidays for her far-flung adult children and her grandchildren. I admire her bravery and pluck, and she's a good neighbour, so when she halloos me, I go over to make social pleasantries of the sort I generally try to avoid.

A minute into our chat, she says, "Remember that real estate agent I told you about a while back, the one who was pestering me about listing my house? He came around to see me again today. His clients have their hearts set on moving into the area, and he wanted to know if I'd thought any further about selling."

"Have you?" I don't want Vera to move away — I like having a pillar of the block nearby, a reliable source of neighbourhood memory, someone who can recall the year that the hundred-year-old elm tree that once graced my property fell down and crushed two cars parked on the street, someone who refers to the twenty-year-old maple planted in its place as a sapling.

"I hadn't, not seriously," she says, "not until he showed up today with a bouquet of flowers."

I gesture to her garden. "That was a bit of coal to Newcastle, wasn't it?" One of my mother's old expressions, that one, that I wouldn't use with anyone but Vera.

"I suppose so, but he meant well. And he brought me spring flowers — tulips, which made me think about how long and cold the winter will be."

"The winter *will* be long and cold, but moving away — and where, to a condo? — would be such a radical step. You'd have no garden then. And I'd have no nice neighbour to call when the power is out or I've lost my keys."

"I'd miss you too, dear," she says, a little perfunctorily. "But every so often, radical steps need to be taken in life, don't you find? Why, twenty years ago, when I started menopause, I was hit so hard with the hot flashes and the insomnia and the night sweats and the mood swings that I had to develop a whole new daily routine to cope. I had to change everything!" She eyes my sallow skin and slouched posture. "You must be about menopausal age now. Has yours started yet?"

I stand up straight. "Not yet." Except, possibly, for the mood swings.

"Well, good luck with it when it comes. Menopause will make moving house look like a piece of cake."

Yeah, I can't wait.

I go inside my house and spend an hour at my office desk doing paperwork. I would like to stay put and eat my usual salad for lunch, have my usual nap, but at twelve-thirty I force myself to put on my architect attire (dressy daytime version) and drive off to a luncheon at the home of a client named Suzanne.

The full-scale restoration of Suzanne's Queen Anne Revival house in midtown was completed a few weeks ago, Suzanne is still speaking to me, and she has invited me and her socialite/charity volunteer friends over to lunch to celebrate. My lack of keenness to attend is due to my nap longings, my disinclination to small talk, and because Suzanne is a young (early thirties), sophisticated, wealthy, and unfailingly nice woman who has so far proven herself incapable of an honest or discouraging word. Throughout our working relationship, from her mouth came a string of platitudes and graciously worded comments that were awe-inspiring in their consistency and in their apparent — because who can talk like that all the time and mean it? — falsity. Our professional time together was smooth and stress-free, but I don't trust her sincerity for a second. I'm waiting for the real Suzanne to emerge, when she decides that the ground floor flow is off, or the stair riser height too high.

I'll endure this lunch in order to maintain good customer relations in the hope of future referrals. Also because the other guests are potential clients, the food will be precious and tasty, and my interior designer friend and collaborator Danny will be there, to deflect attention from me and rightfully take praise for the way the house now looks — classy, elegant, and accessible. Like Suzanne, except for the accessible part. She moves in the rather restricted circles in which she met her husband, a junior scion of a wealthy family whose surname is known even to allergic-to-society me. A surname Suzanne has, of course, taken as her own.

I ring the bell and am admitted by Suzanne's eldest child, a tow-headed girl of about age five, name of Tory, dressed in a balletic getup, complete with dollar-store tiara on her head. Tory is louder in voice and plumper of body than I imagine stick-thin, perfect-complexioned, artfully highlighted blonde Suzanne would like her to be, though I am impugning Suzanne to say so. She has never given me any indication of dissatisfaction with Tory's look and attitude, has always spoken to her and of her in loving and affectionate tones. Maybe she'll slip up today.

Within my immediate view on entry is an arty and lavish flower arrangement — sent on in advance, I'm sure, by Danny, who knows how and when to spend money to prevent a client from falling prey to a nasty bout of cognitive dissonance over the size of the decorating bill. The flowers are displayed on a massive round mahogany table positioned in the expanded, light-filled (courtesy of new window wells cut into the exterior brick wall) centre hall, created by eliminating an old closet and a powder room. Never mind that the table, sourced by Danny from England for thousands of dollars, is of a style and period that predates the house by about a hundred years. Or that a warren-like collection of cupboards and closets around the front door was the standard in houses of the time. My clients tend to go for a beautifully restored exterior (with new windows) and an interior designed for modern practicality, with maybe one room decked out in wide plank wood flooring and refreshed wainscotting out of respect to the house's origins. Authentic my restorations are not. If they were, I'd have no clients.

Suzanne floats into the hall, says to Tory, "Thank you for answering the door, sweetie-pie. Did you say hello to Mrs. Harada and offer to take her coat?" Before Tory can answer or I can object to being called Mrs., Suzanne's face lights up with joy — there is no other word to describe how happy she looks — at the sight of my tired face and hunched right shoulder, the side of which I am gripping with my left hand in the belief that touching the sore spot will make it better.

"I'm so glad you came," she says, all sweet breath and breathily sweet, and I am struck anew by how pretty she is, how small her head, how shiny her hair, how slim her shoulders, how perfect her clothes: a silk sweater in the season's "it" colour, a necklace made of small, shiny precious stones, and black pants cut short to reveal tanned slim ankles and small feet clad in fashionable shoes.

My arm stops aching for a second, and I understand why the junior scion married her — because I want to, too.

I hand her the hostess gift I've brought — a jar of *fleur de sel* — and as she thanks me prettily, the doorbell rings again. Suzanne excuses herself to open it and greets the next arrival, a woman styled like her, only with long chestnut-coloured hair instead of blonde. Suzanne's face lights up, the picture of pleasure once more, she says, "I'm so glad you came," in the same joyful way she said the same words to me, and the spell is broken. How could I have forgotten? She is a robot, programmed to be pleasing.

I move toward the kitchen, from where I can hear Danny giving a guided tour, speaking in full voice about the marble this, the cherry that. On the way, I nod at little Tory, who lurks in a corner of the hall, tiara askew. She sticks out her tongue at me — atta girl — I return the gesture, and I head for Danny, a roomful of fake smiles, and two hours of bullshit.

When I was in my mid-thirties, and suffused with the arrogance of youth, I thought women aged fifty were anachronisms from another era. At a time when I was not fabulous, but still believed I could be, my opinion of women that age was that they talked too slowly, told too-long stories, and were too hung up on social conventions like table manners, the wearing of slips, and thank-you notes.

If you'd asked me then to describe a fifty-year-old woman, I would have started with a no-nonsense, short hairstyle, in an undyed shade of gray, the end result of a roller set. Someone that age would wear a blouse and slacks and pumps and pantyhose and use those antiquated words to describe her clothes. She would not ever have smoked pot (and she would call it marijuana) and not know Jim Morrison from Jimi Hendrix, but she would know how to dance, could be counted upon at a wedding to take to the floor and jive away — looking graceful, if dated — with the husband for whom she cooked, cleaned, and ironed.

That was the image I had, but now I'm the anachronism, because somehow, over the course of Jesse's fourteen and three-quarters years of life, the woman I've described has become seventy, and the woman of fifty, surprise, surprise, is me. I'm too tired to dance, good at avoiding housework, and I'm working what I'll call a classic — and someone else might term staid — fashion look rather than paying heed to any current ludicrous trend. This fifty-year-old dyes her hair and wears it long and sometimes wishes she knew where to score a joint — a safe, not-too-strong one. (I'd like a hit of relaxation, not hallucination.) I swear like a longshoreman (and I know what a longshoreman is), I brought up my child the way I wanted, and I'm unmarried, since taking care of a man was never part of my deal.

My foremothers — or, I should say, older sisters — didn't fight the feminist fight so that I could do a man's laundry or heat and serve him dinner when he comes home late from work and tries to delegate evening child care to me, my full-time job notwithstanding. No. What I am, at fifty, is the single mother of a dear and sometimes difficult teenage boy; I'm an independent, self-sufficient, strong woman who answers to no one, who race-walks to her own rhythm track.

That's except for the times when I miss my turnoff because I've put my driving brain on autopilot and forgotten where I'm going. Or when I leave a pot on the stove to boil and forget about it and burn blackened broccoli marks onto the pot's surface and worry that next time I might burn down the house. I am woman, hear me roar, except when I fuck up.

We are eight for lunch chez Suzanne, eight seated around a large dining table dressed in linen, china, crystal, and platters of designer salads that are passed around so that we can help ourselves using Suzanne's antique sterling silver serving utensils.

I'm holding a platter of wild rice salad, made with apricots, roasted almonds, and mint, when the woman on my left says, "So Suzanne tells me your father is a famous artist."

"Was. He's dead. And he wasn't that famous. His fifteen minutes happened in the sixties. Were you even alive then?"

She laughs because I'm so funny. Or bizarre. "I love Japanese art," she says. "And Japanese ceramics. I collect Japanese dishes. They're so delicate and beautiful."

I fork some food into my mouth so that I won't say anything too raw to her, like that I have no time for people who think their fascination with Asian culture is in any way relevant to me. Go be all Zen/samurai/tea ceremony somewhere I'm not, honey. When I'm done chewing, I say, "My father's parents were Japanese, but he was Canadian — born and raised in Vancouver. His art is considered Canadian." And the massive, organically shaped sculptures he's known for aren't delicate at all.

She says, "Is it true that Japanese children are taught at a young age how to handle dishes carefully?"

Is it true that she's obtuse? "I wouldn't know," I say, and either the edge that has crept into my voice or her inability to reconcile my responses to her boxed-in ideas shuts her up.

Silence may reign in my vicinity, but Danny holds up his end of the table conversation with aplomb — he exclaims over every little thing and makes entertaining insider foodie talk about a funky downtown restaurant that serves Maritime-style lobster rolls, but only on Tuesdays, and off the menu. At one point, he even moderates a panel discussion about china patterns.

When the topic of private schools comes up — all the women either have kids in private school or expect to enroll them in the near future — I tune out and try to estimate what time I'll make it home, if I can still fit in my afternoon nap, if a good dessert will be served, or if I will eat my usual square of Belgian chocolate with my two o'clock cup of tea, though at this rate I'll be lucky to be home in time to put the kettle on before three. And in so musing, I miss the first part of a new conversational thread.

Danny says, "To be forever twenty-nine is such a cliché. That's why my inner age is a far more original, believable, and attractively mature thirty-six."

Danny is in his early forties but has kept himself up and could pass for thirty-six, or thirty-eight, anyway. But how old one looks does not appear to be what we're talking about.

The chestnut-haired woman says, "I still feel like I'm eighteen. I'm surprised every time I look in the mirror and see someone older. I read teen magazines in the supermarket checkout line, for goodness' sake."

Another woman says, "I'm stuck at twenty-seven, my age when I got married. I still consider myself a newlywed, and it's been five years."

Suzanne asks the guest on my right how old she feels, which means my turn is coming, in about thirty seconds, when I'll be expected to say something interesting and self-revelatory about this subject because Suzanne's social graces require her to include everyone, even the old bag.

The problem is that I feel forty, maybe forty-one — I often inadvertently describe people in their forties as being my age, having failed to internalize that I've passed the milestone/ millstone that is fifty. I am the oldest person in the room but in denial about it, which is such a tired, leftover attitude from a previous generation of women who acted coy about aging that I can't admit to having it.

So I say, when asked, "Hey, I'm fifty, but sitting here with you lot, I feel more like sixty." I cannot explain where the pretentious "you lot" came from, nor do I quite understand why that sour, strident tone coloured my voice, why I am so fed up with everything and everyone. What I *can* see is that my utterance has cast a pall over the company's hitherto smiling faces.

Danny jumps into the gap, says, "You know what *I* feel like? A piece of that delectable-looking cheesecake I saw waiting for us in the butler's pantry. May I help you clear, Suzanne?" The look he shoots me when his words set the women in motion up and away from the table tells me I can thank him later, but I'm not finished, have become dangerously out of sorts.

In the kitchen, Suzanne tells us to leave everything on the marble counters. "My girl will tidy up later," she says, and I bite.

"Your girl?" My voice sounds awful, rheumy and thick with emotion.

"The nanny," Suzanne says. "She's upstairs with the kids right now."

"Surely if she's old enough to be looking after your children, she's old enough to be referred to as a woman."

There is a pause before Suzanne wrinkles her small, straight nose, smiles, and says, "You sound just like my mom. Your generation got all caught up with the semantics of feminism, but my friends and I are so past that now."

Behind her, where only I can see him, Danny licks his index finger, and racks up a tally point in the air for Suzanne.

After a piece of pumpkin cheesecake (humble pie for me) and a drawn-out cup of coffee poured from a goddamned silver coffee pot, Danny and I say effusive thanks, make our escape, and before we get into our cars, walk around the block and talk while he smokes a cigarette.

He says, "What happened to you back there? Demonic possession?"

I inhale a drift of his cigarette smoke, which still smells tempting, sixteen years after I quit. "I don't know. My arm hurts."

"Your arm hurts?"

"I had a cortisone shot today for this frozen shoulder ailment I have. Maybe sudden rage is a side effect. Though that wouldn't explain why I almost told the doctor to fuck off before she gave me the shot. Or why I had a huge fight on the phone with the cable installer on the Burrows house last week.

A red-faced, furious, shaky-voiced fight. Totally brought on by the idiotic, know-nothing kid I spoke to, by the way."

Danny butts out his cigarette on the sidewalk. "Kevin's been angry a lot lately, too. Maybe there's a rage virus going around." Kevin is Danny's life partner, a lawyer ten years older than he.

I say, "I don't know what was worse: when Suzanne compared me to her mother, or when she said" — I mimic her little girl voice — "My friends are so past feminism, you know?"

"Look at it this way: you cracked her veneer for once. That's some feat, right there."

"Thanks for not attributing my behaviour to hormones, and for not saying maybe Kevin and I are turning into old farts."

"Come on, now. Fifty's not old, it's the new — "

"Please don't."

He pauses to light another cigarette. "So did Suzanne's place look fabulous or what? I went over this morning and dressed it."

"It did look fabulous. You're a design genius and a social genius. I predict you'll net at least two new clients from today's lunch. Unlike me, whose reputation as the blunt bitch architect will only be enhanced."

"You jazzed up the proceedings, though. Nothing like a little tension to make an event more talkworthy."

I might as well have pushed back the chairs, rolled up the rug, and started to jive. Or maybe Charleston.

By the time I arrive home, the dull ache in my shot-up arm has turned into a searing, stabbing pain that made me gasp all the way there. I manage a one-handed car exit and house entry, find and swallow some extra-strength ibuprofen, and stagger to my desk to check my messages and emails over the sound of the whimpering noises my gasps have turned into. One of the messages is from my friend Sylvia, who has coerced me into agreeing to help chaperone a dance at Jesse's school this evening.

Sylvia's son Ben and Jesse are both out of town, an opportunity Sylvia suggested we seize, in their absence, to put in a volunteer stint at Westdale Collegiate. Ben is at a soccer tournament. Jesse is off on one of his quarterly weekend jaunts to New York, where he'll be treated to courtside basketball tickets and trendy restaurant meals by his dad in exchange for being cordial to his stepmother, Henry's second wife, a thirtysomething ex-journalist named (shudder with me, now) Bryony, who's trying to use her fecundity (two squalling kids so far, born a year apart) to keep Henry committed. Normally, I take Jesse's periodic absences as welcome solo time and have a quiet evening in, but not tonight, thanks to Sylvia.

Her message says she'll pick me up at seven and to call back only if that's not okay. I call her back. "I'm not sure I can make it tonight."

"Why? What's wrong?"

I tell her about the shot in the arm, the pain, and the gasping and whimpering, but she won't have any of it.

She says, "Have you taken serious painkillers?"

"Five minutes ago."

"Did you wash them down with a glass of wine?"

"No."

"Drink a glass of wine, let the drugs take effect, soak in a hot bath, eat a light dinner, and be at your door ready to go at seven. I'll honk."

I'm too pain-addled to argue.

At seven, I slide into Sylvia's car and into her not-unpleasant scent of perfume and powder.

"Feeling better?" she says.

"If you call a state of chemically induced relaxation better, yeah. I hope there won't be any heavy lifting required tonight. Or fast thinking."

"There won't be. The most we'll have to do is take a few tickets and patrol the back halls on the lookout for clandestine cocaine snorting and underage sex."

"Why are we doing this again?"

"Because it'll be educational and we'll collect evidence from which we can extrapolate information about how our own children behave in similar circumstances."

"But Jesse has no interest in this sort of occasion." The dear child of my antisocial heart has so far avoided hanging out with girls and appears to care only for rap music, basketball, and computer games.

"That's what Ben was like six months ago, but when I drove him to the bus this morning, he complained at length about the school's stupidity and lack of foresight in scheduling a dance for the same weekend as his soccer tournament."

"Did he really use the phrase 'lack of foresight'?"

"I think his exact words were 'the administration sucks.' The point is that by observing the boys' peer group at play, we can better understand their world and be better parents to their sensitive souls."

"Uh-huh." Not long ago, Jesse was a child who gave me wonderful, long-lasting, heartfelt hugs, and walked hand in hand with me in public, and kissed me goodbye in front of his friends. He was an affectionate, loving sweetheart, the light in the window at the end of a long day.

Now, when he speaks to me, it's to ask for food or if I want to hear a good line from a rap song, a line that cleverly rhymes with *pussy, ho,* or *gun.* Or it's to tell me to stop nagging him about his homework, because he'll do it when he feels like it and not before. There are still moments when he relates, of his own

volition, a heartwarming anecdote about his daily life — like
that some girls got into a fight after school and five police cars
came, or that one of his friends got drunk on malt liquor in the
park, threw up, and caught the barf in his hands. But the sweet,
sensitive mama's boy I cherished seems to be slipping away.

Sylvia pulls down the visor and checks her lipstick in the
mirror. "If all else fails, we can have some vicarious fun at this
dance, relive a moment or two from our youth."

I throw her a suspicious look. "Is Mr. Sutherland going to
be there?" Mr. Sutherland is a tall, single, said-to-be-straight
English and drama teacher at Westdale, a man toward whom
Sylvia has on more than one occasion professed lustful feelings.
He does nothing for me.

She flips up the visor. "Maybe."

"And does Ed know you've gone out flirting for the night?"

"Ed's home supervising Kira and a friend on their sleepover,
while I put in some helpful volunteer hours at Westdale. And
anyway, if it's just a little flirting, what's there to know?"

This is one of the many things I value Sylvia for: her ability
to provide me with timely reminders about how pointless
couplehood can be.

She says, "It wouldn't hurt you to flirt now and then.
Even better, you could actually try to meet someone new and
consider dating. Say the word and I'll find someone to set
you up with."

This is what I *don't* value Sylvia for: her desire to pair me up,
to convert me to her two-by-two ranks. Why can't she accept that
I'm content with my single lot in life, with the one-person
dwelling I've built to my own particular and peculiar specifica-
tions? Why can't the coupled-off leave us solo acts alone to live
out our solitary, tea-soaked existences? I do not need to be saved.

I say, "You have me confused with someone who doesn't
want to die alone."

"All I'm suggesting is that you open your eyes to the opportunities around you." She laughs. "Except for the Mr. Sutherland opportunity. He's mine."

The vice-principal at Westdale in charge of discipline, a stocky, short-haired, tie-wearing, shirt-tucked-in man of about fifty-five named Mr. Harkness, refers to females as ladies, whether he's talking about Sylvia and me, as in, "Thank you so much, ladies, for coming in tonight and helping out," or addressing the girls attending the dance: "Would you ladies form an orderly line to the right, please?" He doesn't leer or make suggestive comments to us or to the scantily clad girls, I'll give him that. But the gleeful gleam in his eye when he picks out for ejection a grade nine boy who, from the smell of him, must have poured one bottle of beer over his head while drinking another, is the gleam of someone who gets off on exercising authority. A type I can't stand.

"Zero tolerance is our policy here at Westdale," he says, after the boy's parents have been called to come pick him up, an incident report written, a suspension promised. Sylvia and I nudge each other at this, though our thoughts probably do not match. The "thank god that wasn't my son" parts may, but I'm not sure she'd be as quick as I am to classify Harkness as a power-mad asshole.

I position myself at the other end of the ticket-taking table from him, at the hand-stamping station, and try to act cool. I do not display on my face the shock I feel when a boy I know from Jesse's year, a thin, nerdy kid who always excelled at academics, shows up with his arm draped around a hot-bodied girl dressed like a debauched pop star. I do not tell the boys that they look cute but vulnerable in their pressed khakis and polo shirts or silly and poser-like in their gangster wear. I do not hold my nose at the strong smell of musk-noted aftershaves in the air.

Most of the kids I know seem to appreciate the impersonal treatment, to tacitly agree that, under the circumstances, better to disavow previous acquaintance and avoid acknowledgement of how often I've car-pooled them over the years. Except for Spencer McKay. Spencer sidles up to the table with a posse of two girls and three boys, looks me in the eye, and in the ringing voice he used to spellbinding effect in last year's school production of *Romeo and Juliet* (he played Mercutio), says, "Hey, Emily. How you doing?"

I take his ticket, check his face, see no obvious signs of inebriation. Spencer is a year older than Jesse and has never been a close friend, but they worked on class projects together in the split grades in elementary school, played on the same teams, and attended each other's birthday parties before they became too old for such things.

"I'm fine," I say, evenly. "How are you?"

"Ready to party." He shoots his crew a knowing grin and leads them into the gym.

At my elbow, Sylvia mutters, "There goes trouble."

"You think? He looked sober to me."

"Yeah, but you know Spencer. If he can't find a ruckus, he'll cause one."

An hour later, the incoming traffic has slowed to a trickle. So when Mr. Harkness says, "Would either of you ladies like to take a break from ticket-taking and do a girls' washroom check?" I say yes right away. I need to pop another painkiller: my arm ache is sharpening, the previous pill wearing off.

I'd also like to escape from the sight that is Sylvia's crush-object Mr. Sutherland. His long hair is tied in a ponytail, his denim shirt is rolled up at the sleeves to expose his hairy forearms, and two buttons are undone to show off his hairy neck. He has emerged from his post inside the gym and sits perched on the edge of the admission table, ready to pontificate. Any minute now, he will start quoting Shakespeare, and I will gag.

I signal my departure to an oblivious Sylvia and set off down the hall for the women's staff washroom, where I use the facilities, wash my hands, take a pill. When I emerge, I hear voices coming from the adjacent girls' washroom. Does my chaperone role really require me to stick my head in there and act officious and super-visory? Maybe I could wait out in the hall and nod at the exiting girls when they appear, pretend not to notice the cloud of cigarette smoke that surrounds them or to see the telltale outline of minia-ture liquor bottles through the thin fabric of their tiny purses.

The loud voices have turned into low-volume murmurings in the short time I've stood there, but no one has come out. I'd better do my duty, get it over with. I push open the swinging door with my bad shoulder — ouch — and walk into a tableau in which Spencer, surrounded by four girls, enacts a drug deal. At the moment I open the door, Spencer's right hand, holding a clear plastic bag of pot, is extended toward a girl I have also known since Jesse was little, a tough cookie named Jill. Spencer's left hand grasps the bills she presses into his palm.

I stare for a second, a girl in a pink top says, "Oh, shit," I step back out, and I let the door close on the scene. My impulse is to walk away, fast, and blink away the image. But when I turn to do so, I spot Harkness strolling toward me from the other end of the corridor. I turn back, open the door again, slip inside.

In a strained whisper, I say, "Harkness is coming. Girls, out now. Spencer, take cover. Hide. Go!"

A thought snail-paces its way across my tired, drugged brain that I'm not supposed to be abetting feckless youth, I'm sup-posed to be the responsible, policing parent here. But it's too late to change my approach now.

I hold open the washroom door and half-push, half-follow the girls out. They run straight into Harkness, who holds out his hand like a policeman directing traffic. Jill is in front, at the point of the birds-in-flight V formation the girls have formed, her face hardened into a defiant but impassive expression that I wouldn't have had the guts to wear when I was her age.

"Can I help you?" Jill says. Sounding in the air is a warning that if Harkness dares to harass Jill, her lawyer father will be all over the school administration the next day, weekend or not.

Harkness falters. "Where are you ladies coming from?"

Jill relaxes — there's no threat here. I wouldn't put it past her to yawn. "Where do you think?" Understood: moron. "We were in the girls' washroom. And I hope you're not going to ask what we were doing in there, because it's personal."

The girl in pink emits a stoned-sounding giggle and earns a punishing over-the-shoulder glare from Jill for the eruption.

Harkness looks at me. I make a nonsensical thumbs-up sign from my post at the washroom door, rub my now-throbbing arm, and will Spencer not to choose this moment to come out of hiding.

"Carry on, then, ladies," Harkness says. "Enjoy what remains of the dance. And stay sober, please."

Jill grunts, flips her hair, and leads her friends down the hall with the swagger of a teen movie bad girl who bests the doofus vice-principal daily. Mocking bursts of laughter float our way from the now out-of-danger pack.

Harkness watches them go. "I don't like that girl's attitude," he says.

"I don't know. Seems to me like she's got serious leadership potential."

He turns to see if I too am lipping him off and notices my door-barring stance for the first time. "Is anyone else in there?"

"I'll go check." I slip through the door again and almost trip over Spencer, not hiding but sitting on the floor, his back to the wall. He flashes me a peace sign and a grin, I mime to him to wait three minutes then leave, and I return to the hall, where I escort Harkness back to the gym doors without blowing Spencer's cover or angering Harkness further.

A new pair of volunteer moms are sitting at the admission table, and Sylvia stands, leaning, against the wall, ready to go. "You two were gone a while," she says, when Harkness has entered the gym, probably in search of couples dancing too close that he can separate. "Did you have fun back there?"

"Don't make me sick." I grip my arm, which is aching in rhythmic pulses now. "What happened to Mr. Sutherland?"

"He's back inside. And our shift has ended anyway. I'll go to the washroom, then we'll leave, okay? But I'll be quick, unlike some people."

I find my jacket, put it on, sling my purse over my shoulder, and am headed for outside and some fresh air, when Spencer saunters into the foyer, walks over to me, and stands too close.

"Hey, Emily. Thanks for covering my ass." He fixes his hooded eyes on mine. He's never suffered from a lack of confidence, this kid.

I already regret having saved him from Harkness, but I'll never be old enough to betray my youthful self and play narc. I can't be bothered to chide him now, to issue some Mother-Knows-Best admonition about what he should or shouldn't be up to in his spare time. His own private spare time. "Good night, Spencer."

I step away, but he comes after me and places a friendly hand on my back, as if we are familiars. "No really. I appreciate what you did. Props, man." He tilts his head to one side and forms his hand into a fist, offers it to me. And in the same way that it's impossible to refuse a handshake or a hello kiss without seeming rude, I raise my own fist and brush knuckles with him, though the movement hurts my arm *and* my hand.

Sylvia bustles out, Spencer melts off, and Sylvia says, "What's he up to? I thought I saw him coming out of the girls' washroom when I went down the hall."

"He's slippery, all right, but he's not our concern. Let's go home."

When I go to bed on this fun night, the capper of my fun day, I lie awake longer than usual. I can find no reclining position that does not pain me, and there's the racing mind to contend with, the recriminatory thoughts to air — I should have walked away; Jesse will not be happy when he hears about this; Spencer is a devil, why did I protect him? To distract myself, I try to visualize the design for a bed that would allow people with sore arms to sleep standing up. I almost have it worked out when I remember that Dr. Joan gave me a task to do when I came home from her office, a task I should have performed this morning.

I get up, shuffle into Jesse's room, turn on the light, grab a pencil off his desk. On a wall in his bathroom, we've been charting his growth — the latest mark, made four months ago, in June, has him at five feet, eleven and a half inches. With pencil in hand, I reach up to a blank section of the wall and draw a line at the highest point my right arm can touch, a full four inches lower than where I can touch with my left.

"Make a mark on the wall when you get home," Dr. Joan said, "do your exercises several times daily, see if your reach improves, and check in with me again in three months. Do you understand?"

Yes, I understand. I also understand that according to the writing on this wall, Jesse's still on the incline of life, but I've already crested the mountain and am making my slow, hobbled way down the decline. I get it. And now I'd like to get some sleep.

~ CHAPTER TWO ~

I drive out to the airport on Sunday evening to pick up Jesse from his New York trip, and when I see him waiting at our agreed-upon curbside spot — his hair messy, his jeans baggy, his eyebrows knit in a poor imitation of nonchalance — my heart does its usual salmon-spawning leap. The primal mother in me will always be relieved to find him safe, uninjured, and not crying after we've been apart, even when he's thirty, I should live that long.

In the car, I take his hand and hold it for a moment, and the old, sweet, affectionate Jesse squeezes back. The newer, more independent Jesse ejects the Brandenburg Concertos CD from the car stereo and says, "How can you stand hearing this same old classical shit over and over?"

"It has a certain mathematical precision that I find soothing."

He isn't listening, meant his question to be rhetorical. He inserts his own CD in the player, turns up the volume, and does not fasten his seatbelt until I remind him to five minutes later.

"How was the flight?"

"Okay."

"Did you get something to eat?"

"I had a Caesar salad at La Guardia, only I forgot to ask for no croutons so I had to pick them out, but don't worry, I didn't eat any crumbs."

"Have you had any cramps?"

"Relax, I'm fine."

Jesse's celiac disease — a lifelong allergy to the gluten in wheat, barley, and rye — has weighed on me since he was diagnosed with it at the age of eighteen months, but I am not otherwise unrelaxed. I watch the road (I must get some new eyeglasses for distance), listen to him rap along in his tuneless voice to the music, and wait a verse's length of time before saying, "How's your dad?" It's difficult not to modify the word *dad* with an adjective like *pompous* or *puffed-up*, but I manage.

"He's okay. He's put on some weight."

"Bryony isn't watching what he eats?" Bryony is a size zero, eats only fruit and lettuce, I'm convinced, and runs twenty miles every morning on a treadmill at seven o'clock with a trainer while the au pair minds the kids and Henry reads his first five newspapers of the day.

"She tries to get him to eat healthy, but he does what he wants."

Henry always has.

There are doubtless more fascinating details Jesse could tell me about his weekend, like that he saw a NBA player up close at a game and how cool that was, or that one or both of his half-brothers was an out-of-control brat. But he will dole out tidbits of information later, when he's in the mood — or not.

He says, "How was your weekend?" as if reading a line from a play spoken by a character more well-mannered than he.

"I did that chaperoning thing at your school dance."

His archness drops. "Shit, I forgot about that. How'd it go? Tell me you didn't do anything I'll be hearing about on Monday at school, like say one word to my friends."

I see again the cocky look on Spencer's face by the gym doors and feel him touching me. Since I neglected to tell Spencer to keep our encounter — too grand a term for what transpired — confidential, and I didn't swear the girls to silence either, the story may be all over the school population by now, courtesy of instant messaging. "Actually, there was an incident." How to present this to minimize Jesse's disapproval? "Nothing major."

He covers his face with his hands. "Fucked for life, that's what I am. Fucked for life, because my mom had to go and volunteer at the dance."

"Calm down. All that happened was that I told Spencer McKay to hide when I found him in the girls' washroom dealing dope and Mr. Harkness was around the corner." Much as I want it to, this summary does not sound like a description of nothing.

"Are you kidding me? What do you mean that's all that happened? What more could have happened?"

I could have beckoned Harkness over is what, and said, "I think we've got a live one here," Spencer could have been suspended and/or handed over to the police along with tough cookie Jill, parents could have been called, and endless earnest discussions about drug use could have ensued, and I had prevented all that, more credit to me. I say, "You've still never smoked dope?"

"It's called weed, Em. And no, I haven't. I don't drink, either."

We drive on a minute in silence. "Why not?"

"Shut up."

"No, really. If everyone else is doing it, why don't you?"

"You know why — because I'm an athlete."

I should be happy that Jesse's dedication to athleticism has given him a reason not to drink and smoke, but how long can he resist what I think of as the inevitable rites of teenage passage? Rites I underwent repeatedly at his age.

He says, "I'd better stay home from school tomorrow, so I don't have to see anyone who was at the dance."

"You're overreacting. I'm sure it's all forgotten now. And would you prefer that I'd ratted him out?"

I wish I'd used a different expression, one that sounds less like Edward G. Robinson issue, but he doesn't mock me for it or complain. Instead, he ejects his CD from the car stereo player, says, "You can put your classical shit back on," places his CD into his Discman, plugs his headphones in, and turns up the volume, shuts me out.

A few minutes later, I reach inside my jacket pocket for a tissue, touch something unexpected, examine it with my fingers inside the pocket, mutter, "What's this?" Luckily, Jesse's music is playing too loud for him to hear me, so I don't have to explain that what I'm touching feels like a foil packet about two inches long and one wide. Luckily, I have the presence of mind to leave the mystery packet in my pocket. If it's what I think it is, it can only have been placed there by Spencer.

The packet burns a hole in my mind all the way home and is still giving off heat when we go inside the house. Jesse heads up to his room right away, and when I can hear his music playing and know he's settled in at his computer, I deke into the kitchen with my jacket still on, pull out the packet, unwrap the foil, count three thin, neatly rolled joints, and wrap them back up. I hide them in a deep green ceramic vase that has stood untouched on a high shelf for months. I could flush the contraband down a toilet or bury it deep inside a garbage bag, but my subconscious murmurs that the painkilling effects of weed might one day be of help with my frozen shoulder. And my immediate objective is to keep from Jesse any reminder of my collusion with Spencer.

Soon after, Jesse forgives me for the dance incident; that is, he forgives me after he chats online with friends and finds out that the main gossip story of the night did not involve my actions or inactions but was about two boys who had a fistfight, during which wannabe thug x had metaphorically kicked wannabe thug y's ass by bloodying his nose. According to eye-witness accounts, Harkness, ever ready to face conflict and terror, stepped into the fray and his shirttails became untucked, and oh, the drama.

The threat of social ostracism due to my parenting removed for the moment, Jesse resumes his normal behaviour. He drops his clothes and belongings all over the house, is appreciative of the chicken cacciatore I made him for dinner, and spends two hours on his computer doing thirty minutes' worth of math to the accompaniment of loud hip hop music. At one point, he entreats me to enter his room and listen to a song when I pass by in the hall, and he hugs me — payment for my servitude — when I bring him the fresh pineapple and cut-up apple he requests as a post-dinner snack.

At ten-thirty, when I remind him it's bedtime, he's watching television. He tells me to chill and let him watch one more play — always one more play, one more possession, one more batter, one more pitch, to the end of the quarter, there's less than a minute left, see? — and when we've watched the one more together, he gets up, brushes his teeth, goes to his room, dives into bed, and waits for me to come say good night like I've done every night since he was a baby.

I stand in his doorway and lift my bad arm, reach up and stretch it in the doorframe, try to breathe through the ache. "Did you get all your homework done?"

"Most of it. I can finish my reading for English at lunch tomorrow. Or in my history class. The history teacher's boring as shit, anyway."

"That's an excellent plan. Maybe you can save more time by eating your breakfast in the shower. Or sleeping there."

"There's no need for sarcasm, Em."

"What do you have left to do?"

"Read another chapter of *The Catcher in the Rye*. I read some of it on the plane."

"How are you liking it so far?"

"I can't stand the guy. What a boring wuss."

Such is parenthood: a favourite, formative novel from my youth, one of the few books I read in an English class that I liked, is to Jesse boring, its hero weak.

I don't know why I bother, but I say, "Holden Caulfield is considered to be one of the truest voices in American literature."

"True to who? Weird loners everywhere?"

Well, yes.

I wasn't always a loner. In high school I had a set of equally alienated friends to get stoned with on weekend nights, in university I found fellow students who shared my disregard for modern architecture, and when I was a newly minted young professional, I had work friends to grouse about the office with, over drinks or at brunch. In the year or so that Henry and I were together before Jesse was born, in the first, self-sacrificial stage of our relationship, we socialized like mad: we went to and gave dinner parties for his writer/artist/journalist friends, we attended book launches, theatre performances, and art gallery openings, we heard jazz musicians play in smoky clubs, we behaved like the other couples of our circle.

Jesse's squalling, demanding infant presence put an end to any inessential adult outings on my part for a few years, but by the time he could be left with a babysitter for more than two hours without either of us breaking down (not until about age three),

I'd lost interest in arts talk, political talk, most talk. Spend time with the same people, I find, and topics, points of view, and anecdotes tend to repeat. Spend time with the same people and the radical ways in which I differ from them — in opinions, attitudes, and tolerance for repetition — become apparent. The many ways in which they irritate me crystallize into clarity too, and sooner or later (lately sooner), I express that irritation, say something obnoxious or critical, regret my words, and want to crawl under a rock afterwards and never come out in public again.

I sometimes fantasize about living alone, in the wild, where I would see no one and I could drop all pretence of conforming to societal normalcy. I could let my hair grow out long and grey and wear it in braids. My eyebrows could get scraggly, I could wear shapeless clothes — the same ones every day — and no makeup, and talk to myself out loud, and eat and gain weight and not care, and keep whatever irregular sleeping and waking hours I chose, and never worry about opening my mouth and saying the wrong thing, because there'd be no one to hear me act the fool, or be rude, or reveal the gaps in my education, or blurt out my prejudices.

The loner in me enjoys entertaining that fantasy, but the pragmatist that I also am knows it's a crock of implausibility. I hate the wilderness, and where would I get the food that would make me fat, and I'd bore myself to death with no company but my crazed own, and braids would give me a headache, and I'd need some human connection, at least for short periods between restful bouts of solitude.

If only I didn't find most of those connections so awkward and irksome.

On our next Wednesday morning walk, Sylvia says, "So I think Ben's started drinking now, for sure."

"Why? What happened?"

"I went to unpack his bag from the soccer tournament and I found a can of beer wrapped up in one of his soccer socks, inside his shin pads."

"That's a clever way of hiding it."

Sylvia glares.

"I meant, maybe he was carrying it for someone."

"Or maybe it was the one left over after he drank five others in his hotel room with those punks on the soccer team."

"Did you ask him about it?"

"I left it there and told him to unpack his bag, waited until he had, and searched his room the next day and couldn't find it anywhere."

"You see — he *was* carrying it for someone."

"What would you do if this happened with Jesse?"

"Jesse can't drink beer. He's allergic to the gluten in malt."

"What if he was drinking vodka, then?"

"I guess I'd think it was quasi-normal teenage behaviour but be worried to death every time he went out."

"What I can't get over is that Ben had a whole scheme worked out in advance for hiding the beer so the cans wouldn't clank around. This from the kid who's incapable of doing a homework assignment at any minute but the last."

"Why are you so surprised? What were you doing at his age?"

"Harbouring unrequited crushes and feeling insecure, of course. Weren't you?"

"Yes, but if we didn't start acting out until we were sixteen or so, that's only because time moved slower then, back in the Chaucerian era."

"So I told Ed we needed to sit down and have a talk with Ben about drinking and partying and whether he wants to throw his life away or succeed."

Sylvia is a big proponent of the kind of heart-to-heart talks featured on sappy family television dramas. My equally ineffective approach with Jesse when issues arise is to employ the one- or two-minute whiny plead tactic.

"And the worst thing," Sylvia says, "was that when I talked to Ed, he chuckled and said, 'That's my boy!' and asked me if Ben was dating anyone yet."

Ed is a good provider — he's a dentist — but he's also a hearty, bad-joke-telling bore. I don't know why Sylvia married him, but I invariably fail to see the appeal of my friends' mates.

"Lately," Sylvia says, "Ed's been making Steve Sutherland look more and more attractive."

"You call Mr. Sutherland by his first name now?"

She waits until a woman with a dog walks by us before she says, *sotto voce*, "I'm thinking of calling and asking him out for a drink or a coffee the next time Ed goes away to one of his conferences."

"Why am I afraid you're not joking?"

"Because I'm not. Ed is so — Why this weekend, he — I — Okay, listen to this: he insists on reading aloud to me from the Sunday newspaper when I'm trying to have my morning coffee. Twenty years we've been together, he knows I hate being read to, he knows I hate being talked to at all in the morning, and still he does it."

"That would piss me off, too." It would.

"Whereas Steve doesn't seem to have a single unattractive trait. And he was pretty heavily coming on to me the other night at the dance. "

"So, you'd have coffee with Mr. Sutherland and then what?"

She flushes. "A little necking in a car might be nice, some making out. Don't you think?"

In the four years since Henry left, I have tried not to think about necking, making out, or any other form of sexual contact, and have been fairly successful at suppressing and denying any urges of that nature. But why Sylvia, who already has a live-in sex provider, wants to tangle with someone else, I don't understand.

She says, "For years now, I've thought I was happy enough with Ed, that his good points outweighed his bad, and I never thought about cheating. But now it's like I've become enveloped in a cloud of fairy lust. All I can think about is how sexy Steve is, and what I'd like to do to him, in graphic detail."

"Graphic detail that you'll spare me, I hope."

"You're such a prude sometimes, Emily, honestly. But do you know what I mean? Has this ever happened to you?"

What did she call it? Fairy lust? How immature. "No, I can't say that it has." Not that I would admit, anyway.

I'm standing inside my door at 8:38 a.m., dressed and ready to go. I try not to tap my foot while I wait for Jesse to finish wandering around the house the way he does every morning, picking up his various items for school. If he were me, he would pack up the night before, but he's not me.

"Have you got your phone and your wallet?" I ask this every morning. It's part of our scripted routine. "And your lunch and your bus tickets?"

He says yeah and yeah, then, "Wait. Is it Thursday?"

"Yes, and can you please get going? I'm in a hurry."

"It *is* Thursday? Fuck. Basketball tryouts are today after school." He runs upstairs. "Do you know where my Jordans are? And my sports bag?"

I set down my briefcase, walk to the mudroom at the back of the house, and retrieve his basketball shoes and sports bag from the built-in cupboard designated for this purpose, the cupboard Jesse can never bring himself to use. I meet him in the front hall, where he throws a T-shirt, shorts, and his ankle brace into the bag, shrugs on his jacket, and says, "What? I'm ready. Are you?"

"Let's just go."

In the car, he says, "Where are you rushing off to this morning, anyway, that you're so freaked out about the time? Going for a walk with Sylvia?"

I'm dressed in my business-type clothes and I have my briefcase. "Do I look like I'm going walking to you?"

"Forget it." He turns on the car radio and switches the channel to his station.

"I'm teaching today," I say, above the music. "In Leo Antonelli's class. Remember, I did it last week?"

"Then where are your slides?"

"I packed them in the trunk earlier, when you were still asleep. After I read the newspaper and had my coffee and before I took my shower and made your lunch and breakfast."

"Are you done talking now? Because I'd like to listen to this song."

I want to ask him about the basketball tryouts — if this is the first or has he missed one, and when is the next, and what time should I expect him home, and is it the same coach as last year. I need to know if I should worry about this aspect of his life. But the moment isn't right. And I can always interrogate him tonight, when he comes home for dinner, turns on the television to watch while he eats, and will be even less inclined to talk.

I pull up in front of the school at three minutes to the bell. Jesse opens the car door, shrugs on his knapsack, turns around, and looks in the back seat. "Oh shit," he says, more sheepish than angry.

"What?"

"You're not going to like this."

"What?"

"I left my sports bag at home."

"For fuck's sake, Jesse."

"Can you bring it at lunch? Please? I get out at 11:45."

If I hustle, I can make it home and back to school after my lecture by noon. I don't want to, but I can.

He says, "Can you?"

"I could meet you at 12:05, not earlier."

He hops out of the car. "Thanks, Em, you're a doll. I'll meet you at 12:05, right here."

Leo Antonelli made his name young, designing homes in the Post-Modernist idiom — he's known for a handful of steel-framed, glass-walled, flat-roofed residences built in locations that afford panoramic views. In the mid-seventies, he took up a teaching position at the university's faculty of architecture, where he still lectures, wears striped bowties and suits of English tailoring, and sports the startling, out-to-there eyebrows some men of his generation affect.

When I was a student, he took a kindly interest in me. He admired my spunk (his word) and called me a spitfire, which I've always considered a euphemism for a woman who's energetic in an off-putting, mannish way, but he meant it as praise. After I graduated, he encouraged me to keep in touch and he followed my career progress. When I left the big firm, started Harada Restorations, and was struggling to make a go of it, he invited me, one term, to give a few guest lectures, for pay, to his students, about nineteenth-century Canadian architecture and the challenges of restoring it. When the lectures went well, he charitably suggested I repeat the series of three one-hour talks each term thereafter.

I'm nervous every time I go in, but I've come to enjoy standing up in Leo's classroom on an infrequent basis. For all my avowals that solitude is my preferred and natural state, that I would rather hide alone in my study making drawings than have to interact with clients, contractors, or any people other than Jesse, I do become more alive than usual, more peppy and performance-high, when I stand up in front of the students. It helps that the room is dark when I speak, the faces of the students obscured.

Today, when I finish my lecture, I turn on the lights and pack up my things. As the students disperse, Leo strolls into the room from the hallway — he retreats to his office when I come in to speak — and thanks me. "How did it go?" he says. "Did the students hang on to your every word, as usual?"

"Actually, the room felt a little sleepy today. As if some of these kids were having trouble seeing the relevance of old houses to their careers as the next Frank Gehry."

"Were there any difficult questions?"

"No. Why?"

"I have a few feisty students this term, a few who like to question long-held principles simply because they are long-held. One young woman reminds me of you, years ago. But if Autumn didn't make her presence felt today, well and good."

"Your student's name is Autumn?"

"Yes, as in the current season."

"And you say it with such a straight face."

"I learned long ago not to question or remark on anyone's name. Down that path lies accusations of prejudice."

"Also fallen leaves. Big piles of wet, slippery ones, I imagine."

His smile is uncertain. What the hell am I talking about? He says, "Do you have time for lunch at the faculty club?"

"I don't, I'm afraid. I have to drop something off at my son's school."

"Until next week, then. Oh, and you can expect an invitation in the mail to a small party in my honour that's being held in a few weeks' time. I've won some kind of award, it seems."

"You have? Congratulations. Which one?"

He names a prestigious lifetime achievement award given by the national architects' association, I congratulate him, and I promise to attend the party, whenever it is.

Public speaking makes me hungry, but I have no time to stop for food; I race home, throw Jesse's bag into the car, and drive up to Westdale. It's 12:04 when I find a parking spot in front, turn off the car, and try to pick out Jesse's black sweatshirt among the lunchtime hordes that flow on and around the sidewalk and lawn in front of the school.

In the grey light of the overcast day, the Westdale student body glows far less than it did at the dance. Many of the faces that pass by my car window are pale and acne-ridden, and some are badly in need of a shave. Several boys who look to be Jesse's age are smoking cigarettes with all the mannerisms of veteran smokers.

A Goth girl in dark makeup, clothes, and hair trudges past on six-inch-high platform shoes. How much time does it take to layer on her look each morning, how much effort to make her angry/sad, I'm-different-damn-you style statement? As much time and effort is probably required to turn two ordinary, fresh-faced girls into the pink-lipsticked, whorish, dyed blondes who walk by next, in shrunken jackets worn open to reveal their low-cut tops, and jeans so tight the seams must leave deep, detailed imprints on their legs.

How happy I am not to be young at this moment, how relieved to have found my weird loner place in life, to be cloistered away in my late middle age.

Jesse looms up beside the car, opens the passenger door, reaches for his bag, says, "Hey, Em, thanks a million. Gotta run." Behind him is Sylvia's son, Ben, someone I didn't think Jesse lunched with. Ben says hi, Jesse closes the door, and they turn away and walk up the street, are swallowed by the pale and pimply masses. Leaving me to shake off the cloying mist of teen angst that has seeped inside the car and drive home.

~ ★ ~

After lunch and a nap, I sit down at my desk with my tea and square of chocolate, turn on my computer, and open an email from a name I don't recognize — a Thomas Denby. I am about to delete it until I realize that this person is not selling prescription drugs or counterfeit Rolex watches. He knows me.

The message reads:

> Dear Ms. Harada,
>
> I'm looking for the Emily Harada who worked on rescue archeology excavations in Earith, Cambridgeshire, and North Cave, Yorkshire, during the summer of 1975. Are you by chance that person? I obtained your email address from a website about Canadian architects, but no picture or age was given there, so I'm rather taking a shot in the dark.
>
> If you are that Emily Harada, or if you know how to reach her, please advise. I lived in Manchester thirty years ago, but am now an urban planner in Leeds and am on a committee charged with organizing a diggers' reunion in Earith in a few weeks' time.
>
> Yours truly,
> Thomas Denby

I am that Emily Harada, and at the age of twenty I had the good fortune to get a summer job in England. A childhood friend of my mother's lived in London and knew someone who knew someone who helped arrange for me to be a "subsistence volunteer" on a rescue archeology dig, which meant that for four weeks I slept in a tent pitched in a field in the fens of Cambridgeshire, used a chemical toilet, and bathed only on Saturdays, when we bused into town and paid fifty pence to use the public baths.

With my dig mates, I spent nine-hour days in the blazing sun wielding pickaxe, wheelbarrow, and trowel, digging up the remains of a Roman villa that had been unearthed by a backhoe at a gravel quarry. (The pit men stood by, waiting for our crew to finish excavating and recording the site, so that they could, er, quarry on.) In the evenings, we walked for half an hour across pastures, over stiles, and down country roads to the village and its one pub.

I did not think that doing menial labour — ditch-digging, basically — for pennies per hour under primitive living conditions was debilitating, depressing work. I was young and on my first trip abroad — I thought I was living a heady adventure.

My fellow subsistence volunteers were a mix of English and Irish and Scottish students who devoted their summers to the rescue excavation circuit. The dig director was a graduate student from the London Institute of Archeology, a lanky man named Clive, long of leg and charm, a gifted gabber with twinkly eyes, handsome smile lines around his mouth, and defined biceps revealed for my viewing pleasure when he occasionally dropped his supervisory clipboard to shovel dirt alongside the volunteers.

I developed a mad crush on Clive within about a day of meeting him, uncaring that he had a young wife at home and a roving eye that did not rove over me. Such was my devotion that soon before the dig ended, when he mentioned during a tea break that he was driving up to Yorkshire next to do a quick survey of a late Neolithic hut circle site that had come to light when a farmer plowed his field, and did anyone want to join him, he could take and pay three diggers for a few days, I shouted out yes before he'd completed his sentence, like an overeager game show contestant jumping the buzzer.

A smelly but cheery young teenager named Tom, from Manchester, who relished the outdoorsy, camping aspect of archeology, also signed on. So did an Oxford student named Mary, a milkmaidish girl — busty and apple-cheeked and sweet of countenance. Neither a maker nor appreciator of acerbic remarks was she, and therefore, to me, not friend material. Having her along would make the tent-sharing arrangements equitable, though — Tom and Clive would tent together, and so would Mary and I.

The Yorkshire site was remotely situated, the nearest village a cluster of houses grouped around a church and a combination grocery store and post office. Heavy machinery sent on ahead had excavated the field down a few metres prior to our arrival and exposed, on the dusty plain below, five or six round darkened rings of soil that indicated the location of postholes for the posts that had held up the huts of the late Neolithic/early Bronze Age people who had lived in the area a few thousand years before.

Other Bronze Age sites in the area had revealed large earthworks and funeral barrows filled with artifacts, including pottery indicative of the Beaker Culture that emerged in England during that time. There were remains of henges, elsewhere, but our Blasted Heath, as Clive dubbed it, was a dud. The sand flew into one's eyes whenever the wind blew, gradations in soil colour were the only signs of ancient inhabitants (there was nary a pot shard), our toilet was the massive spoil tip of earth piled up at the end of the football field–sized site, Tom smelled, Mary giggled too much, I grew bored of holding the surveyor's staff, and Clive was businesslike with me, did not twinkle an eye or crease a laugh line in my direction.

He twinkled and creased around Mary, though, especially in the closest (ten kilometres away) pub, when we drove over on our last night and startled the locals with our out-of-town presence.

THE RESTORATION OF EMILY ~

(And where lucky me got the chance to explain that despite my look and name, I wasn't from Japan but from Canada. Yes, born there, if you can imagine, of a father who was born there too and a mother who was not Asian but Irish! They couldn't imagine.) A few hours of heavy drinking later, Clive asked a more sober than he Tom to drive home from the pub and stepped up from twinkling at Mary to fondling her in the back seat of the van. The fondling elicited from her a series of delighted giggles and chortles, and from me a stabbed heart and a grim face. In the front seat next to Tom, I stared out the window into the deep rural darkness and turned on the car stereo, though the tape was one of makeout music, so "Stairway to Heaven" blared out, a song I have despised ever since.

Young though I was, I should have known better than to go after the top dog male of any group. I'd been spurned by such golden boys in high school and university, had settled instead, on more than one occasion, and for solid stints of time, for the boyfriend who is cute once you get to know him, versus the godlike quarterback prom king. I should have known better, but I didn't, and the passing-over hurt as much as if I'd never felt it before. More.

I stared out the window, died a few times, tried not to let fall any self-pitying tears, and resolved that if I were asked to bunk in for the night with Tom so that Clive and Mary could fuck their brains out in the women's tent, I would refuse, no matter how churlish and unsportswomanlike that decision would make me seem.

Clive and Mary fucked their brains out all right, but in the back of the van, which had convenient fold-down seats for the purpose. Tom and I slept alone in our separate, newly roomy tents on the sandy soil floor. Or Tom slept — I heard him snore — and I lay awake most of the night, wrapped in a blanket knit of sadness and humiliation.

The next morning, at around six, I pulled on jeans and a shirt over my T-shirt and underwear, stepped into my construction boots, went out to pee behind the spoil tip, and walked back to the tent, my face and head aching from fatigue, all vans and people and farm animals in the vicinity quiet, save for a few very loud birds, including a cuckoo.

When I caught a glimpse of something not sand-coloured on the ground, I crouched down for a closer look. The object was round and ring-like and made of a crusty, heavy, dark metal — bronze. It was a bracelet, perhaps, or a buckle. I picked it up, thereby breaking a cardinal rule of archeology — that finds must be considered in context, in situ. I squatted there for a few seconds longer and thought about putting it back, placing it into the impression left in the dusty soil. I could have taken off my belt and used it to mark the spot, then roused Tom or, if I had to, Clive and Mary, and shown them the object, and properly documented the find according to its coordinates on the field. But I didn't. I swept away the faint circular outline on the surface of the sandy soil with the tips of my fingers, stood up, clasped the ring in my palm, crept back to my tent, slipped inside, and closed the tent flaps.

No one stirred until eight o'clock, by which time I had examined my find closely, turned it over and enjoyed the heft of it, run my finger across its roughened surface, and arrived at two rationalizations: first, that Clive, contemptible and indiscriminate if only because he'd fallen for a simple pack-age of tits and giggles, did not deserve to be handed this gift; and second, that in the world of archeological objects, the armlet, bracelet, ring, or whatever it was, was insignificant, not close to museum-quality, an everyday sort of trinket that would eventually be catalogued by a bored clerk, lumped into a drawer or a box in a storage facility somewhere, and for-gotten about.

I wrapped the object in a bandana, hid it in a zippered pocket inside my knapsack, and said nothing about it when the others awoke and we began the process of striking camp.

Tom and I were both quiet that morning, he presumably due to embarrassment about Clive and Mary's roll in the van — Tom was younger than the rest of us, still in high school. I was preoccupied with thoughts of my hidden treasure and with convincing myself that since artifacts unearthed in archeological excavations are referred to as "finds," the finders-keepers rule can be applied to them.

Clive and Mary acted abashed about their illicit coupling, which they blamed on drunkenness, as if they'd become lovers because they were drunk, rather than gotten drunk so they could become lovers. I was already not caring so much and had my eyes and mind directed toward home. After packing up, we hit the road, drove away from the Blasted Heath, and when Clive dropped me at the train station in York, from where I would proceed to London and a youth hostel and, a few days later, home to Toronto, we were all relieved to part company and say goodbye.

The bronze object was smuggled into Canada without incident and was collected in a shoebox full of souvenirs that I kept of my English sojourn. My journal was placed in there, with a few English coins, some train schedules, my youth hostel passport, an envelope stuffed with black and white photographs, my trusty digging trowel, and, in a square lacquer box, the armlet, as I'd decided to term it, because I liked the sound of the word and the connotations of weaponry and strength it came with.

For all my imagining of the armlet's neglected future without me, it didn't fare much better under my custodianship. The shoebox was moved from my communal student house to my first solo apartment once I began working full-time, then to the two-bedroom I shared for eight years with a boyfriend named Sam, someone I lived with when I was too young to consider marriage but, for reasons that now escape me, thought I wanted to be part of a couple. The shoebox stayed with me when I broke up with Sam and lived alone again, and it was moved to the small house Henry and I shared before we were married.

I didn't gaze upon the armlet again until Henry and I split up. In the course of separating his junk from mine, I came across the shoebox, then some twenty-odd years old, and opened it, and cringed when I read the childish observations I'd kept in the journal of that bittersweet summer. I looked in disbelief at the photos of my slim, young self, hair down to my waist, cigarette in insouciant hand, eyes bigger because the skin around them was tauter. I studied a picture of Clive, Tom, Mary, and me that I'd taken with the camera on timer on our last day at the dig, before the pub night, and, with the objectivity that only years can bring, saw that Mary was wholesomely pretty, that I fell into the interesting-looking category of young womanhood, and that the camera had captured the rogue light in Clive's eyes.

The armlet was still inside the lacquer box, unaffected by two decades of careless storage and basement humidity, and was as dark and crusty as the day I'd picked it up off the ground. The simplicity of its shape, its rustic finish, and its heavy weight all still pleased me, so I brought it upstairs, in its box, and set it on the corner of my desk. I play with the armlet still, sometimes, during long phone calls.

When Jesse asked me about it, I told him the armlet was very old and had a storied history, but I glossed over the finders-keepers aspect in my explanation of how it came to be in my possession. I said I found it in the spoil tip on the last day of the dig and asked and obtained permission from an indifferent Clive to take the worthless piece home. That the piece is of little monetary value is true — I've seen a similar object for sale on an Internet auction site with a price of fifteen English pounds. The part about Clive's indifference was true also. So I didn't lie, or not about anything that mattered.

Thomas Denby of the email must be — is — the same Tom who snored in his tent in North Cave while I fretted in mine that long summer night thirty years ago. I read his email again, pick up the box on my desk, and remove the armlet, hold it in my right palm, lift it, do a few bicep curls with it in my grasp. Tom would no longer be young, and likely not smelly, is probably a respectable and married-with-kids kind of urban planner. I run an Internet search on him, but his name is not sufficiently unique to deliver any meaningful results, and I find no picture.

I spend the next few hours working at my desk, when I'm not looking up and staring into time. Reunions have no appeal for me — I have, in recent years, avoided nostalgic gatherings organized by all of my former elementary school, high school, and graduating university classes. I have no need to revisit the past, but with the armlet in my hand I'm taken back to that summer in England, to the sunny blue and green days, the rolling countryside, the rosy sunsets, the starry night skies.

And to memories of the itchiness of being unwashed, the army of earwigs that invaded the tent, and the way a dinner from the chip shop would coat the inside of my mouth with such pervasive grease that only a gin and tonic or two in the pub afterwards could cut it.

In those days, I ate fish and chips, with pineapple fritters on the side, chased by alcohol and cigarettes, a few times a week, and I didn't gain weight. I also flung my long hair around in an obnoxious fashion, and when I spoke, I tried to attract attention, to amuse, to stand out, and as a result said many regrettable things.

At four o'clock in the afternoon, I compose this reply:

Tom,

I am indeed the Emily Harada who dug alongside you in Earith and North Cave for a few
weeks in 1975, though my memories of that
summer are sketchy (I'm surprised you remem-
bered my name, as I can't recall hardly anyone's).
So much has happened in the intervening years
that that period seems very far away now.

As you've gathered, I'm an architect, living
in Toronto. I don't have much of an appetite
for reunions as a rule, but do say hello to whoever might know me when you go, and I'm
glad to hear you're doing well with the urban
planning and so on.

Cheers,
Emily

Could I be more cold? Yes — I could not answer at all. Will
poor unoffending Tom pick up on the little jabs meant for
Clive and Mary — the bit about not remembering anyone's
names and the implication that my life has been so goddamned
glamourous and action-packed since 1975 that I've forgotten
all about North Cave? Likely not.

The reply is petty, sly, and was fun to compose. Before my
better, wiser instincts can prevail, I send it off, shut down my
computer, and go into the kitchen to cook dinner.

In a commercial break between the hip hop music videos
Jesse watches while he eats, I say, "So I got an email today
from a guy I did archeology with in England thirty years ago.

A guy from the place where I found the armlet that I keep in my office."

His eyes stay on the TV, but he says, "What did he want?"

"To know what I was up to, so he could tell people at a reunion in England."

"What kind of reunion?"

"A reunion of archeologists."

He says, "Remember when you told me that old bracelet thing had magical powers?"

"That old bracelet thing, as you call it, is a genuine Bronze Age artifact. And you were much younger when I told you it had powers."

"I believed in dream catchers in those days, too. I was so gullible."

He scoffs at his own naïveté, but all I remember is how every few nights, for months after Henry left, I woke up at two or three or four a.m. and found ten-year-old Jesse standing by my bedside, looking down at me. "What is it, honey?" I'd say, my mind clouded with its own anxious images.

"I had a bad dream."

I'd take his hand, and walk with him back to his room, and crawl into his double bed with him, and fall back asleep until I woke up an hour or two later, groggy and stiff, underneath the ineffectual dream catchers, surrounded by the dull gleam of the sports trophies on his shelves.

Now, I say, "How do you know the armlet doesn't really have magical powers? Maybe it's the reason I ended up with a lovely son like you."

"Yeah, sure." He turns up the TV volume with the remote. "Hey, this video is sick. You have to watch it."

He's right. The video *is* sick.

~ CHAPTER THREE ~

After I drop Jesse off at Westdale of a morning, I sometimes reward myself for getting him up, fed, out of the house, and to school on time by stopping in at a neighbourhood tea shop called Ruby's. Twinings is available there, the chairs are chintzy and comfy, and the reading material on hand, British tabloid-style magazines, is a fascinating collection of stories about celebrities I've never heard of. Ruby's also has wonderful scones that are baked on-site — not those bumpy things filled with raisins or cranberries but plain, wedge-shaped, floury scones, served warm, with butter.

On this particular Friday, I've finished my scone, wiped butter from my fingertips, and am deep into a photo spread on the eighteenth-century country cottage belonging to a middle-aged woman I'm led to believe is an English television star, when a shadow falls over a picture of her, reclining, in an evening dress, on top of her kitchen counter.

The shadow belongs to Spencer, kid dope dealer, standing next to me with takeout coffee in hand and cocky grin on face. "Hey, Emily," he says. "Come here often?"

His eyes look sleepy under the sideways brim of his baseball cap. Could he be stoned already, at 9:15? Of course he could. I say, "Shouldn't you be in school?"

"I have a first period spare."

I turn a page of the magazine.

He says, "About the other night at the dance — "

"Were you there? I don't recall seeing you."

He grins wider. "Okay, fine. We didn't speak. Nothing happened. And I guess I'll never know if you enjoyed the gift I didn't slip into your pocket."

"There was no gift. I emptied my pockets as soon as I got home and threw all the crap that was in there into the garbage."

He emits an unpleasant yelp that is supposed to indicate merriment. "That's too bad. I hate to see good shit go to waste. But I'm sure you know what's best. Like you did in the girls' washroom. See ya." And he lopes out of the shop, his posture as swaggery as his grin and the angle of his hat brim.

I rub my shoulder, close the magazine, put it back on the rack, and mutter to myself all the way home. I will never chaperone a school function again. Can Spencer be sent away to boarding school, please, right now? And: I'm going to flush those joints down the toilet the minute I get into the house.

But when I walk in the door, my business line is ringing. Calling is my work pal Joe, a builder and real estate speculator who hires me once or twice a year to draw some plans for a redo when he decides (or heritage conservation zoning restrictions decide for him) not to demolish an existing house on a newly acquired property, not to build one of his upscale mock-Georgian manors.

Joe has made a small fortune catering to the desires of the rich and home-conscious, building houses with his and hers dressing rooms and wood-panelled libraries, marble and limestone kitchens, two-sided fireplaces, ground-floor great rooms, and luxurious basements outfitted with home theatres, wine cellars, and spas. But for all his apparent traditionalism (he's my age, was married young to his high school sweetheart, has three kids all older than Jesse, and lives in the far suburbs, in a mansion of his own construction), and unlike other builders and contractors I can name, he's comfortable working with a female architect. He has never made a sexist remark to me. He's never once referred to my Japanese-ness, either, or asked me to put shoji screens into a house. And he gives me work. So I'm always happy to hear from him.

Can I meet him this afternoon, he wants to know, come check out a big old pile of a house for sale in the Annex, a few blocks over from me? He has a new, deep-pocketed client who's thinking about buying it and wants a professional opinion on what could be done to restore and refurbish it and at what approximate cost.

I say yes, we set a time to meet, and I forget all about my aching arm, Spencer, and my resolution to destroy the joints. I'm no visionary, but I can visualize, and I enjoy walking into an old house and trying to see, through the worn carpet and shoddy drywalling and ugly wallpaper and tired drapes, the proud old bones that lie within. When I witness some of the gravity and grace an elderly house can bear, I feel a small spark of the same fire I felt when I visited ancient sites in Europe in my youth. Like when I stood within the Avebury stone circle and was blown about by the centuries of history swirling in the air around me. Or when I crouched down on the ground on the Blasted Heath in Yorkshire thirty years ago and picked up a two-thousand-year-old bronze armlet.

The house where I meet Joe is huge, about forty feet wide, twice as deep, three storeys tall, and adorned with a tall corner turret covered in fishscale shingles. It's the work of a name architect of early Establishment Toronto and boasts the jumble of declarative (now decaying) architectural elements that local historians have dubbed the Annex style: a heavy stone base, Romanesque arches, terracotta embellishments, a red brick upper trimmed with more stone, and a third-floor sleeping porch framed by Ionic columns and turned woodwork.

Someone has clumsily divided the house into odd-sized apartments, now vacant. Kitchens and bathrooms have been wedged into corners and closets, and steel fire doors inserted into hallways, but the house has retained many engaging features — an intact stained glass window still graces the centre hall stair-well, a few original fireplace mantels remain in place, egg and dart ceiling mouldings adorn what was long ago a front parlour.

The real estate agent who admits us parks herself on a stray chair left in a ground-floor apartment and starts making calls on her cell phone, leaving Joe and I to go through the house together. We knock on walls, try to follow floorboards and baseboards from room to room to discern the original layout, lift up corners of broadloom, take some rough measurements, wonder aloud about covered-up back staircases, false walls, and blocked-in chimneys. We venture into the basement and look at pipes and wiring, poke at plaster and note down signs of patching and leaking, take a tour around the outside and examine the brickwork and trim.

We work quietly and thoroughly and quickly, Joe and I, and admire the solidity of the banister and disparage the hack jobs done to install window air conditioners, and an hour after we've arrived, we're ready to deliver a qualified verdict for the client, whose name is Stewart something.

We're standing gingerly on the sleeping porch — its wooden floor is rotting — when Stewart drives up in his expensive sports car. Joe says, "I should warn you: this guy's a bit of a big shot." Below us, an expensively dressed, silver-haired man steps out of the driver's seat, his trench coat flying up behind him, and dashes up the walk to the front door.

My anti-authority sense starts tingling. "He thinks he's King Shit, does he?"

"He acts like he's a player."

"How about if you do most of the talking and I stand there and nod a lot, back you up?"

"Good try, but he wants to hear from an expert, and when it comes to these old houses, that's you."

Stewart is in fighting shape — I can picture him doing his hour a day on an exercise bike, while checking stock prices on a high-end hand-held electronic device — but his face betrays his age, what with the deep lines, the network of spider veins on his cheeks, a nose that appears to be lengthening while we speak. He's around sixty, I'd guess. Ten years and a generation older than me.

He says, "It's a pleasure to meet you. I've seen your work," and mentions a Second Empire showplace I did a few years back for a wealthy woman in Rosedale, a foundation block on which I built my modest reputation. We chat briefly about that house and owner, and Stewart gives me no immediate reason to get my back up, not yet (he does not refer to my ethnicity, for example), but my first impression is that the design of his eyeglasses is too trendy, his dress shirt too white, his jacket lapels too sharply cut, his Italian leather shoes too shiny.

In the house's front hall, I start with a few introductory words about the typical features of the Annex style, and Stewart cuts me off after one sentence. "I'm a little short on time," he says. "Can we get to the specifics, please?" Okay. And strike one.

I lead the way through the ground floor, the real estate agent trailing along behind with Stewart and Joe. I point out what I think the original room layout and finishes were and explain what would have to be done to restore them, with Joe supplying rough estimates for costs along the way. Stewart is the smart sort of rich man — he must have earned his money rather than inherited it — and catches on quickly. He can visualize, too.

When we reach the back of the house and stand near the cramped galley kitchen outfitted for one of the apartments, I say, "The house's original kitchen was not likely located in this area, but that may not be relevant — I'm assuming you'd want a large, modern kitchen that spans the back of the house."

"You should never assume anything," he says, and bares his teeth in what he might have intended as a smile. Strike two, and fuck you, buddy.

My speech about what we could do on the second floor comes out rather clipped, and Joe adds a few sentences to complete my paragraphs. On the third floor, I gesture to the four small rooms lined up along a narrow hallway and say, "These rooms would probably have constituted the servants' quarters when the house was new, and they could easily be converted back to serve the same function again, should you wish to house your staff in an authentic, classist, Dickensian atmosphere where you could deprive them of their civil rights and they could conspire against you. If you have household staff, that is. I wouldn't want to assume."

There's an awkward pause during which Stewart stares me down in an admonitory manner reminiscent of the fish eye I gave Spencer at Ruby's and Joe ahems loudly, possibly in an attempt to communicate that I should stop with the barbed pseudo-jokes. The real estate agent breaks the silence, says, "Or this floor could be made into a group of guest suites with ensuite bathrooms."

I nod. "Quite right. It could be made into anything your heart desires and your bank balance can pay for, I'd say. Joe?"

Joe throws out a range of figures, we talk about knee walls, dormers, and skylights, and I resist the urge to push Stewart through the rotted railings of the sleeping porch and onto the flagstone path three storeys below. If I did, his executive raincoat would no doubt spread out, act like a parachute and break his fall, anyway.

Downstairs, in the front hall, Stewart gives me his best snaky smile and firm handshake, as if he didn't hate me. I've always been inspired by that kind of business-style duplicity. Inspired to run away from any job that requires it or from any client who's good at it. "Thanks so much, Emily," he says. "You've been very helpful."

"You're very welcome," I say. "And best of luck with the house. In the right hands, its former beauty could shine again." In hands other than his, we both know I mean.

"Goodbye, now," he says. And to Joe, "Can I speak to you privately?" The real estate agent says she'll wait outside on the front porch, and I take the hint and let myself out.

Halfway to my car, I realize I've left my tape measure behind, on a radiator just inside the front door. I turn back and mumble to the agent, who's on her phone again, that I've forgotten something. I open the front door, reach inside and grab the tape measure. Stewart and Joe are standing in the hall, on the other side of the frosted glass in the vestibule door, their backs to me, when Stewart says, in a voice magnified by the acoustics of the empty house, "I appreciate the time and advice, and I'll let you know in a few days what I decide."

"It was our pleasure," Joe says, and, my hero, "If you decide to buy the place, I highly recommend Emily Harada as the architect for the job. She really knows these old houses."

"I'm sure she does," Stewart says. I'm letting myself out when he adds, "But she seemed a little hostile. What is she, a lesbian? Or just frustrated?"

I'm mostly at peace with my single state, my ordered existence as the sole adult in my household. If Jesse weren't in my life, I would be more alone, and possibly more lonely, and I will be, I'm sure, when he grows up and moves away to university or wherever life takes him. I'll have to adjust when that day comes, stretch myself out a little thinner to fill my spaces. But Jesse is often out nowadays — rare is the weekend evening when he stays in, and on those nights when the rest of the city moves about in coupledom, I don't feel desperate or sad. I'm content to eat dinner — alone, with a magazine — at my favourite Greek restaurant, a place that caters mainly to extended families or couples on dates. I'm content to sit inside at night, in my armchair, under a good light, in peace and quiet, and read a novel. If I want to watch a movie — in the theatre or on video — I have no desire or need for company to do so. I don't wish for another baby or for a pet.

Sometimes, I wonder about the matrimonial road I no longer travel — when I hear about divorced people remarrying and blending their families or about anyone over forty dating someone new — but I can't imagine expending the effort required to make a relationship work. If Jesse were gone, and if, by a lottery-odds type fluke, I met someone attractive who also found me appealing, and fell in temporary love with him, and we lived together, he would drive me crazy, this mystery man, soon enough.

When I listen to Sylvia complain about Ed or to one of my clients making excuses for her peremptory or inattentive-to-detail husband, I know that if an imaginary future partner of mine didn't exhibit the same deal-breaking habits that Henry had, he'd have others, equally intolerable.

Now that fall is here and darkness comes earlier each day, the spectre of loneliness more often beckons — it hovers in the corners of rooms before I turn on the lights or lurks beside the front walk up to the house, in the flowerbed, where the squirrels have dug up every one of the bulbs I planted in a vain attempt to buy some insurance of cheer for spring.

When I sag, discouraged by the household drudgery, by the certainty that a frayed towel or a broken appliance will not be replaced unless I muster the energy to replace them, that I alone face the never-ending question of what to make for dinner, I remember when I was sixteen and went away for a month to Quebec with a girlfriend to take a summer course in French, for credit. I left a boyfriend behind, a boy I'd gone around with for a year and had lost my virginity to, a boy to whom I wrote long, sucky letters and missed terribly.

I missed him, but when I returned from Quebec, from a month of being independent, irresponsible, and unencumbered, I found his attentions cloying, felt strangled in his presence. His neediness — and he wasn't that needy — sapped my strength, made me crabby and mean. I wanted nothing more than to shake him off, cut him loose, which I did, a bit cruelly. I regret that cruelty now, but I'll never forget how refreshed I felt, how released, by the bracing wave of freedom that washed over me when he was gone, when I needed answer to no one, care for no one. When I was all, blissfully, alone.

I come home cursing from the Stewart meeting but cut short the profanity when I'm hailed on the street by Vera, returning from an afternoon stroll. "I have something for you," she says, goes inside her house, and brings out a small package she took delivery of from the mailman, an obscure hip hop CD Jesse ordered online. I thank her, and she says, "You'll never guess what — I've bought a condo."

"You have? Where?"

It's five blocks north and west, in an older building with a good reputation. It's a cozy two-bedroom, one and a half baths, not all fancy and expensive like the new luxury towers going up nearby. And the deal closes in February, which gives Vera plenty of time to host Christmas dinner for her family, plenty of time to get the house ready for the market. "I'm going to be picky about the buyer," she says. "I've thought of two stipulations so far on the sale: I don't want the house torn down, and I don't want my garden ripped out and replaced with ugly concrete or flagstones, like yours. No offence."

I do not take offence, since the removal of most of the greenery in my front yard (except for the twenty-year-old sapling and the small, weedy heap of earth that is my flower bed) was the work of previous owners, not me. However, I'm dubious about Vera's selling conditions. Her house's vintage — late 1920s — suggests it might warrant restoration, but the design is not a distinctive or harmonious piece of architectural work. A couple of ill-conceived, afterthought dormers mar its rooflines, a clumsy, siding-clad addition has been tacked onto the back, and the spindly porch columns don't match the squared-off lines of the main structure. The interior's no classic waiting to be reclaimed either — the kitchen and baths were last redone in the 1970s. Forget the real estate agent who pursued Vera with the heartwarming story about the couple eager to move into the neighbourhood. Developers and speculators will submit the highest bids once Vera lists the house for sale — people eager to demolish the house and build in its place a stone-veneered, faux chateau monstrosity that would crowd out the small lot. I think this but say only, "This is so sudden. Are you really ready to leave?"

She turns and looks at her house's facade. Does she see the grimy brick, the old sash windows, the peeling paint on the fascia? Or does she see years of her life lived, with children and husband and without, decades of long summers and winters, short springs and falls, come and gone? "If I'm not ready now," she says, "I will be by February."

"I'm not sure I will be."

She winks at me, and I'm pleased to see no tears in her eyes, only mischief. "The real question is: are you ready to take over as the block's official old-timer?"

Such a jokester, that Vera.

I go inside, toss Jesse's package on the hall table, pick up the regular mail from the floor, and find that it contains one semi-interesting piece: the invitation to Leo's award celebration party, requesting the pleasure of my company plus that of a guest. I sit down at my desk, turn on my computer, check the party date on my calendar, and call Danny.

"I've got an invitation to a swanky party to honour Leo Antonelli next week," I say. "You want to be my plus-one?"

I tell him the details and he says he'd love to come and work the room. "All those architects! It'll be great for business."

Now that he's buttered up, I tell him the Stewart story.

"That's crazy," Danny says. "You're not dyke-like at all. Even when you have your workboots and jeans on. Did you have those on?"

"Yes, but we had to go in the basement and attic and crawl spaces and everywhere."

"The guy is undoubtedly the kind of arrogant straight man who thinks the only reason a woman could resist his testosterone emissions is if she's queer."

"I hate him already."

"And anyway, to my mind, you're more like a nun."

"A nun?"

"Or a spinster teacher of a girls' school. Like Maggie Smith in that fabulous movie, *The Prime of Miss Jean Brodie.*"

"You see me as a fascist spinster schoolteacher?"

"Not fascist, but smart, and aside from the occasional shit fit at a ladies' lunch, you're operating on a higher spiritual plane than the rest of us. What with the ascetic life you live and all."

"I'm going to pretend what you've said is comforting." My computer sings the new mail tune, and one of the messages is from Tom Denby.

"Glad to be of service," Danny says, and we hang up, goodbye.

Tom's message says:

Dear Emily,

How good to hear from you. It certainly has
been a long time, but my digging summers
were a highlight of my school years, so I
remember them in great detail. You must recall
that dusty Neolithic site in North Cave that
we worked on for 3-4 days. The Blasted Heath,
Clive christened it. I think it took me a week
of daily baths to wash the sand out. My old pup
tent might have some North Cave dirt in it
still! I'm sorry you can't make the reunion, but
I'll tell people I heard from you. Being an
architect is impressive. Have you designed anything interesting? (I'm joking. Remember how
people always asked us if we'd found anything
interesting when we were digging?)

All the best,
Tom Denby

I smile at his little quip — I understood it before he
explained it. Despite my protestations to the contrary, that summer was also one of *my* life's high points, a memorable period
right up there in the top ten. I reread Tom's message, sift through
it for subtext, find none. He seems pleasant, with no axes to
grind, no grudges to bear — not with me, anyway. I would have
liked him to provide an information update about what has
happened to some of the others, though, to Clive and Mary, for
instance. Is Clive still working in archeology, or is he seducing
graduate students at a university somewhere? Has Mary gained

weight and met her destiny as a ruddy-cheeked, jumper-wearing, tweed-clad, dog-owning mother of four or six, living in the country? I'll never know, I guess, my last email having more or less closed the door on reminiscence and reunion. And maybe I'm better off without making further contact, so no one over there will find out what I've apparently become: a frustrated ascetic with a huge chip on her frozen shoulder.

I decide not to tell Sylvia about the Stewart incident during our next walk. I'm afraid she might not sympathize and might ask how *have* I stood going without sex for so long, and don't I miss it, and what I am doing instead, anyway? I don't want to hear her agree with Stewart that a lack of men in my life is what's making me testy and hostile. Or with Danny's description of me as nunnish.

Anyway, we have other, more interesting topics to cover, like Sylvia's recent assignation with Mr. Sutherland.

I say, "You went out with him on an actual date?"

"It wasn't a date. What happened was that Bunny at the gallery mentioned that the International Authors' Festival was on now, and I realized it was my big opportunity with Steve."

Sylvia is an itinerant bookkeeper, and among her clients is a trendy downtown art gallery that gives her a small amount of cool quotient with which she tries (and fails) to offset the dreariness of keeping the books for Ed's dental practice.

"You know someone named Bunny?"

"Haven't I told you about her? She's the associate director at the gallery. She's young and funny and bawdy and totally up on everything that's artsy in the city. You'd love her."

"Probably not. Don't trust anyone under forty, that's my motto." Especially someone named Bunny.

"So anyway, I happened to drop by Westdale last week, and I happened to run into Steve, and when I did, I asked him if he knew of anyone good reading at the festival, and he said he was definitely going to see such-and-such, the young Scottish writer, so I ran out and bought a ticket for the reading on Sunday afternoon and told Ed the least he could do was watch the kids so I could have some culture in my life."

"And Ed bought that excuse?"

"Of course. So I went down there and listened to an angry young man read a passage about depraved sex and drug use and afterwards I ran into Steve and said, 'Fancy meeting you here!'"

"Was he alone?"

"Yes, why? Who would he be with? What do you know?"

I sidestepped some dog shit on the sidewalk. "Nothing, I know nothing. I just think that if it were me in the situation, if I'd gone to all that trouble, the plan would probably backfire somehow. But you're not me, and I'm glad your plan didn't go awry. At least I think I'm glad. Are you glad?"

"Let me tell you the rest. We go for a drink in a bar that overlooks the lake, and we order frozen daiquiris, and the sun is setting, and the sky's all pink, and the next thing I know, we're making fun of the author reading all these dirty bits with his funny accent, and we're laughing, and my hand's on Steve's shoulder and his hand is on my knee and I say it's getting late, I should get home, and he says — are you ready? — 'We should do this again sometime.'"

"Wow." I can't think of anything else to say. Anything else that isn't snarky, I mean.

"So, remember how Ed is going to that five-day conference in Palm Springs?"

"No, but okay."

"He leaves next Monday, and I plan to see Steve while Ed's away."

I suppose I should be happy for her, support her in her endeavours, no matter how misguided. A good friend wouldn't lecture in this situation, wouldn't say, "So, fie on your marriage vows, is that the idea?"

I say, "And are you excited? No, stupid question. I can see you are. Are you really going to go through with it?"

"I don't know. Will I? Can I? Have I got the nerve? Will it be worth it?"

"But," I say, slowly, "what if — hear me out a second — what if you end up having sex with him? Don't you think the odds are better than good that it won't be enjoyable, that it'll be awkward and unpleasant in some shameful way, so why put yourself through that?"

Shit. I've gone too far, pricked her balloon, done the equivalent of telling her she resembles a fascist schoolteacher. "Maybe you're right," she says, and I regret stomping on her adulterous desires and projecting my risk-averse, spinstery doubts onto her.

She perks up a mere second later, turns hyper once more. "And maybe you're wrong." She sticks out a defiant chin. "I'll have to find out which."

"Okay, then. And good luck, I guess."

She breaks the slightly cool silence that follows. "So will I see you at the basketball game tomorrow?"

"Yes, though Jesse would prefer I not come. Every time I try to find out about the team, he says to stop asking so many questions and what do I care, anyway. Does Ben tell you what's going on?"

"Only that this is an exhibition game, that the team hasn't been set yet, and that there are a couple of new players."

"Playing what position?"

"I have no idea."

Why didn't I know there were new players on the team, why is Jesse clamming up more lately, and what was the significance of my seeing Ben and Jesse together that day at lunch? I asked Jesse about that afterwards, asked why he was with Ben and not with his old friends, and was told to back off. "Tell you what," he said. "From now on, I'll keep you informed on a need-to-know basis."

I say to Sylvia, "Have there been any further developments with Ben and the drinking?"

"None that I've noticed, but then, soccer's over. And he usually stays out overnight at a friend's house on weekends, probably so I won't see him drunk at the end of the night."

Oh, wonderful. Jesse announced this morning that he's going out Thursday after the game — there's a school holiday the next day — to sleep over at his friend Mark's house. But I needn't worry. Assuming Jesse's I-am-an-athlete philosophy still governs his behaviour. Does it? Maybe I do need to worry. I could start right now.

Sylvia says, "I feel like I'm a teenager again."

I don't. "What? Why?"

"Because all I can think about is Steve. If I had a notebook, I'd be writing my name and his in a heart shape on every page."

She says this as if re-experiencing adolescence is enjoyable, but when I looked at those kids in front of the school the other day, all I saw were awkward moments and betrayals and disappointments and foolishness and heartbreak. I have no desire to be a teenager again and hate that poor Jesse is now enduring the agonized state in his turn, but one look at Sylvia's rapt expression tells me to shut my outspoken mouth on the subject, at least this once.

~ CHAPTER FOUR ~

W hen I give my third lecture of the term to Leo's undergrads, they are attentive and laugh at most, if not all, of my jokes — I might have to retire the one with the Joe DiMaggio punchline. They seem to enjoy the slides, to be amused by the silly, pretty Victorian gewgaws and furbelows, impressed with the Second Empire boulevard-styled city houses, and stupefied by Richardsonian Romanesque. So my arm is not throbbing with tension-caused pain when I turn on the lights and ask if there are any questions, though I am doing some performance-induced sweating under my jacket.

A pause ensues, a mass hesitation; the wall of faces is silent. A little more sweat collects in my armpits and seeps into my shirt. The students don't like me after all, aren't interested in these dried-up old houses, why would I think they were? I'm about to wrap up and get out of there when one young woman, what we used to call a strawberry blonde, raises her hand in a manner I hope I'm imagining is aggressive.

"Yes, in the middle there," I say. "Do you have a question?" Can her hair colour possibly be natural? When I was in university, young women didn't dye their hair, with the result that power accrued to those blessed with glorious colour like hers. In my creaky day, people like me, whose natural hair colour was a dishwatery mud-like shade, had no choice but to live out their predestined dishwatery mud-like lives.

"A comment and a question," she says, and at the word *comment*, a slow, quiet throb begins within my shoulder, like the faraway rumble of an oncoming train.

"Go ahead."

"It seems to me," she says, "that the houses you supposedly 'restored'" — she makes the ironic fingers in the air sign for quotation marks — "weren't restored at all. I mean, maybe a new wood floor would be laid in the old style, and you'd recreate some plaster detail on the walls or ceiling, but where's the integrity of the project? The people who lived in the house when it was built a hundred years ago wouldn't recognize it today, what with the monster kitchen and the ten bathrooms and the two-storey addition on the back that overlooks the outdoor water feature, now would they?"

Heads turn, the crowd shifts in their seats. This must be the feisty girl Leo warned me about, the one named after the season. Had better be, because I'm in no mood to face any others as confrontational as this, cannot handle her, am hoping an imaginary class-ending bell will ring. When it doesn't, I say, "The question is: where is the integrity in restoring a house if it isn't restored to its original state?"

"So what's your answer?" the feisty girl says, and now I'm angry.

I could explain that if she wants to see a true-to-period room in a true-to-period house, she can visit some here in the city in what are called museums, and that while people may enjoy glimpsing how our predecessors lived, few want to live that way now, amid those muted colours. I could tell her that when she grows up she'll realize that houses and buildings, like people, are meant to age, to adapt, to attain a patina that speaks of history and lives lived. And I could let her know that one way to describe idealism is as innocence unsullied by experience.

I could tell her that in the nineteenth century, there were lots of pretty brick houses trimmed with graceful gingerbread, but indoor plumbing was limited, racism and sexism were accepted belief systems, and children worked in factories and died young of incurable diseases.

I could give this whippersnapper with the gorgeous hair any number of solid reasons why trying to relive a romantic vision of the past is a fool's game, why being old should not be about trying to recreate youth, because youth can suck, too, doesn't she know that yet? But I say, "Take it from me: Integrity is overrated."

Amid a few surprised titters, and before she can bluster back, I add that we're out of time, thank everyone for listening, and wish them all good luck with their degrees and careers. They clap politely for me and get up and begin to leave, and when the strawberry-haired girl has flounced out with a few theatrical sighs and well-I-never looks, Leo looms up — how much did he hear? — and says, "That was interesting."

I laugh off the incident, claim I wanted to stir things up, set the students thinking, and I half-apologize. I expect Leo to tell me there's nothing to be sorry for, that a little provocation and a real-life perspective are good for the students. He does say that, in his way, but he uses the word *spitfire* again and makes odious comparisons between me and the girl, the Autumn of my dread.

I thank him for the gig, say I'm looking forward to his award party next week, and break away as soon as I can. I walk briskly to my car — I'm in such a hurry, so busy — get in, drive out of the university district, start crying at the first stoplight I come to, and cry all the way home.

My face is puffed up like a blowfish after the crying. My under-eye bags have inflated, the whites of my eyes have become pinks, the eyelids are swollen as if I have sties on each. I try applying cold, wet teabags and cucumber slices, and I lie down with an icepack on my face for about five seconds before I whip it off, convinced I'm getting freezer burn. Two more tears, one from each eye, flow down the sides of my face and land on the pillow.

I look like shit, and I care what I look like because I'm going to Jesse's basketball game and I'm not thrilled about the idea of anyone I'll see knowing I wept like a depressive old woman today. I need to go to the game to find out what's happening with the team, to see if I should take Jesse's silence about it as ominous, if he's getting some minutes, if he's holding his own. And I must go because he phoned me at lunchtime and left a message asking me to bring some specific items of clothing and some money when I come, so that he can go out afterwards. He'll grab dinner somewhere, he said, and see me late the next day, long after the partying and the sleepover.

I could wear sunglasses indoors, the big, black, sixties bug-eye kind, with a white scarf wrapped and tied around my hair. Except that I don't own those items, and I'd look like an idiot if I did wear them, and Jesse would be pissed off that I called attention to myself. To him, it's cause for complaint that I ever show my normal, unswollen face anywhere near the school.

I could claim an allergic reaction to a bee sting or to, wait, what allergen is around right now? Outside, maple leaves litter the back yard. How about leaf mould? There's a passable excuse. Leaf mould it is.

I get to the gym ten minutes early. Various and sundry students are collected in the spectator gallery, taking up too much room with their coats and their backpacks. They tend to hang out for the first quarter or two of a game, pay no attention to the action, kibitz on the sidelines, and leave when they are bored. I nod at a few parents of my acquaintance among the spectators and keep my distance. On the far side of the gallery I see Sylvia, but her head is turned away from me. She's deep in conversation with Mr. Sutherland.

I lean in a dark corner against a post, hope I can hide out here the whole time, talk to no one, make a quick handoff after the game to Jesse of the bag I've brought, and flee.

To the accompaniment of loud hip hop music, the team warms up. Jesse is not leading the drills, which I thought he did last year, when he was captain, or were there several captains last year who alternated leading the warm-ups? That must be right. I mustn't assume the worst, just because I'm a little shaky today. A lot shaky. Sylvia calls my name above the din, waves, beckons me over. Mr. Sutherland has left, and she persists with the beckoning, so I abandon my newly beloved post and weave my way through the noisy, lounging kids and sit down beside her.

She says, "Emily, what happened to your face?" Then, quieter, "Did you have a peel?"

I had not thought to blame my puffball face on a cosmetic procedure, but admitting to extreme youth preservation measures seems no less embarrassing than admitting to a sob session. I say, "It's an allergic reaction to leaf mould. I took an antihistamine but the swelling hasn't gone all the way down yet."

Sylvia appears to fall for this explanation. "Are you feeling okay?" When I nod, she says, "It's not that noticeable." This kind lie makes me wonder if her belief in my leaf mould allergy is also bogus, but I'm not going to press her and find out. I say, "How'd your conversation with Mr. Sutherland go?"

"You saw me talking to him?" Her face is the picture of guilty pleasure. She leans toward me and whispers, "We're meeting for a drink next Tuesday night." She hugs herself, and she looks so euphoric, so spun around by romance, or lust, or a flattering amount of male attention, or a combination of the above, that I hasten to change the subject. I've never liked to view large emotions close up. "So which are the new players, do you know?"

She points out first a tall kid, six-four at least, therefore a forward, probably, and no competition for Jesse, who is a point guard. Next she indicates a black kid, maybe five-seven, who looks quick and keen in the warm-ups and who, at that height, would likely want to play Jesse's position. I ask his name. It's Akeem.

The buzzer sounds to signal that the game should start, and the team collects in a huddle. Jesse stands on the outer edge of it, head turned inside but eyes on the floor. Anytime I've asked him afterwards what the coach said in these situations, he's said, "I don't know," or "I wasn't listening." Which could just be another way of telling me to back off and leave him alone. The huddle breaks up, the starting five walk onto the gym floor, and I heave a secret sigh of relief because Jesse is starting. So is the Akeem kid, but I can handle that.

What I have more trouble handling is that Jesse is benched halfway through the first quarter. When he sits out the rest of the first half, is not put on for a minute, dismay rises within me like water inside a blocked toilet. He starts and plays most of the third quarter but sits out the fourth, bringing his total playing time to less than fifty percent of the game. Compared to last year's eighty percent.

Around me, the parent spectators (the kids are all gone) stand up and say what a good game that was — Westdale won, damn it — and I try to contort my still hot, tight-skinned, angry/sad face into a bland expression of general contentment with, I'm sure, minimal success. Sylvia is no help — she's chatting with another parent, not at all bothered that Ben played fewer minutes than Jesse. I hear her say, "Ben's really a soccer player. He's happy just to be on the team." And the new kid Akeem, by the way, played more than Jesse, much more.

I take Jesse's bag of clothes and go wait near the locker room door for him to come out. When the coach walks by me, I nod, but I'm seething inside. I also have no idea what to say to Jesse when he appears. My instinct is to hug him and say, "My poor honey. What happened?" but since when — take my morning in Leo's classroom, for instance — do my instincts serve me well?

Jesse comes out of the locker room at last — the sixth or seventh player to do so — his face carefully blank. Wordlessly, we walk out to the parking lot to do the bag exchange. We pass some teammates and parents on their way out, someone says, "Good game, Jesse," and he mumbles a thanks. At the car, he drops his backpack inside the trunk and says, "Have you been crying?"

"No, my allergies are acting up. I was putting some leaves in bags to be left at the curb" — great, now I'll have to do this before he comes home tomorrow — "and I was overcome with this huge eye-watering and sneezing fit and I had to come inside and take a pill, but my eyes got all puffy anyway."

"Uh-huh."

Phew. "What'd you think of your game?"

"I got no playing time. And I played like shit."

"No, you didn't. You played well. You took those two charges. You hit that three-point shot."

His shakes his head. As in thanks for trying, but you know nothing, so stop embarrassing us both by pretending that you do. "See you later."

"Where are you going for dinner? What will you eat?"

"Don't worry. I'll find something. I'll call you tomorrow morning. Or by noon, anyway."

"Have fun. And don't stay out too late. Or do anything crazy."

One side of his mouth curls up slightly. "Who, me?"

He goes back into the school, and I put my twin aches — one in my maternal heart and one in my frozen shoulder — into the car and take them home.

I was equally as dismissive, or more so, with my own parents when I was Jesse's age. They had me late — at my birth, my mother was forty and my father fifty-one — so to my teenage eyes they were nothing but old. That they were both artists — my mother did finely detailed pen-and-ink drawings of obscure subjects like an insect's-eye view of blades of grass — with distracted, lost-in-their-art temperaments, didn't help me relate to them any better.

I picture them staring at me in gentle bewilderment when I was an infant, without the faintest idea what to do and with their fingers and minds itching to get back to their work. But in their absent-minded fashion, they raised me well enough — when I was little, they clothed me, fed me, and sent me off to school, and they made sure I was put to bed before they dined at nine, often with their bohemian artist friends, at the big old wooden kitchen table adorned with empty Chianti bottles used as candelabra.

Once I reached the age of fifteen, they became hands-off parents. They knew nothing about my social activities, set no curfews, allowed me to smoke cigarettes in the house, offered me wine with dinner (I refused to drink with them, would only do so behind their backs). They didn't care about my dope smoking or that I was having sex with my sixteen-year-old boyfriend. They often slept late after staying up all hours in their creative fervours and relied on me to get myself up in the mornings, fix my own breakfast, get to school on time, do my homework, keep track of my life.

When I started graduate school, they announced that they were selling the house and retiring to Vancouver Island, where a balmier clime and an active artists' community awaited them. I eventually realized they'd wanted to go for years, had waited for me to get settled until it was almost too late. They died out there, not many years after, my father at age eighty-two, suddenly, of a stroke, and my mother at age seventy-three, of colon cancer, with me at her side during her awful final weeks.

They never saw Jesse, never saw me staring at my own infant in my own bewilderment, and they didn't live long enough to see that though I am in some ways permissive, in most others I do not emulate their parenting technique. I did not make my child walk to and from school from grade one onwards, no matter what the weather, or the books, projects, and sporting equipment to be carried. I did not leave him alone in the evenings to amuse himself at age eight while I tooled around in my studio with the door closed. I know the names of his friends and what nefarious activities they're up to.

Jesse was not and is not the centre of my existence, but he's the reason I get out of bed every day whether I'm sick or well, optimistic or discouraged, the reason I cook balanced dinners instead of subsisting on random pleasing foods like cauliflower cheese one night, tomato sandwiches the next, the reason I schedule my work appointments during his school hours whenever possible, the reason I know anything at all (though not much, Henry is more learned than me) about basketball and rap music, both subjects I would happily be ignorant of if I were childless.

My needs get satisfied after Jesse's, not before, and I'm at peace with my parenting philosophy, secure in it, always have been, until recently, until Jesse's unwillingness to admit me into his current life has started to overcome any affection or bond he feels for me. Now, as I drive home from the game, I consider, for the first time, a revisionist take on my childhood: that maybe my parents were wiser than I am, for not needing their child, for living their adult lives at a remove, for following their own stars.

Tonight was not the night to go to one of my favourite restaurants and read an architecture journal alone at a table while young people made lively conversation around me. Tonight may not have been the night to order in vast quantities of Indian food either, but I did, and now sit, stuffed and grossed out, at my kitchen table, surrounded by the meal's detritus.

I watched a cooking show on television while I ate, and I intend to make, soon — maybe for lunch tomorrow — the comforting-seeming recipe for creamed mushrooms with shallots and Marsala that was featured, but what to do now? How can I pass the rest of the evening, until a reasonable bedtime? (Six-thirty, the current time, does not seem reasonable.) Jesse's basketball laundry needs to be removed from the washer and hung to dry. That ought to be exciting. I could do that, and tidy up the dinner mess, and see if there's any mindless movie — nothing disturbing or upsetting — on television to watch while I do my arm exercises. If I had some energy, I could do some paperwork in my office, but no, I don't think so.

I'm clearing the table when I remember the dusty green vase on the high shelf with Spencer's gift to me hidden inside it. The gift of anesthesia.

I carry over the stepstool, bring down the vase, pull out the package, unwrap the joints, hold one between two fingers, roll it back and forth. I place it on the table, put the stepstool away, and call Jesse on his cell phone.

"Just checking in," I say. "Where are you?"

"At Mark's house." I hear raucous laughter and yelling in the background, and Jesse yells at someone to shut up, then says, "Sorry. What?"

"Did you eat?"

"Yeah. Takeout sushi."

"Are you still hungry?"

"I'm fine."

"What are you guys doing tonight?"

"We're going to hang here for a while, maybe go out, I don't know."

"Okay, love you. Be good. Be careful."

The background noise has started up again. Over it, he yells, "Later," and clicks off.

My plan is to smoke a joint. I'll lower the blinds, dim the lights, and find an ashtray — I might have one in the basement, a leftover from years gone by, from when I smoked two packs a day. I'll look for it, and I'll set myself up in a comfy chair with a joint, and I won't care for a few hours about my depressing stage of life — about my advanced age, emotional instability, and increasing irrelevance.

About a year ago I had some invasive dental work done that I was assured was necessary unless I wanted to eat on one side of my mouth for the rest of my life. I seriously considered the chewing-only-on-the-right approach for weeks but ended up paying the thousands of dollars required to get the problem fixed. Far too many hours of downtime later, one of the memorable things I took home from the procedure — other than a new empathy for road surfaces under jackhammers — was the oral surgeon's explanation, in his overview of painkilling alternatives, of the effect of nitrous oxide: "If I give you that," he said, "you'll still feel some pain, but you'll be high, so you won't care."

I signed up instead for the multiple needles in the mouth freezing process, the complete numbing down of the entire area, and said, to the various friends and acquaintances I may have bored on the subject, "Can you believe that? Who'd want to be in pain and stoned at the same time?"

I grasp the concept now, though, and it seems like an excellent idea.

I go down to the basement and root around in my storage boxes for a big glass ashtray that was once my constant companion. It's in the second box that I check, but the first contains videos and photo albums of Jesse's early years that I haven't looked at in ages. A selection of those comes upstairs with the ashtray.

For all his pseudo-intellectual affectations — tweed jackets, moleskin notebooks, wire-rimmed glasses — Henry could never cope with smoking materials, couldn't strike a match to light a candle, let alone a joint or a pipe. When we were together, I operated and programmed the VCR, and I handled all fires. I use both these skill sets now — I pop the cassette into the machine, settle into my chair with the applicable remotes in hand, and masterfully light up the joint.

Less masterfully, I cough and splutter at my first intake of smoke since before Jesse was born. The taste is raw and harsh in my throat, and my puffy eyes squeeze shut in protest when the smoke comes near. After a few healing breaths I try again, take in a bit less this time, feel it flow through more easily.

On the TV screen, Jesse is a gurgling infant of about four months old, lying on his changing table. Henry is playing with him, repeating idiotic phrases in a high voice. "Who's the baby?" he says, "Who's the baby?" I'm wielding the camera from over Henry's shoulder, zooming in on Jesse's chubby cheeks and blissed-out smile, recording his blurpy chuckles. "Who's the baby?" Henry says again, and I can be heard, normal-voiced, issuing instructions: move back and to the side, play hide-and-seek, see if you can make him laugh again. I'm the boss/director of the family, in other words. But Jesse is adorable.

The joint has burned halfway down and may have begun to take effect. The sound from the video is magnified, echoey, like it's coming at me from a great distance, unless the old tape is screwed up. I take another toke. The smoke isn't harsh anymore but smooth as it goes down, almost cool in my throat.

Ten minutes later, I've put out the joint, am struggling to keep the hallucinatory sights, sounds, and sensations churning on the edge of my consciousness at bay, and am staring, slack-jawed, at the television. On the screen, I am ice-skating around an outdoor rink — ice-skating! — carrying a snowsuit-clad Jesse in my arms. This was the first time we had him on bobskates, at age two, about six months after his celiac disease was diagnosed, so he looks healthy and thriving, has lost the malnourished look he had when the gluten in his diet damaged his intestinal lining and made him develop a distended belly like you'd see on a starving Third World child.

He is already stouter and stronger here, and he wears a woollen cap that Henry's mother knitted for him, a funny thing that exposes his face but covers his ears and has a pompon on top that makes him look like the letter *i*, especially with his eyebrows raised in excitement at the *whoosh*, the speed at which we're moving. Henry is doing the videotaping for a change and makes encouraging noises when we pass by, as if he were an involved and loving father, which he was for maybe an hour a day when he still lived with us and still is for a weekend each quarter and a week each at Christmas, in March, and during the summer.

At one point, Henry ineptly zooms the camera in on my face before moving its focus to Jesse, to his lovely cold-flushed cheeks. I tsk at this because it's Jesse I want to see, Jesse the sweet, cuddly, uncomplicated toddler who sat in my lap and asked me to read him his favourite book, the one about trucks.

But when the camera pans close to my face for a few moments — to my thirty-seven-year-old, exhausted-by-

THE RESTORATION OF EMILY

motherhood face — I look almost pretty. My eyes are brighter, my face less block-shaped. Could it be that I once possessed some small bit of beauty, nothing head-turning or ship-launching, but enough to merit a second look?

I rewind the tape, watch the two-second zoom again. Oh, right. Or wrong. That wasn't prettiness I saw, that faint glimmer of something — it was youth.

I'm not a good sleeper, never have been. It takes me forever to fall, the smallest noise — a car door opening and closing on the street, Jesse sleep-talking in his room down the hall — wakes me up, and I'm often troubled by bad dreams, dreams that intensify in anxiety if I try to sleep late in the mornings. That's why I rise at six.

But on the night I smoke Spencer's weed, there is no slow, agonized descent into unconsciousness — I pass out like a drunken frat boy. After the videotape ended, I crawled upstairs, laughed at the sight of my destroyed face in the bathroom mirror, brushed my teeth, and fell into bed.

So far am I under that the bedside phone rings four times and goes over to answering before it wakes me. It begins again while I struggle to open my eyes, peer at the clock — it's 12:42 a.m. — and reach for the receiver, too late. Was it Jesse? I sit up, turn on the hurtful way-too-bright lamp, and check the call display. It *was* Jesse, on his cell. The phone rings again. I pick up. "Jesse?" My voice is froggy. I clear my throat. "Are you all right?"

There's noise in the background again, but not as loud as the last time.

"I'm fine," he says. "Why didn't you answer before?"

"I was asleep. Why are you calling?"

"I know this is crazy, but could you come pick me up?"

"Of course. Where are you?"

"Mark's house."

"Are you okay? Is something wrong?"

"I'm fine. Come."

"I'll be there in twenty minutes."

Mark's house is only a ten-minute drive away, but I need to shake off some sleep before I go, and I think I'm still a bit high, and shit, the living room probably reeks of pot. I stand up, pause to see if any yellow submarines are floating around in the sky of my mental landscape — no, hurray — and run downstairs to remove all signs of illegal drug consumption. The roach is flushed down the toilet. The two leftover joints go back in the green vase. I wash and dry the ashtray and return it to the memorabilia box in the basement. The entire first floor gets sprayed with air freshener. I run back to the upstairs bathroom, spritz some perfume on my hair, wash my hands with lots of soap. When I'm finally ready to go, I pop into my mouth two pieces of the extra-strong peppermint gum that Jesse favours, throw a coat over my pajamas, and run out to the car.

I see the first knot of prowling teenagers two blocks away from my house. There are five of them, including a couple of girls in short skirts. Within the group, one boy and girl hold hands. All they appear to be doing is walking outdoors late at night, but I regard them with suspicion anyway. Same for the four boys standing on a street corner a few blocks on, one of them with a cell phone to his ear, another holding a lit cigarette.

By the time I arrive at Mark's house, I've passed six groups of wandering teens. I understand why they'd rather be on the street than home in bed — I do remember, vaguely, my own urges at that age to go out, to do something/anything, to make a/the scene — but I can't relate a whit, not anymore. Or can I? I flash on an image from a dream — a pleasant image from a pleasant dream — I must have been having when Jesse's call woke me, and I blush. The image was a corny romantic one of me kissing a boyishly handsome forty-year-old movie star who's on all the magazine covers at the supermarket right now.

What stupidity. The pot must be to blame, and anyway, the moment has passed. I'm tired and cold and shivery and all I want to do is to bring Jesse home, creep back into my bed, sleep all night and half the next day.

"You smell like perfume," Jesse says, when he gets in the car. Like me, he's chewing gum, which could be a sign he has consumed something he shouldn't. Or that he likes to chew gum.

"What happened? Why didn't you stay over at Mark's?"

"It was boring there. We watched a movie and played some video games and the next movie they wanted to watch was horror, and I hate those."

I'm sorry he didn't have more fun, and relieved that his friends' idea of thrill-seeking is to watch a scary movie rather than to do hash on hot knives in the kitchen then walk on railroad bridges as if they were balance beams, but I wish he hadn't gotten me out of bed and the soundest sleep I've had in years because he was bored.

He says, "Sorry I woke you up and made you come get me, but the movie was really creepy and gross and I didn't want to sleep over."

Guilt weighs down on me for denying him anything but full support, even in my mind. "It's okay. You can always call me if you're in an awkward or bad situation, you know that. And you know how much I enjoy driving around in the middle of the night, checking out the packs of roaming teenagers."

He turns on the car stereo, puts on his station. "I love you, Em."

The car is warm now. I pat his knee, and over the sound of his music, I say, "Me too, honey. Now turn that down."

~ CHAPTER FIVE ~

Leo's party is being held at a lakefront house he designed in the sixties for a swinging fashion designer who furnished it with swinging sixties furniture and used it to hold legendary parties, complete with go-go dancers, martinis, and the wearing of Pucci prints. The house, built into the erosion-prone bluffs that overlook the beach at a time when zoning regulations still allowed building there, has a flat roof, floor-to-ceiling panoramic windows on its two sprawling floors, and a zigzaggy, asymmetrical footprint of the sort that I find wearying. About ten years ago, a rich art gallery owner purchased the house, had it meticulously restored to its former questionable glory, filled it with her collection of modern art, and now uses it to lavishly entertain for only the best causes and the richest patrons, which is why I've never been invited before, have only read about the house and seen pictures of it in shelter magazines. But it makes a perfect venue for the party.

At six, I give Jesse his dinner, tell him to do his homework and that I should be home by nine, and I drive over to Cabbagetown to pick up Danny. Danny says he's looking forward to seeing the party house though he's not a fan of the period, relates an amusing if catty story about Eames chairs and one of his current clients, and does not comment on my choice of wardrobe for the occasion until we pull up to the house and I hand my keys over to a parking valet.

When I smooth down my black jacket over my black pants, Danny says, "You look crisp," which I take to mean like a schoolmarm, but little does Danny know that I eschewed my usual starched white cotton shirt (I don't want to get confused with the wait staff I presume will be at the party) and opted for a light blue sweater under the jacket instead, which, for me, is like wearing something frilly. Plus I'm sporting a necklace of small silver and pale blue agate beads that is not at all chunky or architectural in design but borders on the delicate.

Five minutes later, we have greeted, kissed, and congratulated Leo, who, with his wife, is doing reception line duty in the house's slate-floored, teak-panelled foyer. We've been given a glass of champagne each by a white-and-black-clad waiter and shaken hands with the art gallery owner, a thin, unsmiling woman wearing a sleeveless black cocktail dress and pearls, circa Audrey Hepburn in *Breakfast at Tiffany's*. Upon hearing my name, she professed to be pleased to meet me and said that one of my father's sculptures was featured in her garden, a dramatically lit Japanese-y space viewable through the picture windows. "Really?" I said, "How nice," and drank half my champagne.

On our descent down the open staircase into the main level of the house, we pass an Andy Warhol lithograph and Danny whispers, "Do you think there'll be marijuana and LSD passed around later, or am I thinking of the wrong part of the decade?"

I smile at his joke as if I haven't smoked some reefer myself lately.

The throng already chatting and drinking below us is lively and numerous and contains several people I know. I stop and chat with a guy from my year at architecture school whom I didn't recognize at first, having taken him for an older man, due to his full head of white hair. Also present is one of my former clients, an arts patron who laughs loud and lives large and must have been invited because of her bold-face status in the society pages. She wears me out in about five minutes. When she's moved off to laugh loudly elsewhere, I look around for Danny, spot him across the room talking to a good-looking interior designer who has his own television show on cable, and am wondering where I can get another drink, non-alcoholic this time, when someone behind me taps me on the shoulder.

I turn around and face Nils Grayson, a former student of Leo's.

He says, "Hey, Ms. Harada. I thought it was you. You look the same."

This is unlikely, since when I lectured to Nils's class, I was a mere child of forty-four, my skin was tauter, and so was his. He must be what? twenty-nine now, or thereabouts, and he doesn't look the same as he did six years ago. Forgive me for noticing, but he looks older. Not worse, but older.

"Hi, Nils. Call me Emily. How are you?"

In incredulous tones, he says, "You remember my name?"

Thankful that he doesn't know why I remember him, I ask what he's up to now, is he employed in the field, where is he working.

In the deep voice I remember him having, he says he's working for a large developer that builds suburban subdivisions. Prompted by my questions, he explains the company structure (he's low on the ladder but trying to work his way up), describes the models they build, and tells me the names of the developments, which are all generic and unknown to me.

I keep him talking about his own, more adventurous architectural ideas beyond the subdivisions, ideas he one day hopes to see realized, and I paste an attentive expression on my face, check him out from behind it. His hair is longer, and it suits him. His hazel-coloured eyes still scrunch up and disappear between his dark eyelashes when he smiles. The shirt and jacket he is wearing are of a fashionable if cheaply executed cut that does not flatter his slightly soft physique.

He says, "What about you? Are you still restoring old houses? Still guest-lecturing in Professor Antonelli's class?"

"Yeah," I say, "I'm the same." Except for having divorced Henry, and my child having turned into a teenager, and my body and soul disintegrating like old masonry. "Good to see you, again, Nils." I lift my empty glass. "I need a drink."

"Me, too," he says, and points to the far end of the large room. "The bar's that way."

He places his hand lightly on my back to steer me in the right direction, and through my sweater and jacket, I can feel the heat of his palm. His face is sweating, too — there are minuscule beads of moisture at his temples and on his forehead, and though the room is crowded, I am as cool as the pale blue of my sweater, and glad I wore it, and the agate beads, too.

Nils and I are separated at the bar. After I've been handed my mixed orange and cranberry juice, an architect of my acquaintance says hello and asks whatever happened with a job we both quoted on, do I know? I talk to him, face the room, and watch Nils, drink replenished, move through the crowd and stop to speak to a young woman his age who could be his date, or a former fellow student, or someone influential with whom he should network like he just did with me. To my chagrin, the slight thrill I felt while in Nils's company departs with him. Sweaty and soft or not, it seems that he still exerts some power over me.

~ ★ ~

At the end of my first lecture in Leo's class that year, Nils came up to me, shook my hand, said something like, "I enjoyed the lecture. That High Victorian Gothic brick work is great," smiled, and walked out. I thought no more of him.

The next week, Leo gave me a thirty-second tutorial on a new high-tech touch-screen lectern that had been installed in the classroom and left me alone with the class. When I had difficulty with the equipment, Nils jumped up from the front row to help me, pressed the correct button, and lowered the screen I had mistakenly raised in mid-talk. He smiled again when all was fixed, and this time I thought I saw a flash of — and this sounds so hackneyed and *Death in Venice*-y, but I can find no better word — beauty in his face. He is not typically handsome, and his hair was short and wiry then, spiked upwards in an unfortunate style of the time. Plus there was some paunchiness to his body, a lack of definition around the chin. But something about his physical presence jolted me — not sexually, but aesthetically. His smile gave me a pleasure akin to what I feel when looking at a lovely painting or a verdant landscape or a beautifully proportioned house.

Throughout the rest of that day, while I performed my pro-saic tasks — buying groceries, visiting a renovation site, watching then-eight-year-old Jesse play house league softball at the park, feeding him dinner, and helping him with his homework (Henry was out somewhere, as usual) — I was suffused with a force that didn't feel like lust or sexual attraction but which I could not otherwise identify. In the week that followed, I honed a keen desire to see Nils again, to talk to him. I constructed a strange, limited fantasy that consisted of looking into his eyes and then … nothing. Did I want to kiss him? I thought not. Nor sleep with him. I wanted to stare at him more than anything else. I would have liked to watch him and be unseen, to sit in the booth next to his in a restaurant and spy on him from behind a fern.

I arrived early for my third and final class of that term, was happy to see he had too, and sought him out as soon as I'd dropped my things on the desk at the front of the room and brushed off Leo's greeting on the pretext of needing Nils to review with me the visual aids system.

He was then about twenty-three, young enough to be my son without having to factor in a teenage pregnancy. He had to stand close to me to demonstrate the equipment, and I could have easily touched him — in a friendly way — but I didn't, thank some shred of sanity that still ruled my actions.

I was all too conscious of his gaze upon me during my lecture (only natural for a student to look at the teacher who's speaking, but I was incapable of any sensible explanations for his behaviour or my own) and took care not to glance his way more than once or twice.

My custom is to end my last lecture of a series by putting up a random set of slides I haven't shown before and asking the students to identify the architectural style by calling it out. To my satisfaction, Nils was the first to blurt out the style of more than a few of the ten or twelve slides in question, and I allowed myself to banter with him, publicly and briefly, when he did.

He was friendly but not flirtatious, and I, I can only hope, was the same, and did not betray that the image of his face had occupied my thoughts to an alarming extent in the previous week, that I had become a stalker in mind, if not in deed.

The class ended, and Nils stood up with the rest, said good-bye, and walked away, out of my life.

One day soon after, I said to Sylvia, "It's funny, but there was one young guy in the class I taught who — That is, just the sight of him — and he wasn't very good-looking — I don't know. I found him quite mesmerizing."

Sylvia said, "Youth is so sexy, isn't it? So much sexier than our middle-aged husbands."

What? No. My fascination with Nils, my desire to look at him, wasn't about sex. What I felt was not what Sylvia would later refer to as fairy lust but something less tawdry. And not some sort of sick youth worship, either, I hoped.

The memory of Nils's smile faded more quickly than I expected. Two weeks after I'd seen him for the last time, I had difficulty bringing his face to mind. I was relieved to forget about him, to be freed of a preoccupation that was wrong on a number of levels: because I was married then, because he was so much younger than me, and because I've always despised old men who covet much younger women, so what did my adulation of Nils make me? Worthy of self-loathing.

The saving grace of my short-lived Nils obsession was that I hadn't acted on my desires, had gone temporarily insane only in thought. I had not, for instance, followed through on the terrible idea that came to me late one night that I could ask Leo if the helpful young man in his class might be interested in some part-time office work, because I could use a clerical assistant to manage my files for a few hours a week.

I was proud of my restraint then, and I'm happy now that while I may not be fully resistant to Nils's magnetic charge or whatever pull it is that he still exerts on me, I made the first move to end the conversation a few minutes ago, and I will soon leave the party without speaking to him again or manufacturing one more moment of contact. I'm a pillar of strength, I am.

Leo has been presented with his award and made a gracious if too long speech, the crowd has thinned, and I've exhausted the interesting conversational opportunities, am ready to go home, take off the clothes that bind, nag Jesse about his homework, and cut up some fruit for his bedtime snack. I spot Danny by the wall of windows, give him a head signal to meet me at the foot of the stairs, and wend my way over there.

Nils looms up in my path. "Emily, Emily, Emily," he says. "You going already?" He's still sweating, is more flushed, and, judging from the slight swaying of body and slurring of words, is drunk.

His drink — Scotch, it looks like — is sloshing around in his glass. I grab it and hold it steady for a second, though it will only slosh again as soon as I let go. "Yup," I say. "It's time."

"Wait a minute. Don't go yet. I want to tell you something."

I'm not generally amused by drunkenness — I don't drink enough myself for that — but my past fascination with Nils places him, for a moment, on the very narrow appealing side of the drunk behaviour spectrum, so I stop moving away and say, "What's that, Nils?"

He gulps for air before speaking. Any minute now, he'll hiccup and complete the cliché. "Did you know," he says, "that I used to have a major, and I mean major, crush on you?"

The background music — Frank Sinatra from his grey-haired toupee-wearing period — that I have not heard a note of all evening, did not realize until now was playing, starts to wah-wah in and out of my ears, like the television volume the night I was home alone and stoned.

"You were so cool," he said. "And cute and smart and accomplished. I guess it was a typical student crush on a teacher, but the fact that you and Antonelli had clearly crossed that barrier in the past made you all the more attractive."

I splutter, "What do you mean, Leo and I had crossed that barrier?" Indignation over the idea that I was ever romantically involved with Leo, my surrogate father figure, is warring with the shock engendered by the news that Nils had a crush on me.

He leans in close and breathes his hot, boozy breath on my face. "You're not still sleeping with him, are you?"

I am so repulsed by the idea that I step back. "No, I'm not, and never was, and now I'm leaving." I turn on my heel and give him the cold, nay, frozen, shoulder, but he follows me, drink sloshing, tongue wagging.

"You're not? You weren't? Are you sure?"

"Good night, Nils."

He shakes his head in sad, drunken wonderment. "I was so certain you were an item, or had been, back in the day."

We have arrived at the bottom of the staircase, where Danny leans against the steel railing. "Ready to go?" he says.

I nod and try to make the grand gesture, sweep up the stairs away and out, but Nils wrecks it by yelling after me, so the whole room can hear, "I'm sorry, Emily. So sorry."

Outside, Danny says, "What was that about?"

I tell him Nils was drunk, and made an off-colour remark about me and Leo, and apologized for doing so, then I ask Danny how he liked the party. He fills the car with chatter all the way back to his house — he may have talked his way into a guest appearance on the decorating TV show — and I devote the precious few private solitary minutes that remain of my drive, after I've dropped him off, acting like a lovesick teenager, recalling Nils's words, one by one, and allowing myself to speculate whether, if he liked me once, he might like me still.

Jesse's dinner things are in the sink, and he's up in his room, at his computer, music blaring, instant messaging windows chiming and opening. When I appear in his doorway, he covers the screen with his hand but does not ask me to leave, so I remove some clothes from a chair, turn it so I cannot see the screen, and sit down, ask him how he's doing.

"Fine." He reduces the volume of his music to a level that's still too loud for me.

"Did you do your homework?"

"Yes."

"Anyone call?"

"No. Don't you love this song?" He re-ups the volume and I listen to a marble-mouthed rapper speaking over a jazzy, tuneless music track. I don't love it, but I shrug and say it's okay.

"Tell me something," he says. "Is there any music you've liked since the Beatles?"

There most certainly is. At his age, I was known to jump about, a dancing fool, to songs by Creem and Blood, Sweat and Tears and the Rolling Stones, all of whom Jesse would probably deem too rocky and mainstream for his taste. Later, in my twenties, the decade I spent learning that "anything's possible if you work hard" was a big lie, I listened to Joni Mitchell. And, I say now, "I liked Bonnie Raitt." I liked songs about self-destructive women who chose the wrong men and made mistakes — nice, upbeat, sad, cautionary tales of that type.

"Who the fuck is Bonnie Raitt?"

A messaging window chimes. He looks at the screen, makes a quiet laughing sound, and types something. He types very fast. He may have a future in typing.

I say, "You didn't ask me how the party was tonight."

He looks at me for the first time. "What party?"

"The party for Leo, remember?" I grab from his bookshelf a dusty old stuffed animal, a little dog, and throw it at him. The last time I tried to sort and organize his belongings, he insisted we keep it.

He catches the dog and throws it back at me. "So how was it? Did you drink cocktails and chat with people?"

"Yeah. And listened to some Frank Sinatra." And became re-obsessed with Nils, I fear.

"Sounds like a real blast."

Nils is much less jailbaitish, now that he's almost thirty. Though the twenty-one-year gap in our ages still exists and always will. Unless I can convince myself that I'm as old as I feel, which right now is pretty near jailbait age myself.

Jesse carries on multiple online conversations while I sit by, in my daze. "I have a basketball game tomorrow," he says. "Do you know where my uniform is?"

"In your drawer." I get up, pull out his jersey and shorts, lay them on his bed.

He laughs again, at something said on the screen, something more interesting and entertaining than me.

"How have practices been going? Will you get more playing time at this game, do you think?"

He covers the screen with his hand. "Any way I could have some privacy here?'

I go downstairs, tidy up the kitchen, turn off the lights. Before I shut down my computer for the night, I look up the company name of Nils's employer, which is the pedestrian Belvista Homes. I search through the company's dull website about its dull subdivisions and find no mention or picture of Nils or any other architects on it (the site's purpose is to sell houses, what do you know). Not that I expected to find one, or don't already regret looking.

The next morning, around nine-thirty, I'm home, working at my desk before I head out to meet Sylvia for our Wednesday walk, when my business line rings. The call display screen shows the unforgettable because it's so forgettable name of Belvista Homes. From where who but Nils could be calling?

I flex my fingers — once, twice — and let it ring. I squeeze together my shoulder blades a few times (one of the exercises I should be doing thrice daily) and stare at the message light on the phone for the too many seconds that pass until it illuminates. The moment it does, I lift the receiver and dial the retrieval sequence.

"Hey, Emily," Nils's deep voice says. "I wanted to apologize if I acted like a jerk last night. I was a bit drunk on all that free liquor, and anyway, I was an ass. So, I'm sorry."

Is that it? After a pause the length of which would have me saying, "Hello? Are you still there?" if this conversation were live, he says, "Maybe I could make it up to you, take you out for lunch sometime, and have a normal, adult conversation? If you like. Call me. And forgive me." Click.

I exhale the breath I've held since I began playing the message and play it again. And once more, before I save it, wrap up its content, tuck it inside one of my mind's pockets, and go to meet Sylvia.

Sylvia comes out of her house looking how she looks when she's mad at Ed. Past triggers for this glum facial expression have included the way he drinks a beer (a *glug-glug* sound is involved, I believe, and a pouring action down his throat), and his insistence on asking her where she keeps the sugar. "He can't seem to say, 'Where's the sugar,'" she told me once, "or 'Where do *we* keep the sugar.' No, it has to be 'Where do *you* keep the sugar,' like it's understood that my role in life is household manager and cupboard stocker and his role is big-buck-earning lord of the manor, and I can't fucking well take it anymore."

I don't mind hearing people complain about their loved ones — I'm comforted by any confirmation that I am not the only easily detonated explosive device in the neighbourhood. In anticipation of some juicy complaints, I give her a "How are you?" opening, and she says, "Not good."

"Is it the kids?"

No.

"Is Ed still away, and is he okay?"

Impatient nods, yes and yes.

I take a break from mentally fondling Nils's phone message to remember that last night was the night of her illicit rendezvous. "And how did your date with Mr. Sutherland go?"

She shakes her head. "Not well."

You see? I say to myself. Clandestine meetings with younger men, pretentious, hairy ones or not, are doomed to failure. Listen and learn. "Tell me what happened. From the beginning."

The beginning of her story is that he suggested they meet at eight, at an uptown pub near his gym.

"He works out?"

"Of course he does. How do you think he keeps in such great shape?"

I let this one go, and don't comment about the tackiness of the pub, either, which is one in a chain all called The Fox and the Wolf. Beyond tasteless.

"It wasn't the most romantic of settings," she says.

"Though I could think of worse places. Like a laundromat, or a donut shop, or a fast food restaurant, or a bowling alley — any of those would be really depressing." If I do meet Nils for lunch — that's such a big if I should express it in the subjunctive. Were I to meet Nils, it would be somewhere classier. I'll make sure.

She says, "But after a few tequila sunrises, the red brocade wallpaper and the red pleather in the booth started to look quite rosy."

I imagine Nils and me, side by side, in a red booth, tipsy, leaning towards each other, and bumping body parts, like shoulders — though that would hurt. Forearms, then, and thighs, and knees. Oh dear. "So who made the first move?"

They stayed in the pub for a few hours, Sylvia says, and had four or five drinks. (This makes me think of that Dorothy Parker quote about how after three martinis she's under the table, and after four under the host, but sensing that this is not the time for comic verse, I spare Sylvia a recital.)

They nuzzled in the booth for a while, then left so they could continue nuzzling in the darker and more private, er, street. (Sylvia had left her car at home, had travelled to the pub by taxi. Mr. Sutherland, presumably, had his gym bag full of sweaty clothes with him, which would have added to the evening's ripe atmosphere.) They stumbled outside, found an alleyway, leaned up against an oft-pissed-upon brick wall, bits of restaurant and bar garbage strewn underfoot, and began to neck and grope in earnest.

"Make no mistake," she says. "I found all this quite exciting."

A sentiment I actually understand, since, apart from the piss-scented setting, I no longer find her attraction to being romanced so unfathomable. Except for the Mr. Sutherland part.

She goes on. Between necking bouts, he whispered that his bachelor pad was within walking distance of the alleyway and suggested they repair there. When they arrived at his not luxurious (no doorman) but not shabby (freshly painted exterior) high-rise building, they took the elevator up to his floor, entered his apartment, and he kissed her again in his tiny foyer, up against the wall.

We are halfway along our usual walk route when she gets to this point in the story. "That was when I realized that, drunk or not, I couldn't go through with it."

What the fuck? "Why not?" If she'd come this far, endured and enjoyed the jolly pub, the overconsumption of alcohol, the sloppy necking, and the obstacle course walk to his apartment, why stop now?

"Because the apartment was a poky little one-bedroom like the one Ed lived in when he was at dentistry school."

"So?"

"So I started thinking about Ed and everything we've been through, and the kids, and how we talk about moving south when he retires, and how could I ever consider giving all that up for one or two nights of cheap sex in a bed made up with cotton blend sheets?"

I feel like I'm the one with a case of blue balls here, now that I've come around to her way of thinking on this fling business, but I struggle to be supportive. "And probably the towels were threadbare and the shower curtain mouldy, and there were dirty clothes piled on the floor."

She stops walking. "You don't get it — I didn't not sleep with him because of his housekeeping."

"I know." I do. "You didn't go ahead because the payoff wasn't worth the risk."

"And because sleeping with him would be wrong."

As would me seeing Nils. "You're right. Someone our age should not have a relationship with a younger man."

"That's not it at all. I don't give a rat's ass that Steve's younger than me — we're both consenting adults. It would be wrong because I'm married, and I should only have sex with my husband." As if speaking to someone slow of mind, she says, "I'm not single like you, Emily."

She has a point. If Sylvia wants to trade off Ed's boorish beer-drinking habits and insensitively worded questions about the location of household staples for companionship and the promise of golden years to come in Arizona, that's her choice. And if I want to go out for an innocent, friendly lunch with a young colleague, that appears to be mine.

I've made a lunch date with Nils for next Friday, at Bar Sorrento on College Street. When he suggested that location on the phone, I almost confessed that I frequented the joint in my

THE RESTORATION OF EMILY

university days, when it was a mere restaurant, before it became a hip, trendy spot in the nineties, which, is it, still? But I stopped short of admitting I knew it from *before he was born*, and said only, "Sure, sounds good."

"Then how about we meet there at one o'clock that Friday? I'll be the idiot at the bar with my foot in my mouth."

I attempted an amused chuckle, which came out sounding like a nervous laugh. When I found my tongue in the confusion, I said, "Let's agree right now to forget the past, pretend it never happened." Also to forget how much more of a past I have than he does.

"Pretend what never happened?" he said.

My chuckle was more convincing on the second try.

"It'll be good to see you," he said, and I came back with the lame and businesslike, "I'll look forward to it," hung up, smote myself on the forehead, and wrote the time and place of the meeting in my datebook.

An hour after the call, to disperse the nervous energy coursing through my bloodstream, I take a trip to the supermarket, a destination that can be relied upon to deaden the soul and spirit and slow down the circulation, especially when such items as milk, paper towel, and laundry detergent are on the shopping list. At around two o'clock, I return home, begin to unload the groceries from my car, and hear a faint but insistent tapping noise. The street is unusually quiet — no leaf blowers are roaring, or garbage trucks rumbling by, or work crews cutting flagstones, which is why I can hear the noise at all. I pause in mid–bag hoist. What is that? There's a Morse code–like feel to its rhythm. A woodpecker? No, there are no birds on the tree branches above me, and anyway, the sound is muffled, isn't magnified through the outdoor air like a woodpecker's pecking would be.

I give up, take out the last two bags, and close the trunk, but when I turn to go inside, the tapping speeds up, takes on a frantic rhythm. I look around me, the full 360 degrees, and when my gaze sweeps by Vera's house, the tapping stops a second, then renews with vigour. I stop and peer. Is that a movement I see through one of the sidelights that flank Vera's front door? I set down my grocery bags and start across the street. When, halfway there, my short-sighted eyes focus in on a dark shape through the glass that appears to be Vera, sitting on the floor and waving something at me that might be a furled umbrella, I break into a trot, run up her walk, press my nose to the window, and call through it. "Vera? What's going on? Was that you tapping?"

She uses the umbrella tip to open the brass mail slot and I bend down, talk through it. "Are you all right?"

"No." She sounds quavery and weak, nothing like herself. "I've fallen down and hurt myself. Can you get my key and come in and help me?"

"I'll be right back." I sprint across the street and into my house and retrieve Vera's key from the ceramic key holder (Jesse's day camp handiwork from long ago) that hangs on a wall in my front hall. Another sprint takes me back to Vera's, where I insert the key in the lock. Vera is sitting on the floor of the tiny vestibule, on her bum, legs bent in front of her, feet close to the door. "Hold on a second," she says when I open the door an inch, "I have to move back." And with great effort and face contortions, she pushes on the floor with her hands and works herself backwards far enough that the door can swing open to admit me.

I slip inside, crouch down on the floor beside her. "Are you okay? What happens if you try to get up?"

"It hurts horribly is what happens. I think I've broken my hip." She's crying, silently, tears flowing down her face. I smell piss, and there's dried blood on her forearm, also a large bruise.

Wait a second. Dried blood? I take her hand and hold it. "When did this happen? How long have you been on the floor?"

She lets loose one big sob, but only one. "Since the mail came at ten o'clock this morning. I heard it drop through the slot, I came to get it, and I slipped somehow, in the hall, and fell down. I couldn't get up or reach the phone and it took me half an hour to push myself into the vestibule, and I've been here, tapping on the glass whenever anyone walked by, for hours. I thought no one would ever hear me. Thank god you did, Emily."

She's been here, alone, stranded, injured, immobile, for four hours, and if I didn't work at home, if I hadn't gone out to buy groceries, if the usual sources of noise hadn't happened to be silent, she might have sat here all day and night.

I'm still holding her hand, which feels withered and boneless. Also cold. "You feel cold. Are you cold? Let me get you a blanket." I release her hand, pick up a knitted afghan draped on her living room couch, wrap it around her, and rub her shoulders through it. "I think I should call an ambulance and get some paramedics to come and find a way to transport you to the hospital safely and get that hip looked at. What do you think?"

"An ambulance is so dramatic."

"I know, but I don't think we should risk moving you without help. Can I get you some water? Let me get you some water."

When I come back with a glass from the kitchen, she seems a little calmer, but the tears are still running. She takes a sip of water and gives out a big, shuddery sigh. "Alice will be angry. She's always telling me I do too much and need to slow down. She doesn't understand why I'm still in this house, with all the stairs. The house that she grew up in!"

Alice is Vera's fiftysomething married daughter who lives in Boston and comes to visit once or twice a year. The last time she was in town, she told me she'd been trying to convince Vera to move to Boston and live with her, but Vera wouldn't hear of it.

"Alice won't be angry, she'll be concerned. I'll get in touch with her as soon as we know what's what, but right now I think we should get you to the hospital." I go into her kitchen and pick up her cordless phone. "And the stairs had nothing to do with your fall. It could have happened to anyone, anywhere." It could have happened to me.

"What a mess I'm in," Vera says. "A mess of urine and blood and having to depend on my saintly neighbour for help."

I dial zero and wait for an answer. "Yeah, that's me. Saint Emily, protector of fallen women."

"If only fallen were all I am. If only I weren't also so bloody old."

"Oh great, it's an automated answering system. Forget that. I'm dialling 911."

"I'll tell you one thing," she says. "I'm not moving into any nursing home because of this, for sure not. Do you hear me, Emily?"

I hear her. I also hear some bells tolling, and I think they're for the both of us.

~ CHAPTER SIX ~

I accompanied Vera to the hospital and stayed with her for several hours, long enough to find out that she *had* broken her hip, needed to be put in traction, and was scheduled for surgery in the next day or two. When I called Alice, she said, "I knew this was going to happen," and mobilized the family troops. I was free to go home when an adult niece of Vera's showed up to take my place as hospital companion, though Vera protested that no one need stay with her, what did we think she'd broken, her hip or her brain? Alice would arrive by plane the next day and take over all things Vera-related.

Before going to the hospital, I had the wit to pick up the groceries from my front yard, take them inside, and leave Jesse a note and some instructions for heating up leftovers. When I call him on my way home at seven o'clock, he assures me all is well — he has eaten and did not burn the house down. And he inquires after Vera, a small act of selflessness that surprises me.

I give him an extra long hug when I get home, he suffers my embrace, and I defrost some minestrone soup, make that my dinner. After I've eaten, I sit down at my desk, check for emails and messages, find nothing of any consequence, glance at my open datebook, flip it back a page to this week, and stare unseeingly for a few moments at the space for today's date, on which I have written the words "J's report card." When my mental fog is penetrated by the meaning of the notation, I jog upstairs and into Jesse's room (the door is open). He sits at his desk, computer chiming and music blasting as usual. I say, "How was school today?"

"Okay."

"Were you given anything to bring home to me? Like your report card?"

He reaches slowly for his backpack. "You're not going to like it."

"Why didn't you show it to me as soon as I came home? Were you hoping I'd forget about it?" Like I almost did.

"I figured you had more important things to worry about." He gropes around inside the bag. "And you know how you always say that academic achievement is overrated and getting good marks is about learning how to work the system?"

I sit down on the foot of his bed. "How bad is it?"

He withdraws a large envelope and holds it close to his chest. "Here's the good news: I passed every course."

"Good. Now turn down that music."

I take the envelope from him, scan the blue sheets inside. I left my reading glasses downstairs on my desk, so I have to squint, but the bottom line is clear enough. "Your average is sixty-six percent?" Jesse has been, until now, with little effort, more of a seventy-eight/eighty type of student.

He squirms a little, but he's still instant messaging while we talk.

"It's all bullshit," he says, his back to me.

"How? Why?"

"I can explain everything."

"Okay, shut down that messaging screen and go ahead. Explain."

He goes through the report course by course. The history teacher hates him because once at the beginning of term another kid spilled a coffee all over the floor and Jesse got blamed when he had nothing to do with it, though he did laugh, loudly, when it happened. In math, he blew the big test because he was sick the day the test was announced and didn't know to study. A student teacher marked the science group project and was such a hard marker, it was nuts. And so on.

When he's finished his litany, I say, "You've got to learn to manage people better, Jesse, give them what they want. And you should know by now that it's not a good idea to laugh at the obnoxious acts of others." I'm one to talk about how to ingratiate instead of irritate, but let him wait until he's a bit older before he follows in my footsteps and alienates the world.

"I've got it all under control, Em. And this report doesn't really count, anyway. It's an interim one. My next report card, at the end of first term, will be better."

Yeah, and I'll mellow with age instead of turning vinegary.

"What about this seventy percent in phys. ed.? What's the story there? Didn't you have ninety in gym last year?"

"The new teacher, Mr. Dawson, doesn't like me because I don't run over like a little bitch at the end of the period to help put the balls and equipment away."

"Like a what?"

"Little bitch."

"That's what I thought you said."

"This guy Sean in my class? You should see how he sucks up to Dawson. Guess what he got in gym? Ninety-eight."

"Isn't Mr. Dawson also the basketball coach?"

"Yeah, so?"

I hate being a parent at report card time. Hate it. The prospect of talking to any of the teachers whom Jesse has angered, of having to hear them say that he talks too much, or has a lippy attitude, or is a smartass, is horrible, especially without the cushioning that higher marks have provided in the past. A report card like this obligates me to run that gauntlet, to take multiple doses of shit on Jesse's behalf, to swear that he's really a good kid, and to promise to talk to him, nag him, crack the whip at home. That's what mothers are for: to defend their children and to be their falsehood-spouting press agents and spin doctors.

"What about the parent-teacher interviews? When are they?"

"Next Monday. You're supposed to book the interviews online through the school website." Jesse extracts an information sheet about this from the envelope and hands it to me.

I am trying to decipher the woodenly worded instructions — Jesse has returned to the computer, is fiddling with his music files — when he says, "Heard from Dad lately?"

This is an odd question, since Henry and I communicate only when arranging Jesse's trips to visit him and only by email. I haven't laid eyes on the man, or heard his voice, since he moved out. Our post-divorce relationship is not acrimonious, we just don't talk much, or ever. "No. Why?"

"He said he might come up for the parent-teacher interviews. He arranged for the school to email him my report card."

What is Jesse saying? Is this the type of joke he makes that pisses off his teachers? If so, I'm starting to see him from their point of view because he's certainly incensed me — I've gone from zero to angry in less than ten seconds. "Why would Henry do that?"

Jesse shrugs and puts up his hands like he does in a basketball game when the ball goes out of bounds and he wants the referee to fault the other team. "I don't know. Ask him."

Now I'm furious. At Jesse for screwing up at school, and at Henry for choosing this term, this year, to get involved, when he has not attended a parent-teacher interview in Jesse's entire life. I say, through gritted teeth, "Do your homework," and I go downstairs. I sit at my desk, and pick up the old bronze armlet, and think about throwing it across the room and through the glass transom above the front door. Only, knowing my athletic abilities, I'd miss. I place it back on the desk, turn on my computer, and draft a terse email to Henry that asks, in only slightly more polite words than these, what the fuck is going on.

Henry's reply comes the next day:

> Emily,
>
> I should have written sooner to tell you that I was concerned by Jesse's demeanour during his recent visit. He was much less talkative, and less engaged by everything here — his half-brothers, the city, what used to be his favourite foods. The only things that excited him were the rap CDs he bought in an underground music store.
>
> Do you think that Westdale offers a sufficiently stimulating program and learning environment for him? I gave him some excellent books — including some sports-related non-fiction — but he seems to have lost interest in reading. Since returning home, he's also become uncommunicative about his basketball team. Is he still playing? What's happening there? Might he be depressed?

I had his report card emailed to me by the school, and was not encouraged by his results. (64% in English? My god.) If you don't mind, I would like to come up and join you for the parent-teacher interviews Jesse tells me are scheduled for next Monday. (It happens that an actor that I would like to have the magazine profile is in Toronto for the next two months shooting a movie, so I could see him while I'm in town, and also see Jesse, of course.)

Regards,
Henry

My first impulse on reading this is to tell Henry to shut up, to cut the implicit criticism of my parenting and mind his own affairs, of which Jesse has been, until now, not much of a part. An hour or two of fuming later, I remember the words of a wise divorced woman I once met who told me she couldn't ever truly hate her ex, because he was also the father of her children and the only person in the world who could feel the love for and pride in them that she did.

I write back that yes, Jesse has been moodier lately, but doesn't seem to be depressed, and that the basketball situation is a little dodgy, but he played a few more minutes at his last basketball game than at the first. I say that I believe — after consultation with Sylvia, who told me Ben's report card was no picnic either, though Ben's seventy-four percent is less worrisome than Jesse's sixty-six — that Jesse is being normally adolescently difficult, not more so. But if Henry wants to come up for the interviews (and combine them with his star-fucking, you–call–that–journalism? courting of the actor), sure thing, the more the merrier.

It's about time Henry did some of the talking during the interviews, some of the defending. And his own mild celebrity might melt away some of the teachers' animosity. Or deflect it to him. Either way, having Henry at my side would be better than facing the teachers alone.

Within the next few days, Henry's impending visit is settled, the teacher appointments are booked, and some worry about Jesse is abated when he shows me a math quiz on which he scored eighty-three percent — "See?" he says. "I told you I have school under control." I also hear from Alice that Vera's surgery was successful and complication-free, though Vera will have to recuperate in a rehabilitation facility for the next six weeks. "The hospital staff told me she's pretty indomitable," Alice says. "As if didn't already know that."

So now I can concentrate on not anticipating the lunch with Nils.

I tell myself that Nils and I are two professionals in the same field having a friendly meal, two colleagues comparing notes on life and architecture. That's all we are, because no man his age would consider me a dating candidate. The schoolboy crush he admitted to having was only that, and over now, and to think otherwise reveals me to be pathetic, a sad, blowsy divorcee in search of a gigolo.

We'll have lunch as colleagues and I'll be my normal edged-with-bitterness-and-bile self. I'll resist the temptation to imper-sonate my client Suzanne — to make myself likable by acting sweet, smiling, and interested, and by speaking in a high voice. I couldn't pull off an act like that for more than about an hour with-out exploding from phoniness, anyway. So I'll be myself instead, age spots and all. Yes, I've shown regressive tendencies lately, with the dope smoking and the mental replaying of unimportant con-versations and insignificant phone messages, but I still know my way around the deep end of the pool, the old end, where I belong.

On the drive downtown on the Friday, my neck feels stiff and my shoulder is aching. I move my head around and work my deltoids a few times, try to loosen up. I turn on the car stereo, am annoyed by the perky tone of the announcer, and switch over to whichever of Jesse's CDs is in the car stereo. I scroll through the tracks until I hear an opening riff that strikes my fancy, the riff of a hit tune recorded by a gangster rapper that Jesse once liked but has since written off as a sellout. The lyrics are vainglorious and empty, but there's no denying the song has a catchy hook. I turn it up and bob my head, bop along, my bad shoulder throbbing in an offbeat counterpoint.

I find a parking spot close to Bar Sorrento, and I ace the parking job to get into it, though I've developed an aversion to parallel parking, am convinced that the probability of nicking a car — my own or someone else's — is increasing exponentially with every kilometre I drive. All is going well until I discover that Bar Sorrento is not located where it used to be. In its place is a restaurant called Mondo Nuovo, mostly empty, and decorated very Jetsons. A young woman in a midriff-baring top and a six-inch-long miniskirt — dressed like the teenage girls at Westdale, only legal — greets me, and I ask if she knows where Bar Sorrento is. She gives no indication of knowing it was once in this location but directs me a half-block west. I back out and walk ten stores over to the new Bar Sorrento, which is much sleeker and more wood-panelled and glassy than it used to be and is half-full of clients who could not pass for high school students. They're adults, ranging in age from late twenties to late fifties, dressed casually — some with an eye to looking arty, some with an eye only for function. They might be artists or artisans or film crew people on a lunch break. Or shopkeepers or university lecturers. I'm not totally out of place.

My arrival was timed so that I would walk in three minutes after the appointed hour — neither eagerly early nor inconsiderately late — but the location mix-up has cost me two minutes and sped up my pulse. I bite down on the last remnant of the mint I popped into my mouth in the car and spot Nils sitting at the bar as promised, wearing a fugly (a mondo nuovo word I learned from Jesse that means fucking ugly) purple shirt and black pants. A full bottle of beer is in front of him.

I head over, apologize for being late, and don't explain why. He stands when I come close, reaches for me, and kisses me on both cheeks. I am so busy trying to interpret this unexpected gesture that I do not kiss back but press my weathered cheeks in turn against his smooth ones and pick up the scent of cologne. What am I doing here with this stranger? Having a harmless lunch with an acquaintance, remember? So stop acting so bloody fraught, why don't I? I will.

I order my cranberry and orange juice blend, we discuss moving to a table, decide to stay at the bar, look at the menu. I have preselected my meal from the restaurant's website, with a mind to eating gracefully (no sandwiches that have to be lifted with hands) and not trapping any food in my teeth (no salads). I'll have the tortellini alla panna, please, without a starter. Nils orders a sausage and spinach pizza, his "usual," my concerns being none of his. The pretty young female bartender who takes our order, a punky babe with dark hair streaked platinum blonde, seems to know him. When she's gone, he says, "So can I apologize again for acting up the other night?"

"You can, if you promise it's for the last time. And if I can change the subject. Do you come here often?"

He tells me that he is a semi-regular, that he lives in a duplex apartment in a more rundown, less fashionable neighbourhood farther west and south. He smiles somewhere in there, and I raise my glass to drink from it and use it to hide my stunned reaction at his transformation from an ordinary slacker-type guy into a breathtaking beauty. I glance around to see if anyone else — the bartender or the other customers — is equally bedazzled, but no mouths are hanging open in awe anywhere around me. They must all be blind.

"What about you?" he says. "Do you live downtown?"

I tell him about my semi-detached house in the Annex and mention my fourteen-year-old son, because, since this is not a date, I have no reason to hide his existence. Nils asks me what period the house is from (it's an undistinguished Victorian, built in 1888), and if I restored it (some), which leads to me mentioning that I heard this morning I was hired to work on a large mansion-scale house owned by a mogul named Stewart whatever.

Nils has heard of Stewart. "Congratulations," he says. "That'll look good on your resume."

I say nothing, but he quickly realizes he has mistaken me for being his age, at his career stage. His save: "What I mean is, he should be happy to have someone with your expertise on board."

"Actually, I was surprised to hear he wanted me on the job. We didn't hit it off too well the one time we met — he thought I was too blunt and I thought he was a prick." There I am — the real me, tagged in to replace the lovelorn ninny apparently lurking within, the one made woozy by the sight of Nils's smile.

"But I like your bluntness. I liked how when you lectured us in Antonelli's class, you didn't bullshit us, and you joked around and swore and stuff."

I swore (and stuff?) in class? I must have forgotten myself, fallen back on the speech patterns I learned in middle school and never grew out of.

"You were so much more accessible than most of the architecture professors. So down-to-earth. Why do you think I developed that crush on you?"

My accessibility, my bluntness, and my jokes have not often been admired or appreciated, and all of the above are

loving the long-overdue attention, which they and I understand full well is platonic, since the crush is being referred
to in the past tense, where it lived and died. I say, "I figure
you were temporarily deranged by the insane workload of
graduate school."

He looks down for a second, and his long curly eyelashes
sweep the unlined skin beneath his eyes, and — he's gorgeous.
And also not, depending on the lighting, and the beholder,
though this beholder under this lighting sure finds him lovely to
look at. In the same way I'd look at Michelangelo's *David* — a
beautiful and inanimate stone object.

He says, "Maybe I was a little deranged. I built up an
elaborate fantasy about working with you on a project out in
the country somewhere — an old stone farmhouse — and
bonding over the rebuilding of the root cellar."

"That's sweet," I say. It is. And surprising, since I have
been led to believe by contemporary media accounts that
young straight men fantasize about three-ways, dominatrices,
and heterosexual sodomy. "But have you ever worked on a
farmhouse? Rodents are a factor, on an epic scale. And septic
tanks. And broken-down outbuildings. And small-town
workmen who have no respect for female architects who
can't swing a hammer."

"You mean you're not handy? Good. I'm less intimidated
now. I can drink my beer." He takes a long swig, and I watch
him in profile. Like I might study, with the same dispassionate
curiosity, the profile of a marble statue.

Nils says, "I'm not handy, either. My friends are always
wanting me to fix things for them, and I'm like, Hey guys,
you're lucky I can cook."

"You cook?" How has no young hussy grabbed this
guy already?

"My specialties are spaghetti bolognese and chicken curry."

Oh. He cooks and eats student food. Like many people his age, I'm sure. And I'm not distressed or disappointed to know this. Works of art don't cook, either.

"So farmhouses are bad news, are they?" he says. "What's good, then? Will you enjoy working on that new project for this Stewart guy?"

"Enjoy? Doubtful." It's been a long time since I enjoyed my work. "On the contrary, I'll probably develop an intense hatred for the client and have several shit-flinging arguments with him before the job's complete."

"Why do it, then?"

"For the money — so I can pay the mortgage and support myself and Jesse. But it won't be all hard going. I like the contractor on the job — we work well together. And if I'm lucky, I'll get to spend some time alone in the house and take a moment to let some of its aura sink in, to absorb some of its history."

While I said this last bit, Nils regarded me intently like he'd done in class — as if I were intelligent, interesting and thought-provoking. What a courteous young man he is.

He says, "Do you ever wish you lived in another era?"

Huh? "No. I can think of a few time periods I'd like to visit, though. I'd like to swing by ancient Rome, for instance, and see the Forum in its heyday. And Bath, in England, in the early 1800s, might be nice. In springtime."

The bartender places a rolled-up napkin containing cutlery in front of each of us, and I stop myself from reaching over to unfurl Nils's napkin and place it on his lap, like I would for Jesse. "What about you? Where would you go in time if you could?"

"The nineteen-thirties would be worth a trip, to see all the art deco and Bauhaus. And I could get into the sixties."

The sixties? He must have been born — let me do the calculation — in the late seventies, so it makes sense that the sixties would seem far away to him. As far as the forties seem to me. The roadblock here being that the sixties decade basically framed the years of my cognizant childhood, my ages six to sixteen. I could mention that now, act like a boring know-it-all oldster reminiscing about Bob Dylan and psychedelia when they were young, or, here's an idea: I could forget about the age difference and ask him why the sixties. "Why the sixties?"

He smiles, a self-effacing one that still knocks me out. "Because men weren't expected to have abs of steel and biceps like boulders then. You could hide a lot under the boxy jackets and the long hair."

He has body image problems? I'll add endearingly humble to courteous. "But everything old comes back again," I say. "The boys at my son's school are growing their hair long, and it looks good on them." I pretend to notice his hairstyle for the first time. "It looks good on you, too." Fucking hell. What am I doing? That last bit sounded like I was testing the attraction waters, and is there anything worse than someone not on your romantic or sexual interest radar acting interested? If Stewart, for instance, commented favourably on *my* hair, I would recoil in horror. To distract Nils from my misstep, I say, "Maybe boxy jackets will come back in fashion next."

"Here's hoping," he says, and drinks some more beer.

The bartender places a steaming dish before me. "You ordered the tortellini?"

I tuck my napkin into my shirt collar and accept the offer of pepper and extra Parmesan grated on top — that would be lovely, thank you. It's two hours past my usual lunchtime and my appetite is huge, hunger panging in my stomach.

The bartender says to Nils, "You should tuck your napkin in, too, so you don't stain that groovy shirt you're wearing." She leans over and stuffs the napkin inside the neck of his shirt in such a way that her black-painted fingernails graze the skin over his clavicles, and Nils and I both get a good look inside her tank top, at the rounded tops of her breasts in a low-cut, bright blue bra.

Nils blushes and thanks her, she strolls down to the other end of the bar to talk to a customer sitting there, and I can think of nothing to say about her offhanded gesture that won't sound like I'm in envy of her youth and sexual power. A power I never thought I had, or never knowingly exercised if I did.

"In case you're wondering," Nils says, "Amy flirts like that with all the men here. It's part of her job."

"Uh-huh."

"She wouldn't waste her time on me for real; women like that never do." He looks down the bar, at the man Amy is talking to. "See that guy? He's a writer, a novelist. Have you heard of him?" He mentions a name that sounds vaguely familiar. "For years, he's been writing novels and stories about the whole downtown hipster scene. He comes in here to eat once or twice a week, and she's all over him. She hopes he'll write her into one of his books."

I sneak a glance at the novelist, who is lean of build, and dressed with some style, and boyish of face, but has seen forty, is losing his hair. "How do you know all this?"

"She told me the last time I was here. It was a slow day, she was bored, the writer wasn't here, she confided." He lifts up a piece of pizza with two hands. "When I'm not drunk and insulting those I like and respect, I bring that out in people — the confiding."

"Maybe you should moonlight as a psychologist."

"Since I don't have the talent to make it as an architect?"

"I didn't mean that at all. I have no idea how talented you are. And talent is overrated as a component of success, anyway, beyond a certain competency level."

"You think so?"

"In my experience, success is ninety percent bullshit schmoozing. That's why I scrape by with my small client list and small market niche instead of working at a big firm. I have no schmoozing abilities."

He smiles again, and his smiling eyes and eyelashes in combination — fuck the comparison with Michelangelo's *David* — have completely infatuated me.

"I don't know about that," he says. "You're doing a good job of winning me over."

And you me, Nils. And you me.

When I was in grade seven, my phys. ed. class did a unit on co-ed square dancing, during which a male teacher borrowed from the industrial arts department stood on a chair and called out the steps — allemand right, allemand left, and so on — to the accompaniment of a scratchy old LP of fiddle music, spun on a portable record player in a boxy turquoise-coloured case.

Dance, with its even meter and measured steps, appealed to me much more than any arrhythmic sports involving balls and team spirit. I took to square dancing and was chosen to be in a group of kids who would perform a number at a school concert type event, in front of parents. It happened that, for the performance, I was paired up with a cool boy, the kind who went to the necking parties I'd heard the more socially advanced girls discussing in the locker room. But by mutual unspoken agreement, I exchanged not a single word with the cool kid — during rehearsal, performance, or ever after.

I call up this quaint, time capsule–flavoured memory not as an example of my failure to make successful boy-girl connections but because when, over coffee at the Bar Sorrento, two hours into our lunch, after I've relaxed into a state that's almost playful, Nils asks me if I've ever square danced, an image of the grade seven me — skinny, shiny-haired, dressed in a white blouse, plaid pleated skirt, and white knee socks, and twirling — comes to mind.

I say, "You mean square dancing as in swing-your-partner?" He can't mean that, must be referring to some newer activity that uses the same name in a postmodern ironic sense. Maybe he's talking about squares, dancing. Or dancing in a square that's painted on the floor, while wearing a pocket square. Anything but the all-but-lost ritual now only practised by retired couples in pique-trimmed skirts with crinolines (women) and cowboy shirts (men) at fall fairs, on stages decorated with pumpkins.

He says, "Yeah, that kind. Some of the alternative clubs downtown are having square dance nights now. Have you ever done it?"

"So long ago that I can't remember what do-si-do means."

"It's when you do a box step to switch positions with your partner." He demonstrates by walking his fingers around on the surface of the bar in a dorky but sweet way.

"I see I'm talking to an aficionado."

"Not really. I only know the basics. But it's kind of cool to go with some friends and do the antithesis of the usual dance floor posturing, indulge in some low art. You should come out with us sometime."

I want to do the turn around and look behind me move. I settle for pointing at my chest and saying, "Me?"

"Yeah, you. How about next weekend? A club called Hell, on Dovercourt, is doing a square dance night next Friday. Want to come?"

I heard him right. Nils is asking me to go to Hell with him. Why he isn't bored with me already I don't know. I also don't know if he's proposing a group social outing or an actual couple date. But unlike Sylvia, and according to Sylvia, I have no good reason not to jump into a handbasket with him and head on down. So I say, "Sure," and — wait for it — "Hell sounds like fun."

~ CHAPTER SEVEN ~

Henry and I met some sixteen years ago, when he was working on a magazine piece about the restoration of an Edwardian building complex in the west end of the city. I was a lowly member of the project team, only on the job because the architectural firm I worked for had won the contract through its political connections. But on the day that Henry came to the office to interview the boss, his subject was out, said boss being too important to keep his appointments. The receptionist, with whom I was friendly, thought Henry looked like my type and suggested he talk to me instead.

Unschooled about how to handle the press, I spoke frankly to him, listed what I saw as the many compromises being made to the original character of the building — a former mental hospital being converted to office space, condos, and retail — and thereby attracted Henry's attention, armchair crusader and closet firebrand that he was. A less canny journalist might have made hay with my unguarded comments, but Henry didn't use my risible quotes directly. Instead, he turned them into challenging questions that he asked the boss when they finally did meet, and impressed him with what seemed like his in-depth preparation for the interview. Then he asked me out.

I had divested myself of a long-time live-in boyfriend about a year before, and I told Henry on our first date that I was looking to get married and have a baby — I was thirty-three at the time — as soon as possible. He was thirty-six and beginning to tire of the single life, so was undeterred by my directness. He also liked the image he conjured up of us as a sophisticated, culturally advanced couple: a writer and an architect, a WASP and a part-visible-minority person, an articulate quasi-intellectual and a plain-spoken woman who could build houses (which I couldn't and can't do — I design, not build, but Henry liked to think of me as Rosie the Riveter Redux). He told me that his career plan was to write for and edit an important American magazine like *Harper's* or *Atlantic Monthly*, and neither of us understood that our objectives were incompatible.

We fell in love, we had good, frequent sex, we moved in together, we worked hard at our jobs, I survived meeting his family, we had a non-traditional but not obnoxiously alternative wedding. (There was dancing, drinking, and good food in a funky restaurant, but no speeches, no wedding party, few of his relatives, and we wore shoes.) And along came Jesse, a year later.

My desire for a baby was fuelled by a complete lack of comprehension of what life-with-infant was like. I had no friends with children and, being an only child, no nephews or nieces who might have given me pause by acting like normal kids do. So I was knocked out by the reality of new motherhood. I spent my five-month maternity leave trying to adjust to Jesse's infant demands and to having no control over my existence. And I learned how to subvert myself to the care and feeding of a child, an issue that loomed larger when Jesse was diagnosed with celiac disease.

I also dealt with Henry's unmasking as a fifties-style father who needed to "unwind" with a drink or three when he came home from work, who didn't want to have a squalling baby handed to him the minute he walked through the door at seven or eight at night, who thought I should look after groceries, diaper bag packing, dinner preparation, and all other household-related duties because his mind was operating on a higher, journalistic plane. He saw no reason to curtail the incessant media world hobnobbing and travel that he deemed essential to his career-building plans. He kept right on jetting off to Tuscany or Brazil or the Yukon on assignments he'd dreamed up and sold as article ideas to more and more important editors. No reason to stop any of that because we had a baby who cried a lot and needed to be held all the time, because his wife was barely clinging to sanity.

I came to scorn Henry for his self-centredness, his refusal to change for his son's sake, but I fell in absolute mother-love with Jesse, experienced a heady, all-consuming adoration that made the once-romantic bond I'd had with Henry shrink into nothingness. Never would I have fought a proverbial or actual grizzly bear for Henry, nor lifted a car with my bare hands, nor walked through fire, but for Jesse I would have done so daily. As it was, I survived the equally challenging ordeals that are birthday parties for large groups of ungovernable boys, tedious holiday concerts, and overambitious elementary school projects, *and* I mastered the intricacies of the gluten-free diet.

When Henry's accumulated years of ass-kissing and heterosexual man-flirting and networking (okay, and talent) paid off and he got the editor-in-chief job in New York at a men's magazine — a magazine without quite the *gravitas* of *Harper's* or *Atlantic Monthly*, but a big outfit with a big budget and flashy Manhattan offices and A-list athletes and actors on its cover — I had no desire to quit my new solo architectural practice and uproot then ten-year-old Jesse from his neighbourhood friends and school. I didn't yell, "Pack your bags and get out," when Henry told me about the job offer, about the winsome picture of him that would head up his letter from the editor page each month. I didn't tell him he'd outlived his usefulness at the old homestead. I said, "I think Jesse and I will stay here." And overcome with the prospect of media stardom, he didn't need much convincing that this plan was for the best.

It must have been, because look at the pretty picture we now make, of an amicably divorced couple, as we stand in the first-floor hallway of Westdale, outside a classroom, waiting for our next five-minute interview, our last of the afternoon. So far we've seen a history teacher who told us Jesse sits in the back of her classroom, doesn't listen, and talks the whole time to the football players, whom she seems to consider on par with Neanderthals, or maybe Visigoths; a math teacher who said Jesse seems bright but doesn't do his homework and has to be reminded to remove his headphones and turn off his music every single class; and a science teacher who was surprised to hear I'm an architect because he's never met a student who showed less aptitude for physics. I don't hate the drama teacher — she likes Jesse, said he was a great improviser. The computer technology teacher had no complaints, either, because he didn't know who Jesse was.

Throughout the interviews, Henry and I have done our own improvising. I played the supportive spouse while Henry pontificated to the English teacher about the importance of presenting relevant and engaging reading material (something more recent than Salinger and Steinbeck) to grade ten boys before they abandon literacy for life. And Henry nodded in agreement when I pulled out my Mickey Rooney impression and promised I'd make darn sure Jesse does his work from now on, neatly, and on time, too!

Last up is Mr. Dawson, the gym teacher and basketball coach. "I think this guy may be the biggest jerk of them all," I whisper to Henry.

"I'll handle him," Henry says.

Henry considers himself a Renaissance man, thinks he knows art, literature, jazz, philosophy, history, current affairs, politics, blah blah blah, and sports. He was never much of a team player in his youth, being more of a tennis/biking/sailing type of guy, though he does play softball. Like other men of his ilk, he reads Roger Angell on baseball in the *New Yorker*, has chosen a major league team to be sentimental about, and plays on the company softball team. He favours the Yankees, not because he lives in New York or cares for any current individual player, but because of the club's storied past. (And he used to like my Joe DiMaggio joke.)

Henry thinks he knows how to talk to coaches and gym teachers, figures he can do a hail-fellow-I-once-profiled-Joe-Namath routine and make friends. I'm not sure how his act will go over with Mr. Dawson, though it will probably go better than if I reveal my distrust and dislike for coaches and team sports in general, and for anyone who shuns or ignores Jesse in particular.

Our turn. We enter the classroom, smiling like sociable idiots. Henry gives the firm handshake and the respectful smile and introduces us without mentioning the name of his magazine or that he lives in New York, both details that might be a bit too metrosexual for this coach/teacher anyway, who is in his forties, sports a crewcut, a mustache, a gold wedding ring on a sausage-like finger, a grey polo shirt imprinted with the words Westdale P.E., and an enormous, hard, round belly that makes him look nine months pregnant. When I sit down across from him, I feel as if my grade eleven report card, with a mark of fifty-three percent for phys. ed. and the handwritten comment,

"Bad attitude," is branded on my forehead. I also have an urge to light a cigarette, take off my bra, and flip him the bird.

Dawson says, "Harada, you said? That's a Japanese name, isn't it?"

I nod and wait for whatever unfortunate thing he's bound to say next.

"Yeah, I thought Jesse had an Oriental look to him."

Great. The guy is so ignorant, stubborn, or both, that he uses a hoary old pejorative term like Oriental, in this day, age, and multicultural city. Maybe he also coaches the football team and is the head Neanderthal and Visigoth. Maybe next he'll tell me I look exotic.

Henry says quickly, "We know Jesse can improve his mark in gym class, but we're really here to talk about how he's doing on the basketball team."

Dawson sits back and rests his clasped hands on his belly. It looks like twins. "Yeah, Jesse was a starter last year, but this year he's a bench player."

Henry has on a bemused expression that he's worn all afternoon — a non-threatening, non-confrontational, I'm-curious-tell-me-more expression. I want to slap it off his face. After I've slapped Dawson.

I find my voice. "Why is he a bench player? What's changed from last year to this?" Am I being too direct? I don't care.

Dawson shrugs. "There are other boys on the team who are better players, more skilled." He's not apologetic but factual. Two plus two is four and this is what competitive sports are like: survival of the best and abandon the rest.

Henry says, "So what can he work on to improve his game and earn back his starting spot?"

"He can improve his attitude, for one. He's lazy in practice."

I cut in like a cleaver. "I thought you said the issue was his skill level."

"Jesse needs to improve his skills *and* his attitude."

Henry says, "Which skills, specifically? Should he work on his footwork, his defense, his ball-handling, his shot?"

Henry is trying harder than I am to find a solution, to get something constructive out of this meeting, but there's no point. All Dawson sees, I'm sure, is a pushy Oriental woman and a guy with hippie-style eyeglasses, long hair that is taking on an Albert Einsteinian aspect, and the diction of an overeducated snob.

"Jesse could work on all of those things," Dawson says. Oh shut up. Jesse may not be the best player on the team, but he's not bad at everything.

"We'll speak to Jesse," Henry says, "about his attitude and his skills. Basketball means a lot to his identity and his self-worth, so I know he'll do his best to improve." He stands up and offers his hand again, ever the gentleman.

I have no such image to maintain. "What about the tournament coming up in Ottawa? Does he have a chance of playing good minutes in those games if he does well in practice in the meantime?"

I have asked the question that coaches hate, that parents dare not ask for fear of incurring coach wrath, and as a result Henry is probably wondering if he can work a mention of our divorce into the remaining sixty seconds of our interview time and disassociate himself from Emily the Outcast.

"Anything's possible." Dawson's smug smile says the opposite and makes me want to leap across the desk and throttle him.

Out on the street, I say, "No wonder Jesse has bad marks. This place is like any other high school: it's a slave mill, intent on stamping out individuality and turning students into bland, boring cogs. There's no appreciation for anything but the usual, the ordinary, and the expected. And Dawson is your basic racist asshole jock archetype."

In his eternally, infernally mild voice, Henry says, "You wouldn't be exaggerating a little?"

"What, you think those teachers have a clue what they're talking about?"

"I don't think there's anything wrong with Jesse doing his assigned homework or not talking in class. And of course he should turn off his music when the teacher is speaking. These are common courtesies, Emily, and Jesse should learn them."

I know Henry's right. Proud iconoclast that I claim to me, I obey most conventions — I follow road rules, and pay my taxes, and say please and thank you, and don't interrupt or butt in line. At home, I don't make loud noise after eleven p.m. (or ever), and I help Vera shovel her snow in the winter. But being inside the school and sitting at those little subhuman half-desks has stirred up my shallow-seated rebellious tendencies. I stick out my lower lip and say, "Common courtesies, my ass. Jesse's not common."

Henry says, "I'll talk to Jesse when I take him out for dinner tonight, try to make him see some sense. " He starts to do his business handshake on me, considers a hug, and settles for an awkward arm pat. "He'll be fine."

"I know he will."

"And will you be okay?"

"Forget me. What about you? How's the parenting of your other kids going? Are they driving you up the walls of your apartment? And aren't you finding you're a bit old to have toddlers underfoot?"

"On the contrary, Declan and Cody keep me young. And after today, I can't say I'm eager for them to grow up." He tilts his head and goes all compassionate on me. If I were a celebrity being profiled for his magazine, here's where I'd confide my innermost banal thoughts. He says, "It must be difficult for you, dealing with Jesse all alone."

"Yes," I say, "it is difficult," and I run off to my car without much of a goodbye, because goddamn if I'm not about to start crying again.

When I arrive home, Jesse is sitting in the living room, watching music videos on television. "Back already, Em?" he says. "How did it go?"

"So-so." I drop my keys and purse on the hall table, hang up my jacket in the closet.

"What did the teachers say? Let me guess — I talk too much in class."

I sit down beside him on the couch. "You talk too much, do no work, have no scientific aptitude or manners, and you're lazy in basketball practice. Other than that, you're fine."

"I told you they hate me."

"The drama teacher praised your improvisation skills."

"What did Dad think?"

"I'm sure he'll tell you at length what he thinks when he takes you to dinner tonight."

"You're pissed off, right?"

"Yeah. At you, and at your teachers. Some of them seemed like jerks. But you've got to learn how to get along, Jesse."

"Why?"

"So that you can do what you want with your life."

"Be a professional athlete, you mean?"

I wish he didn't have this unrealistic goal. I wish he'd figure out that the odds are against him, and he'll never make it. But I won't be the one to disabuse him of the notion, to take away his dream. "You have to graduate from high school no matter what you want to do. And go to university. That means you should do your homework, pay attention in class, be polite, get good marks. Toe the line."

"Walk the walk?"

"Yeah, sure."

"Okay, I will. I'll do better."

That was too easy. "Just like that?"

"I won't do tons better, just enough to get you and Dad off my back."

"Gee, thanks."

I put my arm around his shoulders, risking a rebuff, but he lets me touch him, lets us be mother and son united, for two whole minutes.

"I'd like this house to be part of my legacy," Stewart says. "And I think the restoration will be seen as a major contribution to the preservation of our city's architectural heritage."

Joe and I are in Stewart's office for a meeting about the mansion, sitting at an enormous board table, in enormous leather chairs. Stewart is at the head of the table, at a right angle to me, his eagle-like profile resplendent. Joe is across the way, the picture of relaxation and affability, since phrases like "my legacy" and "major contribution" do not cause his bullshit detector to go off. I am determined to be a model of adult comportment but am facing odds, based on my recent volatile track record, of about thirty to one that I'll get snippy within the next fifteen minutes.

A house of this size — nine bedrooms, eleven bathrooms, twelve thousand square feet of living space — is a job that will be the source of bread, butter, various other foodstuffs, and living expenses for Jesse and me for the next several months. Provided I don't blow it and piss off the client. I need to heed my own dictum to the feisty student in Leo's class and remember that integrity is overrated and ideals don't pay the bills. I should also follow some of the advice I gave Jesse, how it's important to get along with the people in charge, even if doing so makes my arm ache.

Stewart says, "Let me elucidate my vision for the property." Across the table, Joe makes a note on his pad, in possible violation of what I thought was our mutual understanding to share a private contempt for Stewart. I read Joe's large-scale writing upside down and yes, he's gone over to the sycophant side, written the word *vision* in caps, and underlined it twice. In response, I clench my jaw and draw a tiny perfect square down the left margin of my page, and another below it, and another.

Stewart speechifies on, I run his stentorian sentences through my crap filter, and I make some actual notes, because I can't ignore my few remaining principles and give him what he wants unless I know what that is.

Like most of my clients, Stewart's goal is to restore the house, but his way. Unlike most of my clients — and excuse me while I swallow this bit of crow in my mouth — Stewart wants to keep to the original room dimensions and layouts wherever possible. There'll be no open plan concept for him, no knocking down of walls to make bigger rooms, closets, or entranceways. He does not want a huge kitchen or family room or great room. "I don't cook," he says. "So the kitchen should be of a size that will accommodate the caterers I occasionally bring in and no bigger." He also has no need for a dining room and would rather see the space formerly allocated for that purpose used as a reading room or study, since he either dines *à deux* with whichever local TV personality, party girl newspaper columnist, or new generation heiress he's currently squiring around town, or holds large family gatherings attended by his adult children from his first (long since discarded) wife, with their spouses and assorted offspring — too many people to seat around a table.

"I want to preserve and restore as much as we can of the original plan and finishes, and only update where necessary for functional or safety reasons," he says. "Understood?"

I say, "I think we've got it. Don't you, Joe?"

Stewart's still an arrogant prick, but at least he's a practical prick who knows what he wants and is not bound by such trivial issues as resale value and current decorating trends. Decisive is good, according to my world view. Going one's own way without worry about some of the resulting consequences strikes me as an admirable attitude right about now, too.

Am I approving of Stewart in order to justify my own approach to Nils, to make my acceptance of an invitation to go out dancing with a much younger man more palatable? Maybe a little. A worse fear is that I'm turning into the female version of a prick and becoming a harpy who preys on young men, feeds vampirically on their youth. But when I compare and contrast myself with Stewart, lord of the manor, he of the eagle head, French cuffs, and way-younger girlfriends, I come out as the lesser evil. All I'm doing is going on an innocuous group outing with Nils to an obscure bar in the west end of downtown. I'm no predator — it's Nils who's done the pursuing, and the suggesting, and the making of overtures. And anyway, I haven't been able to bite down hard enough to pierce anyone's skin since I had that dental work done.

The meeting ends, I stand and shake hands with Stewart without having to totally feign civility, I share some relaxed and affable words with Joe in the elevator down to ground level, and we set up a time to go to the house with one of his workmen to do some serious measuring. Maybe this job will be tolerable after all.

~ ★ ~

There's a new message in my email inbox, from someone named Mary Lowell. The subject is "Upcoming Visit to Toronto." It reads:

Dear Emily,

Tom Denby gave me your email address and told me he'd tracked you down in Toronto. Since I plan to be in your city in a month's time at an academic conference (I'm currently the Head Archaeologist for the Northeastern District at the National Trust), I'm hoping we can meet. I'd like to catch up with you, and talk about old times.

I'll be in town December 10–12, staying at a hotel I'm told is close to the university and the museum. Could you meet me for drinks one of those evenings at a location of your choosing? Please say yes, I very much want to see you.

Yours,
Mary

This must be relive-the-past year or something, what with Tom contacting me, and Nils disturbing my equilibrium, and now an invitation from tits-and-giggles Mary, the milkmaid who fell into bed, or rather, the back of the van, with Clive all those years ago. She's not very giggly now, though. She's rather serious in delivery, rather businesslike, I would venture, though it's hard to tell with emails, difficult to know if a person is being stiff or just using language that seems formal.

Why on earth would she "very much" want to see me? Maybe that's a turn of phrase she routinely uses that means little. Or she could be on a twelve-step program and has to seek forgiveness or make apologies or whatever it is that those people do. Apologize for what, though? Getting the guy? No.

I'm surprised and, okay, a little peeved that she holds this important position with the National Trust. I would never have pegged her thirty years ago as an archeologist-to-be. I had her figured as a child-bearing machine who would also be good with animals. More proof that I was ignorant and idiotic when I was young. And still am, much of the time.

What should I answer? I could lie and say I'll be out of town that week, I could plead childcare responsibilities, as if Jesse were five years old. Or I could try to have more of a life that's independent of his.

I could meet her for a quick drink, see how she's aged — that could be entertaining in itself — and hear some gossip about long-forgotten people and places. It could be diverting and fun in a surreal way, like reading about the unknown-to-me English celebrities in the tabloids at Ruby's. And I could find out what possible reason she has to "very much" want to see me.

I write back, pick a day of the three she's given, suggest we meet in a posh bar near the museum that evening, and send off the reply. The new, reformed, less-quick-to-anger me may not last longer than a day or two, but I'll roll with the persona while I can.

It's Friday morning, and I'm driving Jesse to school at eight o'clock to catch the bus to Ottawa for the basketball tournament at which he may or may not get playing time.

"When we get to Westdale," he says, "don't get out of the car. In fact, why don't you drop me at the next corner and I'll walk the rest of the way?"

"With those two heavy bags? I don't think so." We have not forgotten anything today. I have triple-checked that his basketball bag is in the car and contains everything he needs. I double-checked his overnight bag after he packed it, too, and there are no intoxicants in it, though it does contain a cooler bag filled with his gluten-free cereal and crackers and cookies and fruit bars and apples.

"You'll be good, right?" I say. "You'll do what Mr. Dawson says, follow the rules, obey the curfew?"

"This corner right up here is good. Drop me here."

"I'd like you to call me collect from the hotel when you arrive, let me know that you got there safely, you're in a room with Ben, and you've found something to eat for dinner."

"Okay, but don't call me a hundred times in the room over the weekend, okay? It's embarrassing."

"If you call me once a day and give me an update, I promise not to bug you." I clutch his knee. "I'll miss you, honey. I hope the tournament goes well."

He reaches into an inner pocket in his jacket and pulls out a jewel case containing a burnt CD. "Here. I made you this."

I pull up to the school a discreet five car lengths behind the bus and take the CD from him. In his sloppy printing, he has written "Em's Music" on the disc. "What is it?"

"Play it and see. Goodbye." He grabs his two bags and heads off down the sidewalk without looking back.

I watch him get on the bus, insert the CD into the car player, and drive away. The first song is by Bonnie Raitt, also the second, third, and fourth, followed by a Joni Mitchell tune, a James Taylor song, some Jackson Browne, and more Bonnie Raitt. Someone — Henry? I hope not — has tipped Jesse off to the playlist of my twenties, to a time when even the happy songs were plaintive and tinged with sadness.

I'm touched by Jesse's gesture, that he did something thoughtful for me — I really am, I tear up a little — but I can't listen to those songs this morning. They don't fit my mixed mood:

anxiety on Jesse's behalf as I send him into the clutches of Coach Dawson; guilt-tinged pleasure that I'll be alone for the next forty-eight hours and can do what I please, on my own schedule; and fluttery excitement about my night out, tonight, square dancing.

Nils has a car and offered to pick me up and drive me to Hell, but I declined his offer because multiple back-and-forth trips would be required on his part between his neighbourhood and mine and there would arise the possibility of an awkward goodbye on my doorstep at the end of the evening, a situation I'd rather avoid.

I said, "Thanks, but I'll drive myself down and meet you there."

"Are you sure?"

"Yes."

"Great. If I don't have to drive, I can drink more."

Uh, right.

He suggested we meet on a street corner near the club so that I wouldn't have to walk in alone, and that is its own awkward moment, when I drive up to the corner and roll down my window and call out to him and he hops into my car, like a hustler embarking on a trick or a son being picked up by his mother, viewer's choice as to which interpretation is worse.

Above the hum of nervousness in my brain that is so loud I can barely hear, Nils says, "So what's your son up to tonight? What do teenagers do for fun on a Friday night these days?"

I explain that Jesse's at an out-of-town basketball tournament and will watch some other teams play tonight in preparation for his game tomorrow, which is already more information than Nils can possibly be interested in, so I shut up.

Nils directs me to a parking spot close to Hell and ushers me into a dirty old tavern that looks like it was a hangout for down-and-out drunks before the room was painted and given a new name, the bottles on the bar were dusted off, and a huge, angry abstract oil painting (done in shades of hellfire red) was hung on a large wall that I'll bet is seriously cracked underneath.

There are perhaps twenty-five people in the room, all under age forty, all dressed in loose pants and tight tops. I struggled with the wardrobe question prior to coming and settled on black jeans, a long-sleeved black T-shirt, and my black workboots, which all together make me look like a ninja. Or like the fraud I am, trying to blend in with the four youthful people sitting at the table. Nils is at my side, the wattage of his unknowingly killer smile still bright. Next to him is a friend from architecture school, Raj, who is clever and verbal and remembers me from Leo's class (I don't remember him, I'm afraid). "She tells a good story about a talking dog," he tells the others, referring to the Joe DiMaggio joke, but I refuse to tell it to the collected company.

"It only works in the context of class," I say.

Raj says, "Speaking of class, and classiness, I want to warn everyone that no amount of alcohol, money, or persuasive argument will get me to dance tonight, but I'm looking forward to seeing you guys make fools of yourselves." He leans towards me. "Except for you, Emily. Nils says you've done this before, so I'm sure you'll put the others to shame."

Ha, ha, funny, maybe I can leave now.

The other female at the table is a young woman named Melissa, who has a mass of well-tended, well-dyed blonde curls, wears fistfuls of clunky silver jewellery, and speaks and laughs in a smoky, throaty voice that she uses to describe herself as Raj's oldest friend, whatever that means. I avert my eyes at the sight of the generous, jellyish expanse of bare stomach — decorated with both a belly button piercing and a butterfly tattoo — that is on display between her top and jeans. The unrealistic body ideals on which I was raised and conditioned preclude me ever showing my rolls of fat in public like that. Though I wouldn't expose my midsection if it were flat, either.

Rounding out our happy group is a guy named Paul who has an Australian accent and a consumptive air. At one point, a teasing remark is made by Raj to the effect that Melissa picked up Paul in another bar last night, but I can't tell if he's kidding or not, and I don't want to ask.

I don't ask or say much but sit quietly, letting the worlds-apart-from-me conversation of these friends float around while I sip a beer (ordered because that's what everyone else is drinking) and hope the square dancing starts soon. Melissa's stories about her recent trip to Australia are boring, the beer is making me gassy, I'm starting to yearn for my pajamas, my comfortable chair, and a cup of mint tea, and pass me my knitting, will you?

The background music, which has been a mix of laid-back country rock, or maybe folk rock, or country folk, or possibly another genre altogether, stops, and a young man speaks into a microphone on the small spotlight-lit stage. "Five minutes to square dance time. Dancers, if you haven't already done so, please sign up at the bar."

Nils touches my elbow, and for once his hand is not overly warm. "Raj signed us up already," he says. "But I'm going to step out for a quick cigarette first. Want to come?"

I'm tempted by the idea of drawing smoke into my lungs, of tasting tobacco again, but not on the seedy sidewalk outside, and I would probably get dizzy, so I say no thanks, Raj and Paul get up to join him — does everyone young smoke? — and shit, what if Melissa walks out too and I'm left alone at the table, but she says, "Be quick, guys," to them, and to me, "I quit three weeks ago."

I try talking to her about her smoking habits, but she's no more interested than I am in discussing her nicotine patch, and after brusquely answering two or three of my questions, she says, in her husky voice, "So you met Nils when you were his teacher?"

She makes this sound dirty. She makes everything sound dirty, which, combined with the blond curls, pillowy body, and tattoo, is a package of attributes that probably garners her flocks of admirers and has gotten her more sex partners in the last year than I have had my entire life.

"I met Nils six years ago, when I was a guest lecturer in one of his architecture classes," I say. "We exchanged all of five sentences."

She narrows her expertly made-up eyes (liquid eyeliner), as if she were squinting against a plume of smoke from the cigarette she does not hold. "But you thought he was cute as soon as you saw him, didn't you?"

Her aggression is so unveiled that I want to say, "What's it to you?" I don't, though, because she could take me in a fight, easy, and the rings she's wearing could cause real damage. Also because I've realized what I would have seen earlier if my nose for trouble and usual suspicion of all humankind hadn't stepped out together for a smoke themselves this evening — that she's trying to protect Nils from me, the bad guy.

She says, "Do you make a habit of dating younger men, or is Nils your first?"

"I'm curious — is there a sign on my back that says, 'Kick me'?"

"Hey, it don't bother me what you do."

That's right — she said "don't" instead of "doesn't." In case I wasn't already despising her.

"I know what's going on," she says. "I've dated my share of older men, and I've had some laughs with them. Older men don't care that I'm not thin. And they're more appreciative in bed than younger guys, more willing to please me, if you know what I mean."

"I think I do, but I'd rather not visualize it," I say, and her tetchy, "What did you say?" is lost in the noisy return of Nils, Raj, and Paul, reeking of cigarette smoke.

Nils and I are assigned to the same square as Melissa and Paul, which is not a problem, since Melissa has switched from inquisitor of potential cradle-robbers to the life of the party, all hilarious asides and head-thrown-back laughs and what-a-riot-she-is. The dancing begins with a short lesson on the basic steps, and I pick them up quickly, my rusty wiring crackling to life and running along long-forgotten circuits. Nils, who is tipsy-relaxed but not piss-drunk, moves me here and yon and back and forth competently, with enthusiasm if not grace.

I've had better dance partners, but I'm charmed rather than irked by Nils's stiff style. I'm charmed by everything about him, all doubts about the advisability and wisdom of two people our age doing so much as a promenade in Hell together cast aside in defiance of Melissa's comments and her off-putting claim (with its repellent implications for me) that older men are sexually grateful to her when she deigns to fuck them. As we used to say in grade seven, that's just gross.

The dancing starts up properly, and I step and turn and do-si-do with Nils, Melissa, Paul, and four other strangers. The caller, a wiry man with a Maritime accent, calls the steps, the recorded fiddle music plays, I swing my partner, the room begins to revolve, and I'm lifted by the music and the movement and the rhythm to some ageless place where I am joyous and light-hearted, where I become reacquainted with a pure exhilaration I haven't known in years.

We dance (with several breath-catching, water-guzzling breaks) until midnight, and then I become Cinderella by way of Dorian Gray, anxious to leave at once, certain my face will wither into that of a hag when the clock stops striking and the witch's spell I bought (with the sacrifice of my first-born child) is broken. I grab my coat and bag and say nice to have met you to Melissa and Paul, who briefly interrupt their nuzzling at the table to murmur goodbye. Raj is nicer — he tells me my dancing was a pleasure to watch and my company delightful, and hopes we'll meet again. I'm trying to take leave of Nils without seeming too hasty and panicked (I really must go, I'm exhausted and have worn out my social skills, will start snapping and spitting any minute now, the same minute at which my face will revert to its true gruesome aspect), but he says, "I'll go with you," grabs his coat, and comes outside.

An unseasonably warm breeze is blowing, and its touch soothes and lightens and lifts me, or will as soon as I get out from under the hard, bright, neon light of Hell's sign. I blather on to Nils with more thanks, but he says, "It's early — let's go somewhere. You hungry?"

I ate dinner at five-thirty and don't usually eat past six, because of all too valid fears of weight gain brought on by a slow, aged metabolism. But I say, "I could eat. What were you thinking of?"

"It's nice out," he says. "Feel like fries?" and though I try to limit my consumption of french fries to once a quarter, my truthful answer is, "Always." I'll eat some midnight fries, and then I'll go home to bed.

We leave my car where it is, walk three or four blocks to a post-modern chip shop across from a park, and join a lineup of animated young people who appear to be making a pit stop in their full nights, with many more laps to come before they lay their heads down to rest. I hope Nils doesn't run into anyone he knows — I don't want to be introduced and looked over and judged once more as an unsuitable-to-Nils companion, any more than I want to be sexually grateful for Nils's attentions should relations of that nature develop between us. But the crowded shop is full of strangers, and Melissa's insinuations aside, the probability of a physical expression of affection coming from Nils is low in general, lower still once the fries are consumed. So I'm only tense about keeping our place in line until Nils, who is standing behind me, encircles me with his arms — contact occurring at my bicep level — in a hug and drops his chin on my shoulder.

I'm delighted by this gesture — for a few heady, glowy seconds, I feel like I've been declared Most Popular Girl in high school. But the pressure of Nils's arm on my bad shoulder is hurting me, and his chin feels sharp. I squeeze his arm with a free hand — to non-verbally say that I like him too — and as soon as we shift forward in line, I slip out of his embrace and make a show of reading the chalkboard menu, though I've decided what I'm going to have: small fries and a fresh-squeezed orange juice, an early breakfast.

Nils reaches for my hand and holds it, easily, calmly, and this time nothing hurts, and the glowy feeling spreads from my fingers up and down and through my whole body until my extremities are tingling and I've lost all appetite but am grinning because, wrong or not, I like him, damn it, I like this.

The park across the street from the chip shop is the former site of an Anglican college, long since amalgamated with the university and moved to the main campus. The old buildings are gone, demolished in the twenties, in their place a community centre and recreational playing fields. The only remains of the old college are some rather grand concrete and ironwork gates (built in 1851) that frame the drive into the property. Near them are benches that face the street, which is where Nils and I sit to eat our fries and drink our juices and I keep to myself my architectural tour guide knowledge, where we lean into each other in a way that means only one thing to me — sex later tonight — but perhaps not to him.

I once met a man at a cocktail party — a potential client — who told me that he could tell when a woman wanted to sleep with him without a word being exchanged. This jerk claimed to be the frequent recipient of a certain unmistakable come-hither look that spoke clearly of amorous interest, that communicated desire such that all he needed to do if he was likewise interested was to crook a finger in the direction of the woman so inclined.

Nice party talk, huh?

I made sure to avoid this man's eye (and his custom), for fear of having my everyday scowl misread and getting the crooked finger, but since I've never subscribed to sexually tinged gazing, bandying, or touching without purpose, I needn't have worried. In my own prudish way, I'm easy: the only flirting I do is fore-play, and once I'm aroused, I don't dither or see any value in delayed gratification — I go straight for consummation.

So before Nils and I get any further into this night that is already too long, I'd better clear the air, find out where he's at. If he's all hand-holding and no follow-up, I can relax and eat more fries.

I say, "So, back at the bar, when you went out for a cigarette, Melissa asked me some questions along the lines of a back-ground check."

"She was probably trying to make conversation."

"Actually, I think she wanted to know if my intentions toward you were honourable."

His eyes soften (good thing I'm sitting down), he tucks a piece of my hair behind my ear (I stifle a gasp), and he says, "I hope they aren't honourable, because mine aren't for you." Then he leans over and kisses my jawbone, under my ear.

At the touch of his mouth, my body revs into high sex gear, all systems lubricated and ready to go, but I yank on the emer-gency brake while I still can. "I'm completely flattered to hear that. I am. I mean, I could retire to a nunnery now and be happy, but I really think — "

He has pulled out a stick of gum while I'm talking and popped it into his mouth and started furiously chewing, and he offers me one. I take it, chew on it to get it going, then say, "You're very sweet, and really quite gorgeous, but the age difference is such a big barrier between us. I could be your mother."

He removes the gum from his mouth, sticks it on the back of the bench, holds out his palm for mine, adds the chewed wad to his, says, "You're nothing like my mother," takes hold of my face with two hands, and kisses me properly and lengthily, on the mouth, a real Hollywood romantic kiss. I kiss back like I remember how, and as soon as we pause for breath, say, "How far away is your place?"

~ CHAPTER EIGHT ~

A few days ago, Sylvia asked if I'd have lunch with her on Saturday, when Jesse and Ben would be away at the basketball tournament. She said, "We could go to that new restaurant I heard about from someone at the gallery, that place on Bloor Street with the good-looking waiters and trendy food. What's it called again? For Cool People Only?"

Saturday would be the day after the square dancing night with Nils that I had yet to tell her about. I didn't expect anything to happen with Nils that would keep me from meeting Sylvia the next day at noon, but when she asked me, I hesitated. "You mean Ice? If you want to try it, why don't you go there with Ed?"

"Ed hates places like that. And I need him to take Kira to gymnastics."

I continued to hedge, in accordance with my credo of when in doubt, guard the solitude, until she said, "Come on. We old-timers need to get out of our comfortable bistros now and then and dine on the young side. And I could use a non-familial outing to break up my weekend. Last Sunday afternoon, I went to see a bad movie by myself, just so I could escape from the three demanding, spoiled brats I live with."

So much for Sylvia's domestic happiness. "What did they do to piss you off?"

"Nothing out of the ordinary — the usual bossiness from Ed, and whining from Kira, and Ben acting antisocial in his room with the door closed, except when he wants food, which is way too often. Wouldn't it be great to have someone else — preferably a good-looking waiter — serve us a meal?"

"Okay, I'll go. You make the reservation." I'd make sure we didn't linger, and I'd still have plenty of time to be alone the rest of the weekend. Such was my intent, but what I didn't account for was that I would get home at three a.m. from Nils's apartment — a neat, design-y one-bedroom located in a well-kept Arts and Crafts–style house. Or that I would sleep until eleven o'clock this morning, when Jesse called from Ottawa — his one call of the day — and said, "I woke you up? Since when do you sleep in?"

"How did the first game go?"

"We won."

"Did you play?"

"Yeah."

"A lot?"

"No."

"How many minutes?"

"I don't know. I have to go."

"When's your next game?"

"This afternoon. Bye."

Fully awake after that, I crawl out of bed and make it to the restaurant at 12:05, with wet hair and tired eyes.

Ice is done up in shades of white and pale blue — white floor, white chairs, stainless steel tables, pale blue walls. Pale blue shirts and white pants are on the waiters, who are young, scrawny, and to a man have stupid facial hair. A young (white) hostess in clingy white clothes leads me to the table where Sylvia sits, perusing the pale blue menu. A big glass of white wine is there, too, Sylvia's lipstick stains already imprinted on its rim.

"You look bagged," Sylvia says. "Were you out on the town last night?"

She's kidding, and expects me to say no and complain about insomnia, or about the dogs on my block that go on barking jags at odd hours, but here's my opening to confess some, if not all, about Nils.

"Actually, I did go out. I went square dancing, of all things."

A waiter with a goatee that makes him look like a satyr asks if I'd like something to drink and suggests a mineral water that comes in a blue bottle. I disappoint him with a request for tap water, with the house ice.

Sylvia says, "You're joking about going square dancing, right?"

"No, I really went. To a place called Hell. Of all things."

She lets her menu slide onto the table. "Who'd you go with?"

"An architect friend named Nils. I met him through Leo Antonelli, my old professor that I lecture for? I went with Nils and some of his friends."

Her eyes are almost bugging out now, she's so shocked by this news. As she should be, considering how many times I've done anything similar since she's known me. Wait until she hears Nils's age.

She says, "Was this like a date?"

"Yeah, I guess it was."

"And?"

My turn to examine the menu. "And what?" I don't want to tell her that we had sex, and how it went, which was better than I would have expected. Nils made love like he danced — with enthusiasm and little grace. I liked it anyway.

"How did it go?"

147

"The square dancing aspect or the date aspect?"

"The date aspect! Did he kiss you good night? Will you go out with him again?"

I usually cover my ears when Sylvia tries to talk to me about anything sexual, so she does not suspect that I would fuck on a first date, and I can answer her questions semi-honestly. "Yeah, he kissed me good night, a peck on the cheek. And I may see him again. But it's not serious." It may already be over, for all I know. The sex and the attention and the skin-to-skin contact were all nice, but I'm not having any big romance here.

She takes a big gulp of her wine. "How old is he?"

"Thirtyish."

"Thirtyish, as in under thirty or over thirty?"

"Under. He's twenty-nine."

"Oh my god, Emily," she says, in a dramatic shocked whisper that's so loud it negates the whisper effect and makes people turn around and look, as if she yelled.

I give her a keep-down-the-histrionics glare.

"You know what that means, don't you?" she says, and now she's talking so low I have to lean close to hear her. "It means he'll go down on you. The young ones don't mind that."

"For god's sake, Sylvia." What does her saying this mean? That Ed doesn't believe in oral sex? Do I want to know that? A thousand times no.

"Is he good-looking?"

Before I can answer, the waiter returns with my glass of water and recites the specials. Scallops are mentioned, and rutabaga crisps, and duck confit, though not all in the same dish. Sylvia says, "We're not ready to order yet," and as soon as he's gone, "Is he cute, your guy? As cute as Steve Sutherland?"

If I were a more trusting, confiding soul — if I were young and innocent — I might wax on about Nils's ability to look like a traffic-stopping beauty one moment and an ordinary joe the next. I could rave, in a gushy, sappy fashion, about the length and thickness of his eyelashes, the devastating effect of his dimples, the lovely tone of his skin, but I say only, "He has nice eyes."

She drinks more wine. "Holy shit. You're making me have second thoughts about Steve."

Yes, let's get off the topic of me, so I can stop running the shiver-inducing mental replays of last night in my mind, and focus on her. "Do you wish you were still seeing him?"

"No, but my life was sure more exciting for those few weeks. I'll have to live vicariously through you instead. Will you give me all the details, every step of the way?"

I grin. "No."

"That figures, you holdout. Shit, I'm starving now. Let's order."

We make our choices — she wants the salmon, and I choose the lobster club on brioche (I could really get into something rich). We summon the waiter, place our order, then compare notes from our phone calls with Jesse and Ben and learn nothing new, only that both kids were equally terse, which is comforting.

I'm eating some very tasty warm bread and sweet butter (to go with the buttered bread I will have in my sandwich), brought in a white wire basket lined with a pale blue linen napkin, when Sylvia starts a new topic. I think. She says, "Do you know that my father hasn't seen a movie or a play or a television show or new piece of art that he's liked since the seventies? That's when he was in his prime, he says — he was forty then — and formed all his tastes for art, music, and food. He's totally frozen in time."

"He couldn't pick a better period to be stuck in?"

"And he's such a know-it-all and so boring about his antique modern art and bebop jazz and shellfish that I can't stand hearing him talk about them anymore."

Where is she going with this? I say, "Butter always tastes better in restaurants, have you noticed that?"

"I'm telling you about my father because I'm afraid I'm turning into him."

"Don't most people live in fear of becoming their parents?" My father used to wear his reading glasses on the tip of his nose and look over the top of them to talk to people. He looked so affected and asinine doing this that I swore if I ever got reading glasses, I would never wear them except when reading, never read in public, and never look over the top of them. But guess what.

Sylvia says, "I'm worried that I'm freezing, too. I'm becoming a woolly mammoth."

"Come now — you're not hairy, and you do plenty of hot things." As do I, it seems, judging from last night's slate of activities. "You're here now, at this groovy new boîte, for instance."

"Yeah, I'm here, the decor's giving me a headache, the food's overpriced, and I can't stand how the waiter's trying to upsell us on everything. I'd much rather be at one of the five old familiar restaurants Ed and I have been going to for years."

The waiter places our selections on the table, asks if we'd like to pre-order the dessert of the day, a coconut granita with wild blueberries (we decline), and leaves us with an improperly pronounced, "Bon appétit."

I dig in, and Sylvia gestures to a group of young people sitting nearby. "You see those four over there? They probably listen to new music and make new friends and go to see experimental theatre and try new restaurants — that they like! — all the time. They're probably talking about something new and fresh right now."

The two men and two women she's referring to have bed-heads, are wearing ugly retro casual clothes — bowling-style shoes and baseball-style T-shirts — and two of them are speaking at an obnoxious volume level. My fondness for Nils having not cured me of my distrust of other young people, I would describe their facial expressions as arrogant and not be surprised if their conversation consisted at least in part of some mocking of Sylvia and me, two matrons trying to be hip by coming to this with-it restaurant. "Yeah, they're probably talking about something fascinating, like how hungover they are."

She says, "The thing is, I hate experimental theatre. But I don't want to be one of those people who embraces old age either. Will you promise to stop me when I start calling people 'dear' and yelling at the neighbourhood kids to get off my lawn?"

The lobster has been tossed with a lemony, chive-flecked mayonnaise that pleases my palate, whether it's supposed to be newfangled or not. Between bites, I say, "That won't happen, because people who grew up smoking grass don't care about lawn grass. Our generation is different from the ones before, and we'll age in our own different and uniquely aggravating way."

"What do you bet that's what all the previous generations said? Until their hair turned white and they started muttering to themselves about the good old days."

We didn't have dessert, but Sylvia wanted coffee, which she made last until two o'clock, so I arrive home at two-thirty, ready for my nap. I awake from it after an hour instead of my usual twenty minutes, and when I do, I can't remember where Jesse is, or whether I was supposed to pick him somewhere like I dreamed I didn't, and left him, age five or so, standing in front of a huge, deserted, collegiate Gothic school, crying, a child abandoned by his thoughtless mother.

The day outside is blustery and raw, a preview of the many cold, grey winter days to come. I get up slowly, straighten the bed, shuffle downstairs. It's still Saturday. Jesse is still in Ottawa with the basketball team. I didn't dream that I fucked Nils last night and liked it — that did happen — though I seem to be harbouring subconscious guilt about it.

On the conscious front, my main sentiment is embarrassment. Who was that woman who moaned and thrashed about and carried on last night in Nils's bed? What a banshee. Or a hoyden. And how come I had no qualms about exposing my middle-aged naked body to him? For an hour or two, my insecurities ceased to exist, as if trapped in the threads of an insecurity catcher hanging in the threshold of Nils's bedroom.

I put on the kettle to make my afternoon tea, though it's not my regular tea time — at this hour I'm usually thinking about preparing Jesse's dinner. And yet here are the Saturday morning papers on the kitchen table, unread, still wrapped in their elastics, at three-thirty in the afternoon.

The phone rings when I am making my way through the first newspaper and the tea, and in the time it takes me to walk two steps across the kitchen, I become convinced it's Jesse, calling for an unexpected second time this day because he has broken a bone playing basketball, has been caught doing something illegal and suspended from the team, or has been in a car accident. I pick up the receiver at the same time as I check the call display, so I'm already saying hello when my brain registers that the name N. Grayson belongs to Nils, whose call I might not have picked up if I'd known it was he.

"Hey, Emily," he says, "it's Nils."

A woman of my experience might be expected to say something sultry and knowing in this situation, something clever and sexy. Something other than, "Oh, hi."

"I've just woken from a long, satisfying sleep, and I thought I should call the person who kept me up half the night. How are you?"

Embarrassed, thank you. Also made unsteady by the sound of his voice. "I'm okay. I had a nap, too."

"Good. So what are you doing later? I was thinking I could cook you some dinner tonight, if you're up to it. Your son's still away, right?"

I lean against the wall. I thought I wouldn't see Nils again for at least a week, if ever. And now — do I want to see him? Can I face some hearty food when I'm not hungry after my lobster lunch, and do I want to make awkward small talk while he clatters around with pots and pans, and will I have to offer to do the dishes after?

I say, "Jesse's away till tomorrow, but I can't do dinner. I'm going out with my friend Sylvia. She's picking me up at seven." Way to lie, Emily.

"How about after dinner, then? Can you come over then?"

I shouldn't, I won't — I close my eyes and rest the back of my head on the doorframe, and imagine him kissing me again, on my neck, and sucking on my skin, and I say, "Why don't you come here? I'll be home by ten o'clock." And at ten, we can get into bed right away, my own comfy bed, and fuck right away, no polite chatting or eating or dishwashing required beforehand.

He agrees, I give him the address, hang up, sink down against the wall, and sit on the kitchen floor, head in hands, but not for long, now that I have so much to do: finish reading the newspapers, attempt to defunk and beautify myself, put fresh sheets on the bed and towels in the bathroom, tidy up the house and remove all overt reminders of extreme youth and age — Jesse's baby pictures needn't be displayed on every surface in my bedroom, nor should a jar of facial cream called Youth Regained be positioned front and centre on my bedside table.

During a sweep of the second-floor bathroom, I stop in front of the measuring wall and reach my right arm up against it, check my progress against the line I drew six weeks ago, the day I saw Dr. Joan. Today, I can stretch my fingertips out to one inch further than the original pencil mark. Which is better than no progress at all, but awfully slow. I must stretch more, exercise more, especially since I have a new reason to want to be flexible.

Now, what to serve Nils? I poke around in the basement closet I call a pantry, looking for a decent bottle of wine to offer, but nothing there moves me. Hey. What about my dope, er, weed, stash, which has sat untouched since the night of my one a.m. drive to pick up Jesse?

A hit or two of weed (I would go easy this time) might be the ticket Nils and I need to a sex ride free of sophomore slump bumps. That, and — forget the wine — some sambuca, of which I have an old but still potent bottle, a gift from Sylvia to help celebrate my divorce four years ago, her accompanying greeting card having made reference to the flaming out of the old and flaming in of the new, or something similar.

Warming to the theme, I light a fire in the living room fireplace, keep the long matches handy for the liqueur, turn on some low-level lighting. I have no candles on hand, and good thing, too, because they're so tiredly romantic as a concept, and neither will I wear the caftan this setting seems to call for. Anyway, I no longer own the red and purple floor-length Indian print number that I wore at about age seventeen and quite liked in a hippie-princess-for-a-day way. And that, I swear, will be the last arcane reference, for at least the next twenty-four hours, to pop culture touchstones that date from the dawn of the television era.

I'm wearing my usual at-home wear — loose, black, body-camouflaging garments — when Nils arrives at 10:05. We do a shy hello and cheek-kiss at the door, and he exclaims politely about my house, which is not exclamation-worthy, being rather workmanlike Victorian in style rather than ornately decorative or austerely classic, but his stroll through the ground floor gives us both something to do and a subject to fall back on when he asks how my dinner out with Sylvia went and I fudge my answer.

I invite him to sit in the living room, I put on some background music — classical or rap is all we stock in the house, so I opt for low-volume Vivaldi — and I offer Nils some sambuca and a joint, which could be a big mistake if he turns out to be the kind of person who says all he likes is beer, but he knows his way around both substances, which I would like to think proves he's an adult but may indicate the opposite.

Two tokes of the joint and a shot glass of drink later, I sit close to Nils on the couch and lean into him. Nils is still working on the joint, eyes shut against the smoke, but puts his arm around my shoulders so that I can snuggle, an unaccustomed luxury I enjoy.

"About me not staying over at your apartment last night," I say. "I don't know how to say this, but — "

His heavy eyelids make his eyes look prettier than usual. "Don't worry. I understand, and I won't stay here, either. But promise me you'll wake me and make me leave if I fall asleep."

Adept with matches, lovely to look at, intuitive, and easygoing, too? He and I together, like this, apparently in tune, cuddling on the couch, right now, seems like such an unlikely scenario that the only explanation for it is that I am living a horror movie in which everything to do with Nils will be revealed to have been a figment of a madness caused by years of exposure to radon or asbestos in all the old houses I've worked on. Until that revelation comes, however, I'd like to have sex again, so when he's put out the joint, I take his hand and lead him upstairs to bed.

At two a.m., I see Nils out, send him on his way. He was in no hurry to leave, had turned on the television in my bedroom after our second round of sex and lounged in my bed, head propped up on my pillows, naked body half-wrapped in my sheets, completely at ease and channel-flipping, but I was so exhausted that the skin on my face felt like it was falling off. So I said, "I'm pretty tired," and he took the hint, got up and got dressed, as did I, and now we're sitting on my front porch bench, all bundled up, while he smokes a parting cigarette.

"Thanks for coming," I murmur, and he says back, "No, thank *you* for coming. I didn't think you had last night, so I'm glad we were able to sort that out."

"Shush." I'm blushing in the dark. "The neighbours are asleep."

"Not that one." He points to a lit window at Vera's house.

I tell him about Vera, that she fell down and broke her hip, and that her daughter's in from out of town for a few more days and staying there alone and probably forgot to turn off the lights before she went to bed.

"Maybe she's asked some friends over and she's partying."

Fifty-five-year-old Alice has a rather dour outlook that would seem to preclude entertaining guests at two in the morning, but some would say so have I. "Maybe."

He's still looking across the street. "That house isn't architecturally much of a match to the rest of the block. Was it built much later?"

"Yeah, most of the houses on the street date to the 1880s, but that one was built in 1927, by someone particularly uninspired."

"Not necessarily. There's a certain purity to some of those plain brown boxes. They're kind of like a homage to utility. You know?"

I don't know, and don't see what he sees, but fine, whatever, goodbye.

He stands up and effortlessly stretches his arms high and straight above his head, way higher than I can reach. "Can you believe we're talking architecture at this time of the night?"

"I can't believe I'm up at this time of night."

"Okay, I'm leaving." He runs down the steps, stubs out his cigarette on the sidewalk, throws it onto the street, runs back up, and kisses me goodbye. "I'll call you," he says, and I'm not sure how I feel, knowing that he will.

~ ★ ~

On Sunday afternoon, Sylvia and I stand on the sidewalk in front of Westdale, apart from the other parents, waiting for the basketball team bus to arrive. I have hidden the fact that I am so sore in the vaginal area that I can't walk properly and neglected to mention that I saw Nils again last night to Sylvia, though I'm surprised she hasn't somehow sensed my altered sex state. Like in my youth, when the occasional caddish teenage boy would say he could tell by looking in a girl's eyes if she was a virgin or not, then stare at me searchingly, more witch-hunter than pick-up artist.

Sylvia says, "It was strange not having Ben around this weekend. The house was so much quieter without him there refusing to communicate."

I walk over to a nearby tree, raise my arms up above my head and stretch them against the trunk. "Strange better, or strange worse?"

"Strange better. How's your shoulder, by the way? Is it still frozen?"

"Pretty much."

A team mother of our acquaintance walks by, sees me with my head down, my arms up against the tree, says, "Have you been a bad girl, Emily?" and walks on.

I exchange glances with Sylvia.

She says, "I think that was supposed to be an S & M joke."

"Tell me something: are all people but us weird and fucked?"

"No, all people are weird and fucked in different ways."

The bus drives up, the parents converge on it, the boys take forever to file out, blinking in the sunlight, and soon, I'm alone in the car with Jesse. The first thing he says is, "Did you listen to the CD I gave you?"

"Yes, I did. Thank you. It was very thoughtful of you to make it for me. And poor you, having to listen to so much of my music in the process."

"I didn't have to listen to it to burn it. Did you like the last song?"

"I didn't get to the last song yet."

He shakes his head. "You didn't listen to any of it, did you?"

"I listened to some of it but not all. I wasn't in the car that much this weekend so I didn't have a chance."

"You can't listen to music at home?"

"Do I usually?"

"No, but you could. Normal people do."

Normal people exercise common courtesies, too. "Tell me about your weekend, honey. How was it? Did you have fun? Are you exhausted?"

I ask him about the hotel room, and his teammates, and the games, and his minutes, and how he played, and he answers more equably than I would have expected him to, given the CD tension and his general attitudes of the recent past, but five minutes in, he says, "So I quit the team."

"What?"

"You heard me."

"Are you serious?"

"Yeah."

"Why?"

"Because I hate Dawson, and he hates me, and there's no point in sitting on the bench waiting for him to put me in for two minutes, so why the fuck should I?"

I know what he's doing, what he's up to, because this when-things-get-tough-withdraw approach to life is my specialty. I applied it to the chess club in grade five, to my theatrical career after I failed to make the chorus in my middle school's production of *Bye Bye Birdie* (I knew every word of that damned score, too), to visual arts in high school, to the big architectural firm where I developed the tic in my face. I'm not proud that I have a history of giving up on anything I'm not good at (pastry making is another example), but that's the life pattern I've followed. And I don't want Jesse to follow in my footsteps, any more than I want him to lip off to his teachers. Except I do sort of want him to lip off to his teachers.

"Did you tell Dawson you quit?"

"No, but I'm not going to go to practice anymore." He looks and sounds like he's made up his mind. "And don't think about trying to make me."

"When is the next practice?"

"Don't know, don't care. What's for dinner?"

I've picked up some Middle Eastern food, one of his favourite meals — falafel and baba ghanoush and lentil soup and grilled chicken with yellow rice — under the assumption he'd be hungry after three days of scrounging for gluten-free fare at fast food restaurants on the road. I tell him that and quiz him about what he ate while he was away, and I don't bring up the basketball topic again, mainly because I don't know what to say about it or what to do, if anything.

I am reduced, after dinner, to sending Henry an email on the subject, worded as a notification message rather than as a cry for help. I have just clicked on the send button when Jesse comes into my office and sits down in the visitor's chair across from me.

"Yes?" I say, but not unpleasantly.

He opens the lacquer box on my desk and pulls out a key on a curly blue telephone cord key chain. "What's this?"

"It's the key to my new client's house. Put it back."

He drops it back in, removes the armlet, holds it in his palm. "I need homework help."

"What subject?"

"English."

I'd rather help with math, but, "What's the assignment?"

"Write two hundred words on the symbolism of the ducks in *The Catcher in the Rye*."

How many years has it been since I read that novel? Do I remember the ducks? "What do you think they signify?"

"The guy's childhood."

"That sounds promising."

"How am I supposed to say that in two hundred words?"

"When I was in my last year of high school, there was a guy in my English class named Michael who was the class clown, and — "

"Does this have something to do with the ducks?"

"Hold on a minute and listen: this Michael guy kept up a running joke for the whole year — every text we studied, whether it was *Hamlet*, or *The Great Gatsby*, or some long poem or short story, or anything, when the teacher asked what the work's theme was, he'd raise his hand and say, 'Man's inhumanity to man, sir.' And the teacher would say, 'Correct,' without having any idea that Michael always gave the same inane answer. But a couple of us in the back row cracked up every time."

"That's what passed for humour in those days?"

"My point is that Michael would have said the ducks symbolized man's inhumanity to man and he might have been right. Unless they're supposed to represent man's inhumanity to ducks."

"I'm not using that. No way."

"How about saying the ducks represent lost innocence? That's another good generic response."

"Forget it, I'll look up some study notes online."

"There are study notes for the book online?"

"There are study notes for everything online." He has been shifting the armlet from hand to hand but he stops now and returns it to the box. "So what does this thing symbolize, according to your theory?" he says. "Lost innocence or man's inhumanity to man?"

A mental slide of my high school English class, where I sit in my bell-bottom jeans and a gauzy peasant-type top, amused by my classmate's smart-aleck teacher-baiting, is replaced by a more cloudy, dusty slide of me, crouched on the ground in North Cave at dawn, holding the armlet in one hand and deliberately erasing its imprint on the ground with the other.

"A bit of both, I guess."

~ CHAPTER NINE ~

When Jesse was five years old, I took him to the doctor for his annual checkup and a booster shot. He was his playful and talkative self while we waited, but as soon as he saw the hypodermic, he screamed with terror and ran out of the examining room, a nurse and I in pursuit. We had to hold him down — him yelling as if being beaten, me sweating and crying — while the doctor injected him. Maybe he'd developed a needle phobia as a result of the procedures he'd undergone to diagnose his celiac disease. But before every doctor's appointment thereafter — every single one since — he has asked me if the promise I made him that day when he was five, that he wouldn't get another needle for ten years, until he was fifteen, still held true. And every year I've assured him yes.

Now, on a day when Westdale has a late opening, I'm taking Jesse to the dentist, also known as Sylvia's husband, Ed, for an appointment to fill a cavity. This is Jesse's first cavity, and so far this morning, he has made clear his feelings about dentistry, the hardship inherent in rising early on his morning off, and my complete lack of sensitivity for having made the appointment at all. "Why do I have get the cavity filled?" he's said. "Why today? And why by Ed? He grips my jaw so hard, and I hate his stupid jokes. Why can't I go to a dentist I don't know? Why can't I leave the cavity and just promise to brush really well from now on?"

He's worn me down with these complaints, and I'm very close to telling him to shut (the fuck) up. But I haven't, yet. I haven't told him either that my promise of no needles until he's fifteen will be broken because he will have to take one in the mouth this morning, which is the most painful kind I've ever had, though a client's son broke his nose once and when she described to me how he had to get a shot up the inside of each nostril to freeze the area before the bone could be pushed back in place, that sounded worse.

One reason I haven't told him about the needle is that I'm still trying to think of ways to save him from it. Maybe Ed uses some new technique that means needle freezing is no longer required. Maybe if we ignore the cavity as Jesse suggests, it will go away. Maybe if I wish on the armlet, I can somehow escape this whole situation and eject from the car into another life, where I am not a parent, where I don't have a child (or mate or anyone) on behalf of whom I need to suffer vicarious pain or shame or discomfort or defeat. I yearn — again — for that isolated cottage in the woods where all is serene and peaceful and there are no kids complaining. Nor, for that matter, are there bugs buzzing or birds chirping or small animals rustling in the underbrush. There is only blessed quiet.

Quiet is so underrated. And anyone as loud as the morning disc jockey (female) who talks so gratingly on the radio station that plays the discordant progressive rap Jesse likes should not be allowed on the public airwaves or out in public at all. She should not be paid to incite me to thoughts of banishment, to make me want to send her forever to her own cabin, far away from mine.

Or to make me want to render her mute by cutting out her tongue. I push the button to turn the radio off. "I can't stand that woman's voice."

Jesse says, "I won't get out of the car when we get there."

Would I prefer him not to talk at all, the way he's been about the basketball topic since he quit the team two weeks ago? Henry tried to sound him out on the subject, by instant messaging, by phone, and by email, and got no further than I had. Jesse said he hates the coach, the coach hates him, and he won't play anymore, so both of us should shut (the fuck) up about it. I have complied with his request for silence on the subject, and since he quit the team, I've tried not to read as a bad omen his new habit of going out more on non-school nights. For three weekends in a row, he's slept over somewhere on the Fridays (having magically overcome his dislike of sleepovers) and come home on Saturday afternoons for a shower and some food before going back out again for another night of the same. "We hang out," he says, when I ask him what they do, where they go, and he always answers his cell phone when I call him and sounds his usual taciturn and sober self during the thirty or forty seconds that we speak.

His being out so much means I've been able to spend a few weekend hours with Nils, at my house or his apartment, during which we talk briefly, have a drink, and have sex. I've snuck out a few weekday evenings as well, left Jesse at home with his computer for company, and invented various two-hour-long excuses for my absences — a new yoga class I'm trying, a book club meeting I was invited to at which an architectural mystery was being discussed and my expertise sought. For this last fabrication, I went so far as to come up with a prop in the form of a suitable book, but there was no need. Jesse hasn't cared about any of my outings, has said, when I've come home after them, "Where were you again?"

On weekend nights, when I see Nils for three or four hours instead of two, I always sleep alone at home afterwards, in case Jesse were to call me needing a late pickup, but he hasn't, not lately, which I could take as a sign of him maturing if I wanted to try out the glass-half-full approach to my life instead of the usual half-empty one.

Our route to the dentist takes us past Stewart's mansion. In an effort to distract Jesse from the impending ordeal, I point out the house to him. "There, on the corner, the big house with the tower, that's the one I'm working on now."

"What about it?"

"Well" — I don't know where I'm going with this, but anywhere will do now that I have his attention — "get this story: I've been doing drawings of the house, and I came across a discrepancy on the main floor that I didn't notice when I did the measurements: a wall between the living room and dining room was twice the depth it should be."

"Meaning what?"

"Meaning maybe there was something between the walls. Like there could have been a pocket door, only there was no opening in the doorway between the two rooms that I'd seen — it was sealed over."

"Or maybe a skeleton was bricked in there." He doesn't sound excited when he says this. He doesn't sound cynical or sarcastic either. "Or there could be a wall safe hidden behind a painting, like in those caper movies. Did you check for that?"

The story I'm telling really happened, but I'm dramatizing it for his entertainment purposes. And so far, I seem to be succeeding, though the exercise reminds me of the days I thought we'd both outgrown when Jesse was a cranky toddler desperate to get out of his car seat and the only way I could keep him in there without him squirming and crying and turning red for a car ride lasting more than two minutes was to put on some kids' music tape and sing along frantically like a camp counsellor on speed.

I say, "I thought of something like that, too. Because there are some other built-in crannies in the house. There's a hidden cupboard under the front hall stairs, and a wooden bin for mail attached to the inside of the front door under the mail slot, and a box set into the brick wall beside the side door that was used, once upon a time, by milkmen who delivered fresh milk every morning."

Milk was delivered daily to my childhood home, homo milk, in bottles, the cream collected under the silver foil peel-off caps. But to Jesse, jokes about milkmen and housewives, the expression about cream rising to the top — if he even knows those references — are rooted outside his experience. To him, a milkman must seem like a character from a fairy tale, like a cobbler or a spinner of wool.

"So what was between the walls?" He's bored already, wants the punchline.

"Uh, well, a set of pocket doors. Dusty but intact, undamaged oak doors, one on each side, the openings covered with six layers of thick white tape, then painted over with several coats of paint."

"That's the end of the story?"

"Yup. And look, we're here."

"That story sucked. And I'm not getting out of the car."

He says that, but he does get out, and follows me up to Ed's office, where I make him take off his coat and hang it up, and he sits down and sullenly watches a four-year-old boy push wooden beads along curved, coloured wires on a tabletop toy.

After some fevered whispering with the receptionist, I'm allowed in to speak to Ed in private, in his consultation room. "I'm sorry I left this so late," I say, "but is there any way a needle can be avoided? Jesse's a little phobic."

Ed leans back in his chair. "I could give him laughing gas. He'd still need the local anaesthetic by needle, but the gas would lessen his anxiety."

Just what my oral surgeon told me a year ago: he'll still feel some pain, but he'll be high, so he won't care.

"You'd give laughing gas to a fourteen-year-old?"

"Sure. It's safe and its effects are short-term." He stands up. "Shall we offer him a hit, see what he says?"

I'm dubious, but I've always believed Ed to be competent and smart about his work, if about nothing else, so I say okay and follow him out. Ed's hearty opening gambit to Jesse is an unfunny comment about Ben being a slacker to be sleeping in at home while Jesse is here submitting himself to the drill. Jesse greets this with a weak and borderline rude smile, but then Ed says, "Would you like to try some laughing gas this morning, to help ease you through the procedure?"

Jesse's face lights up. "Are you serious?"

"Sure am. Your mom says you're not too keen on needles, so if you like, we can give you some nitrous oxide first, to relax you."

Jesse's glance flickers over to me, as if wondering how I could possibly approve. When I shrug and nod, he says, "Okay, cool."

I say, "Do you want me to come in the room with you?" but Jesse is shaking his head no before I've finished the sentence, and off they go together, to Ed's chamber of dental horror/opium den.

In the waiting room, the choice of reading material is between a pile of celebrity gossip rags, heavy on red carpet photographs, and a self-important newsmagazine, its cover emblazoned with the headline, "Do You Know What Your Children Are Smoking? The New Teen Drug Culture." I'm in no mood to be any further alarmed this morning, so I opt for the trash mags, "read" four different issues, and am searching in vain through the last for a single close-up photograph of an actress or singer over age thirty with a lined forehead, when Jesse emerges with Ed. His cheek and lip are slightly swollen on the right side, but his expression is composed. And he's not crying.

"Everything okay?" I say.

Ed says, "Everything's fine. What a good patient! See you, Jesse."

On the elevator, I say, "So it wasn't so bad?" and I try to touch his cheek, but he bats my hand away.

"It wasn't bad at all. I didn't feel the needle go in and the drilling lasted for like, thirty seconds."

"What was the laughing gas like?"

"Have you ever had it?"

"No."

"It was like, I don't know, crazy. Like listening to one of Dad's John Coltrane albums when you're sleepy."

Like being high on weed. "Can't you compare it to something other than jazz?"

"What can I say? It was trippin'."

"You're not still feeling it now, are you?"

"All I feel now is the freezing, which is weird." He touches his numb lip. "So weird."

"How long will it last?"

"An hour or two, Ed said."

"Hey, now we match." I touch my shoulder. "Frozen shoulder, frozen mouth."

He mumbles, "Sometimes, Em, you'd be better off not speaking," and gently and repeatedly touches the numb surface of his cheek with the pads of his fingers all the way to the car.

When I pull up in front of the school, he rummages around in his backpack. "Wait a second. I need you to sign something."

"What?"

"Hold on."

He pulls out a crumpled sheet of paper, hands it to me, and searches for a pen while I squint at what appears to be a permission form for a semi-formal dance to be held next week at a nightclub located in the adult club district, an area known for regular shootings of club patrons. "You want to go to a semi-formal? Downtown? Since when? With whom? What will you wear?"

"Everyone goes. And you wear whatever you want. It's called a semi-formal but it's not. Just sign it."

The form contains a section that the student must sign to indicate his or her agreement not to commit offenses at the party that are punishable by suspension or expulsion, including being intoxicated, fighting, uttering racial slurs, carrying a weapon, and being in possession of illegal drugs. Lovely.

"What do you mean everyone goes? Will other grade tens go? Who do I know who's going?"

"People. Everyone on the basketball team."

"Including Ben?"

"Including Ben."

"Do you need this today, or can I discuss it with Sylvia first?"

"The tickets go on sale today and I can't buy a ticket without the form, but go ahead, take it home, discuss it with Sylvia, see if I care."

He opens the door and is already halfway out when I say, "Are you sure?"

"Do what you want." Door slammed, euphoria gone. And I hope I imagined hearing him mutter "bitch" under his breath.

I expect a slightly better reception at my next stop, to visit Vera, in an in-patient room that features shades of teal and dusty rose, not my favourite colours, either alone or in combination on a ghastly patterned wallpaper border, but better them than hospital green and stark white, I suppose. Or not. "So this is what a convalescent home looks like," I say. "I've never been to one before."

Vera says, "They're called rehab centres now. And let's hope for your sake you never have to come back to one again."

She says my visit is gift enough and tells me I shouldn't have brought the box of Belgian chocolates and the book about English cottage gardens, but she exclaims over the beautiful cover photo on the book, opens the chocolates, takes one, pronounces it divine, and offers one to her roommate, a gloomy-looking woman with hairs sprouting from her chin who says no thanks. Vera gives me a two-minute master class demonstration in how to receive presents, in other words.

"So how are you holding up in here?" I say, after I've pushed her in a wheelchair to the common room, where we can sit and talk in relative privacy.

"It's tolerable. I do my therapies, I talk to people — there's a group of us that plays cards in the afternoons some days, I watch television. It helps that I know I'll get out of here eventually and I can mark off each day on the calendar that brings me closer to my release date. If this were my permanent home, if I were imprisoned for life in here with a bunch of old, sick people, I'd die."

I have no answer to that and am about to fall back on another interior design comment — to question the wisdom of quite so many potted ferns — but Vera saves us both by saying, "Emily, after everything you've done for me, I hate to trouble you, but could I ask for one more favour?"

"I'm happy to help. What can I do?"

"It's about the house. I want to start the selling process, get it underway as soon as possible. Alice doesn't approve of my timing; she says I need to concentrate on getting better, not on a crazy scheme to control the future of a house that won't belong to me."

I don't disagree with Alice, but it's Vera to whom I have pledged my allegiance. "So you want to go ahead anyway?"

"I want at least to get the discussion started and find out what my options are. Would you consider dealing with the real estate agent I told you about and having him in to do a proper evaluation? I could talk to him on the phone and explain what I want in terms of stipulations and conditions, but if you could take him through the house, I'd be grateful."

"Sure. Give me his name and number and I'll call him."

She pats my hand with hers and I try not to shrink from the soft, wrinkled touch of her skin. "You're such a dear. I always knew that under that gruff exterior was a kind heart."

If only she could convince Jesse of that.

I sign the permission form that evening, after a phone talk with Sylvia, during which we discuss the pros and cons of allowing Ben and Jesse to attend what is, we seek comfort in reassuring each other, a school-sanctioned party, and what Sylvia's research, conducted with other Westdale parents, has led us to believe is a high point in the school social calendar. We pledge as our condition for approval that one of us (or Ed) will drive the boys down to the nightclub at the start of the party and the other (or Ed) will pick them up at the end. And we agree that the boys wouldn't be so witless as to risk getting caught and suspended for drinking, so this night will be one at which they are more likely than most to be sober. Though I'm still hoping against reason that Jesse is always sober, is still hewing to his I'm-an-athlete philosophy.

Sylvia says, "Now that we've got that settled, I have to go help Kira build her rainforest diorama. What about you? Are you going to your, ahem, yoga class, tonight?"

I regret having told her that I was still seeing Nils, that we were having sex, and that I was keeping the relationship a secret from Jesse, but she was keenly interested and badgered me into confessing some if not all details on the state of my temporary union.

"Yes, I am."

"Be careful with all those complicated positions, now!" She chortles and hangs up.

Damn. I should have withstood her interrogation and penetrating tell-me-everything stares. I'd make a terrible unfaithful spouse. Have already proved myself a terrible faithful spouse.

My ability to be a good girlfriend, or fuck buddy, or casual sex partner, or whatever I am to Nils, is also tested, soon after I arrive at Nils's apartment in my yoga outfit. I sit down on his couch, accept the glass of fizzy Italian lemonade he offers me, and almost immediately roll my eyes, because he is waving around a flyer he received in the mail from the faculty of architecture that announces a one-day symposium on post-post-modern architecture to be held in a few weeks' time. And after he's exclaimed that it sounds interesting and the panel assembled illustrious, he asks if I'm going.

"I try to avoid faculty of architecture events," I say. "They're usually attended by retired old bores and underemployed recent graduate bores, both of whom talk too much about their misplaced enthusiasms." I'm rather pleased with the bite of these mauvais mots of mine, until I realize that Nils might be said to fall into the latter category. Apologizing will only underscore that insulting notion, so I point to the ordinary drinking glass I'm holding and say, "This is a nice glass. Is it new?" Maybe next I can retell the story about the pocket doors at Stewart's house, followed by an antic off-key rendition of "Baby Beluga."

"But this one guy is doing some fascinating work with sustainable development," Nils says, unaware that he has pissed me off by using the word *fascinating* without irony. He finds the listing for the admired guy in the brochure and begins to read aloud — enthusiastically — the canned bio of a crusading architect from California who builds new houses out of salvaged building materials, who uses reclaimed floor boards and antique railings, recycled brick and old barn beams, etc.

And here's where I'm being unnecessarily irascible, because the salvage concept is of some interest to me. I just don't want to hear about it right now. Like Sylvia, I'm not keen on being read aloud to under any circumstances, especially when the time allotted for yoga is slipping by. Spare me the reading aloud and spare me the puffed-up symposium filled with posturing egotists jockeying for position and importance, each one taking an hour or more to say what could be summarized in ten minutes. Email me a well-written article on the subject from a reputable newspaper or journal and I'd be happy to read all about successful salvaging (skipping paragraphs here and there if I so choose) and not discuss it, or have to listen to pretentious, self-aggrandizing questions from the floor. I say, "So you plan to partake of this feast of ideas, do you?"

"Definitely. My boss is letting me take the day off work. You should come too."

"I don't think so."

"Why not? Some of these techniques could be the techniques of the future."

"Some of them, maybe. But new ideas tend to be impractical to implement in the field and have an inconvenient way of costing the clients more than the old forest-depleting, fossil fuel–burning methods that we already know and love."

"Clients should be more forward-thinking."

And so should I, he's implying, but if I were, I wouldn't be here right now, living through this relationship with no future.

"You're right," I say. "Clients should have more open minds and wallets. I totally agree." I move toward him, place my hand on his chest, stroke him through his T-shirt, and quickly arouse him, take his mind off anything but responding to my hands and my mouth and my groin pressed against his.

In the past few weeks, Nils and I have learned a little about each other's bodies and preferences, about what spots are to be avoided and which to be given attention, about who likes what and in what order. We've begun to develop a shared tempo, our own rhythm, but tonight, the pace is changed — it feels alternately too slow and too fast, never right.

My mind wanders more than once as we go through the routine we're still working out, and during the big finish, I bite my lip and wonder how much longer this will take, and what a courtesan or geisha or high-priced hooker would do to speed up the process — probably some secret move that guarantees instant satisfaction on the man's part but would disgust me to hear about, let alone execute, so good thing I don't know of any such tricks, old dog that I am.

When Nils comes, his orgasmic shudder and vocalizations seem the same as they have on previous occasions, so maybe it's me who's out of step, who's off the beat. After a polite interval — I count ten Mississippis in my head — I push him gently off me and sit up, get dressed, go to the bathroom and sort myself out, fix my hair.

He has pulled on a T-shirt and boxers, not one to go about shirtless — a quality I admire in a man, no matter what his motivation, which in his case may be a reluctance to display his uncut abs — and he sits in this outfit on the side of his bed until I'm ready, then walks me to the door. "Can't you stay longer?" he says. He sounds like he means it.

"No." I kiss him on the cheek, a neat, dry kiss. "Gotta go."

"What shall we do this weekend? And have you got any more of that weed, by the way?"

"No, I don't, sorry." We smoked the last joint of my Spencer stash a week ago, but could I possibly score some more? For a second, I contemplate going to Ruby's, looking for Spencer, and asking him if he can set me up with a supply.

No. I cannot do that, will not. And I've scared myself by considering it as an option.

He says, "I might know someone who can get some. I'll check it out."

Maybe weed could keep us going a bit longer, get us back on the same beat. As long as I don't have to procure it. "Okay, bye."

He pulls me in for one more hug, but I've had enough, am impatient to go, and stand inert in his arms, waiting to be released. When I finally head out, he calls after me, "Hey, do you think it's time I met Jesse?"

I bristle at the very idea. It is certainly not time, not now and probably not ever. That's as ridiculous a notion as me buying drugs from a teenage drug dealer. Someone needs to start being sensible here. *I* need to. "I'll call you," I say, and I run to my car, to home.

The real estate agent who comes to do a walk-through of Vera's house, a man in his forties named Greg, is wearing a preppy suit, shirt, sweater vest, tie, and loafers combination that may be intended to convey his social standing — or his social aspirations — but which puts me off. I'm not keen on his manner, either. He tsks over the antiquated (not in a good way) bathroom fixtures, says about the kitchen, "I would have thought avocado-coloured appliances weren't even allowed in this neighour-hood," and reacts to the four upstairs bedrooms with, "Oh my god, chenille bedspreads and tiny closets." He pronounces the living room and dining room pokey, and after he opens the basement door, he goes halfway down the stairs and runs back up again. "Nothing to see down there," he sings.

I've been inside Vera's house before, but not lately, and never to look at it from the point of view of a potential buyer. I try to take on the perspective of a young couple who'd like to move into the area with their child or dog, but when I do, all I see is a neat shabbiness, an unmistakable decrepitude. The windows are painted shut and fitted with heavy storms that haven't been removed in years. The wood floors are warped and have been sanded so many times they're splintered at the seams. The house may have worked hard and well for Vera and her family in decades past, but its time has passed. Not only is it not worth saving; it almost begs to be put out of its misery.

Greg meets me in the front hall. "Well, well," he says. "Well, well, well."

"Go ahead," I say. "Tell me what you really think. No shit."

He takes a deep breath — honesty must require extra oxygen intake. "From the outside, on this street, the house looks like it could be a nice little fixer-upper for the right client. But now that I've seen the inside — " He takes in more air. "In my opinion? This is a teardown, pure and simple. Don't you agree?"

I do. As would most people, other than young dreamers who talk about the purity of utility and think symposia are fun. I say, "But Vera wants to write some kind of no-demolition clause into any prospective offer. And she wants her garden preserved. She wants to influence the house's future."

"If she does that, number one she won't get anyone reputable to list her, and number two she won't get any offers. A listing like that is a big waste of everyone's time."

"And what price do you think the house would go for without any conditions, roughly?"

He names a fair-sounding price range that would pay for Vera's condo with a solid nest egg left over. "If a couple of developers start bidding against each other, we might be able to squeeze out a little more."

"Okay, I'll talk to her, explain the situation, see what she says. Thanks for coming by."

"My pleasure. Did you get my card? You did. Good." He slips on his polished penny loafers, the like of which I haven't seen since grade nine. He says, "I don't know how you're going to word it when you talk to her, but here's the top line: this house is damaged goods, yesterday's news. It's obsolete."

"Yeah, I'm sure she'd love to hear that right now, in the convalescent home. I bet the damaged goods analogy would go over really big with her at the moment."

"Well, good luck with that!" he says, and, "Ta-ta!"

It's hard to muster the strength required, using my sore arm, to close the door after him quickly enough that it hits him on the ass on the way out, but I rise to the occasion. I also report to Vera by phone on his visit and give her the news straight, minus any mention of obsolescence.

"He wasn't too keen on the stipulations, but he's sure he could get a good price for the house without them."

"You mean he won't take the listing if there are conditions attached?"

"I don't think so, no."

"Oh." Did a small, sad sigh of resignation escape from her? I'm not sure.

"What does he know, though?" I say. "There are plenty of other agents around. Maybe we should get some more opinions."

"I might do that, but I won't trouble you any further, Emily. Leave it with me. Thank you for everything."

"You're welcome. And I'm still keeping an eye on the house and picking up the mail. I'll bring it up to you one day next week."

"Don't bother. My mail's boring and I don't want you going out of your way to come out here. I have to go now, it's time for my physiotherapy session. Thank you again."

~ ★ ~

"So how was your, uh, yoga class the other night?" Sylvia says, on our next walk, and at least she didn't lead off with double entendres about downward dogs.

"It was okay."

She leans forward, tries to see my face. "That's all?"

"Even the best batters don't hit a home run every time they're up, right?"

"You're at the sports metaphor stage of the relationship already? Gee, maybe I shouldn't tell you this hot off the press juicy story I've got."

"Is it about Mr. Sutherland?"

"No. Who's he? No, it's about you and your guy."

"I don't like the story already."

"You'll like it, you'll like it. So. You know Bunny that I told you about at the art gallery? The young woman who parties all the time and knows all the hot spots?"

"The young woman I dislike on description alone?"

"Will you stop? She took me for lunch yesterday to a roti place that's a few blocks away from the gallery. It's one of those hole-in-the-wall restaurants, everyone there is recovering from all-night raves or whatever, and the cook takes forever to make each roti to order, but the food's quite tasty."

"What does this have to do with Nils and me?"

"Let me finish. Bunny and I are sitting in this not-the-cleanest-place-I've-ever-seen, waiting for our roti, and watching the cook pour half a cup of whipping cream into the sauté pan with the cauliflower and potatoes, and that's for my portion alone — no wonder I'd put on a pound the next morning. But anyway, we're sitting there, and Bunny starts telling me about this guy friend of hers who's dating a way older woman, and she's worried about him because he's getting serious about her, and she thinks that's a big mistake, because what if he wants to have kids, and this woman seems to be exploiting and objectifying him because he's young and virile."

"Hearing that makes me want to break up with Nils right away so that no one would ever think of me in those terms."

"A little touchy on the subject, are we?"

"What did you say to her?"

"I said, Funny you should mention a May-December romance, because a friend of mine is dating a younger man right now, and he went after her."

"A May-December romance?"

"I mean, you're not one of those cougar women you read about in magazines. If there's any feline you're like, it would be, well, let's see. You're not like a fluffy Persian, or like the cute grey tabby I had when I was a kid. I know — you're like one of those ancient Egyptian royal cats, all haughty and standoffish."

If I suspect she considered comparing me to a Siamese cat for a few seconds, I'm grateful she didn't express the thought out loud. I'll also not take offence at being described as haughty and standoffish if this story isn't about Nils and me specifically but is part of a discussion about older women and younger men in general. "So what did Bunny — and with a name like that, talk about someone begging to be compared unflatteringly to animals — say to your defense of me?"

"She said that maybe my friend was innocent, but she'd met the woman her friend was squandering his youth on, and not only was she a cool customer, she was you!"

I'm confused. "What?"

"Her friend is Nils. She described you as an Asian architect named Emily. She met you square dancing. She said you were 'steely.'"

Quite the descriptors I'm collecting today: haughty, steely, December-like, and my perennial favourite when it's the first that comes to someone's mind, Asian.

"I don't understand this story. I've only ever met one female friend of Nils's, and her name wasn't Bunny."

"Oh, right. Bunny's her nickname at the gallery because of some legendary and hilarious incident at a costume party a few years ago. Her real name is Melissa."

"Melissa, I've met. Dyed blonde, husky voice, fleshy body, bit of a bitch?"

"I've always liked her."

I give Sylvia a reproving look. She shrugs and says, "She's lively and laughs a lot and is a great gossip."

We walk on, I resist asking Sylvia how she could like a person because she laughs a lot, and I sort through what I've heard. I toss aside Melissa the interfering busybody along with the animal comparisons, faulty assumptions, and minor insults, and grab onto the most depressing part of Sylvia's story: "Nils is getting serious about me?"

"That's what she said. But that's not bad, is it? I thought you'd be happy to hear that."

If I were Sylvia and a believer in coupledom as the key to long life and happiness, I *would* be happy to hear this and might begin to think that Nils and I could one day forge a stable, successful, long-term relationship, critics like Bunny Melissa be damned. But I'm me, a weird loner who thinks the whole long life concept is overrated. So all that this unreliable third-hand reportage does is unsettle me for the rest of our walk and for much of the day that follows.

One of my favourite childhood games, Arrows, a variation on hide-and-seek, called for a band of kids, armed with a piece of chalk if they were lucky and assorted pieces of a broken red clay flowerpot if they weren't, to set off on an ever-changing circuitous route through the side streets and back alleys and garages and laneways of the neighbourhood where I grew up. A first group marked its path with strategically placed (semi-hidden, and at intervals) arrows, scrawled, with the chalk or clay, on the street or the sidewalk, on a brick wall or a wide old tree or a flagstone. A second group followed the snaky arrow trail and tried to catch up before the first group made it back to home base.

The best routes were the trickiest: those that called for climbing over backyard fences and slipping through narrow passageways between houses. Cutting through a block down a little-trodden path, sneaking through a garden at the risk of rousing a dog or a bad-tempered old person, finding a through-way where it wasn't expected, inscribing an arrow where it could be found, but not easily — these were the thrills of the game, the satisfactions.

I have an affection for throughways still, but many of the lanes I once knew and used, in my old neighbourhood and others, are blocked off now at one end, by a new house or a wall, and provide access no more. Schoolyards that were designed to be entered from either end are now fenced off on one side, for safety reasons. Same for some grand old buildings on the university campus: originally laid out with back and front and side entrances, they can now be entered though only one set of doors. The others are locked, used for exit only. On an old city street I know, a set of rowhouses have closed off a space where a footpath once provided semi-secret egress between the backs of two cul-de-sacs.

The restoration of Stewart's house provides me with the opportunity to reverse the trend, to reopen back stairs and recreate second doorways that have been drywalled over and hidden away. The intention of my labour is to restore the past, but one late night at my desk, I get carried away and work into the preliminary plans two new features that didn't exist in the original design.

181

The first wrinkle calls for the replacement of a utilitarian metal fire escape with a wrought iron Art Nouveau–style balcony joined by a graceful winding staircase to a proposed new terrace railing (that I imagine festooned with climbing roses and morning glories) below. The second idea is to create a byway behind a series of aligned closets on the second floor, a dimly lit path with multiple hidden access points of the sort that would be most enjoyed by amateur magicians or practical jokers who wanted to entertain guests with an occasional mysterious disappearance and reappearance. Or by children wanting to re-enact scenes from fifty-year-old English storybooks of the type I read as a child.

There is no reason to think Stewart read or valued those books, is inclined to magic or jokes of any kind, or will find appealing my suggestions to impart a playful or romantic quality to his mansion, but I enjoyed working through my ideas (my current preoccupations with parenting and my sex life put aside), so I present them to him and Joe anyway, at one of our project management meetings. I make sure to contain any eagerness I might feel when I describe what I have in mind, though if I'm given a word of encouragement, I'm likely to dream up a few more nifty schemes, the layout of the house's mammoth basement having already started my brain spinning in fanciful turns.

Stewart listens with the appearance of attention while I present the entire plan in my best deadpan and succinct style. I conclude with, "Those last two things are just some features I came up with for a lark." Did I say lark? That's about as retro as Vera offering me a cutting of violets from her garden. Good thing Stewart's old, so there's a remote chance he knows what a lark is, in this or any other context.

Across the table, Joe has on his usual easygoing facial expression. He's too much the diplomat to offer an opinion pro or con about my little initiatives until the boss does.

Stewart says, "I don't mean to be thick, but why?"

"You know what?" I say — and I hate that expression. "How about if I leave this with you to look over and see what you think? You can get back to us, let us know what you decide."

Stewart says, "I'm sorry, but I don't see the point of these little embellishments, what purpose they serve, or what rationale there is for them."

I've spent the last ten minutes giving a rationale, and I don't plan to give it again. "Well, then," I say, and to convincingly pull off indifference and a sense of humour in defeat here, I have to draw on my poor acting skills and my vast store of experience in dealing with clients I hate, apply the lessons learned from years of giving way, and force a smile through my next words, "the balcony and the closet passageway are hereby nixed and will never be spoken of again. All in favour?"

Across the table, Joe raises a quizzical eyebrow at me, but I'm so fakely unbothered and indifferent and living by the code that there's no "I" in team — like Jesse, I'm such a fucking team player, so ready to kiss ass and help put away the gym equipment — that I'm practically burbling with glee (or maybe with hysterical laughter that will signal a straitjacket-required breakdown). "Moving on, let's book our next meeting. How about two weeks from today — same place, same time — does that sound good for everyone? Great!"

Joe and I walk out of the building together to our cars, though he's not Danny, so there will be no cigarette and bitchy dis walk around the block, much as I would welcome the chance right now, much as I need to vent.

I say, "That was awkward."

Joe looks at his boots. "I liked the closet idea. Though I can see why Stewart wouldn't."

"Because his head's stuck up his ass, you mean?"

"Because he's conservative and traditional."

"I prefer the head-in-the-ass explanation. And to think that he's wrong and I'm right, but it's his house, so what do I care what he does with it?" What was I thinking? And how can I stop myself from thinking that way again? "Anyway, Joe, sorry about my little digressions. I'll behave from now on and hoe my row in my best yes-massa manner, I promise."

"Oh, Emily," he says. Like I'm his difficult child and he's having trouble remembering why he loves me. Though he doesn't walk off in a huff but stands and waits patiently for our conversation to be over.

"How do you it, Joe?"

"Do what?"

"Put up with arrogant clients. Stay married for twenty-five years. Not be in a constant state of rage mixed with despondency. How do you stay so calm?"

He looks across the street at a bland high-rise apartment building. "I'm on antidepressants."

"Oh." Way for me to be rude, intrusive and rude, on top of difficult. "I'm sorry. I didn't mean to — I'll slink back into my cave now and never speak again. Bye."

He smiles. "It's no big deal. My doctor prescribed them about a year ago when my father died and Susan had her bout of breast cancer and I started thinking too much about my own mortality. The pills are supposed to make me less anxious."

"Do they work?"

"I guess so. I still don't sleep very well. But you think I'm mellow."

"Compared to me, you are."

"You shouldn't let people like Stewart bother you."

"I know I shouldn't, but I do."

He gives out a small chuckle. "Though there is something funny about watching you go at him. Like a terrier attacking a bear."

Hey, now I can add dog to my personal comparative menagerie of nuns and cats. And I'm sure there's a good joke to be made somewhere in there: one that begins with a Mother Superior, an Egyptian cat, and a terrier walking into a bar.

"You know what gets me, though?" I say. "A few weeks ago I was happy that this project was a true restoration, happy not to be working on one of those adaptive reuse jobs that make so many concessions to contemporary extravagance that they end up retaining only a few square feet of the house's original character."

"Like my usual builds, you mean?"

"I'm sorry, Joe, that's not what I — "

"It's okay. I know what my product is."

"But what gets me is that if I was so pleased to be working on a restoration with integrity, why did I try to come up with ways to makeover the house that would realize an inauthentic vision?"

"Because not everything old is worth preserving in its original state."

"Yeah, but young isn't necessarily better than old, either."

"Young? You mean new?"

"Young, new, modern, whatever. They should all go away and leave us alone."

"I don't know about that. I wouldn't mind branching out a little sometimes, finding a few more interesting and more varied projects to work on. You know" — he smiles here, and his mid-sentence pause is like the *ba-dum-bum* of a stand-up comic's snare drum — "for a lark."

"Go ahead and make fun. I'm glad I can be a source of amusement for you."

"All kidding aside," he says, though he's still smiling at his joke, "the problem is that I'm a prisoner of my own success. Every time I decide to take a break from building six-bedroom mock Georgians, someone offers me big bucks to build one exactly like the last. You must know what I mean — aren't you tired of restoring old houses?"

On a Wednesday evening, not the day of my fictional yoga class, Nils implores me to meet him for drinks at a groovy new bar called Park Place, part of a major renovation of a former fleabag hotel in the west end. He's fired up about the symposium he attended today and wants to tell me about it. "Come on, Emily," he says, "can't you get away for an hour or two?"

He calls me at six to ask me this, when I'm cleaning up the kitchen after my early dinner with Jesse, and I've had a bad arm day, and the house and I smell like the roasted peppers and leeks I made to mix into the homemade tomato sauce I used on my pasta, Jesse having had rice spaghetti and the same sauce, with ground beef added and the vegetables omitted. I was aggrieved to see Nils's name on the call display and am even more aggrieved by his request.

"I don't know," I say. "I'd have to dream up an excuse to go out." And take a shower to rid myself of the cooking smells.

"You could bring your son along if you like. He'd love Park Place."

How does Nils know what Jesse would love? And what a great idea, regardless, to introduce a fourteen-year-old to hipster night life. Maybe Nils would like to slip him a drink or three while he's at it. But his suggestion decides me. "Jesse has homework to do, but I'll figure something out and meet you there at seven-thirty."

I'll tell Jesse I have errands to run, that I'm going out to do some shopping, then I'll meet Nils at the Monopoly game property, suggest it's time we take a break from each other, not go to his place for goodbye sex, and be home by nine, alone, unburdened.

~ ★ ~

Whoever did up Park Place had a big budget and was aiming for the New York boutique hotel look in the sleek exterior and sleeker two-storey bar. I have troubled to shower, do my hair, and put on some eye makeup, but I was in no mood to pick from my closet any clothing worthy of this fashionable scene (I have none that would do anyway), so I'm wearing jeans, a black turtleneck, and a winter coat (it *is* December). The bar's patrons — numerous, loud, average age thirty-three — wear clothes whose fashion statements are punctuated with of-the-minute accessories, the women in pointy high-heeled shoes and boots that make my feet hurt just to look at them.

I stand in the doorway, try to locate Nils in the crowd, and the assault of the din, the lighting, and the overheated air only worsen my mood.

There's Nils, at a table, deep in conversation with his friend Raj. He does not look his best — he's had his hair cut since I saw him last and wears the fugly purple shirt he wore when we met for lunch at Bar Sorrento.

Raj jumps up when I arrive in their corner, flashes me a friendly smile, says he was saving my seat, bids Nils adieu, and suggests that we go out to dinner sometime, we three, with Melissa and whoever she's dating now. I say sure and nod like this would be a great idea. When he's melted into the crowd, I turn to Nils, who from the smell of his breath and the glaze in his eye seems to be on his third or fourth beer, and I yell in his ear that we should try to find a place to sit where we can hear each other speak.

There is a slightly quieter mezzanine level to this space, furnished with sets of leather club chairs grouped around marble-faced cubes. We repair to one of these nooks, I sink into the too low, too soft chair, set my glass of soda water on the cube, and listen to Nils talk about the charismatic salvage guru he heard speak about sustainable architecture and about how he met some other young architects (why does he identify them as young?) who are forming a collective (which seems to be what was called a partnership in my day, but collective sounds so much more bullshitty, I mean, virtuous) and have invited him to join. "Raj is going to be part of it," he says, and lists a few more names I don't know, "and a woman who's still in architecture school but is really smart, named Autumn, and — "

"Autumn? Strawberry-blonde Autumn?"

"Do you know her?"

"Yeah, we've met, and why she isn't named Spring I don't understand."

"What?"

"Nothing."

"So anyway, I was going to ask everybody if you could join, too, but I thought I'd better check with you first. Do you want to?"

That he would think I might be interested in joining such a group only adds fuel to my let's-end-this fire. "What exactly will this 'collective' do?"

"Get the word out, bid for jobs, and maybe get one or two."

"And if the group did get a job, and you began to work on it in a collective fashion, how would you find the time to do that and hold on to your real job?"

"But that's the beauty of the collective concept. We could each do our share in our spare time, one or the other of us could take a leave of absence for a few weeks or months if necessary, and if the business builds, we might one day all work together full-time."

The concept, or should I say pipe dream, sounds poorly thought out and unrealistic to me, but was I asked for my opinion? No. "Well, it sounds like you had a great day until now,"

I say. "An inspiring day. Good for you." I feel like I'm being shown a kindergartner's fingerpainting. Here, in all insincerity: take this gold star. I also feel like I'm suffocating. "There's something else I need to talk to you about."

"So you're not interested in joining the collective?"

"No."

"Okay, shoot with your something else." He lays a hand on my knee, a hot, sweaty hand. "How was your day, by the way?"

I ignore that sally and fall back on a stock line. I rehearsed other options in the car on the way down, but clichés exist for a reason. "I think we should stop seeing each other." That was weird. I shortened my pre-planned sentence, left off the "for a while" part that I rehearsed. But getting the words out has eased the pressure on my lungs, made me breathe easier.

His face closes up right away. "Where did this come from?"

"Look, Nils, I knew when we started this that it wouldn't work out. We're too far apart in age. You should be with someone who's younger and has more energy, someone who cares about causes, and likes coming to places like this." I gesture to the fabu room and the think-they're-fabu people making much noise about nothing.

"I don't mind the age difference, so why should you?"

Fuck. What do I tell him now? I don't think he would take kindly to hearing that his beautiful-in-the-right-light face isn't enough to keep a relationship going. Or that the sex isn't good enough to make the maintenance work required of being a couple worthwhile.

"You're right," I say. "It's not only the age difference that's the problem. It's also that I'm not good with people, period. I'm more of a loner. Always have been. Impatient. Crotchety. Irritable. Does not work well with others, my performance appraisals used to say. I'm not a joiner of collectives, and I'm not good one-on-one, either."

I've never seen him angry before, but he seems pretty pissed off now. "That's the best excuse you can come up with?"

"It's the truth. I'm sorry, Nils. I should never have let this thing start, but you're so good-looking and sweet, and I was infatuated, and I lost my head." And the rest of my body.

He pouts, not a good look for him. "Melissa was right about you."

The weight of the guilt sitting on my chest shifts a little, and some crispness creeps into my voice. "Oh? In what way?"

"Never mind."

"No, I'd like to hear. Especially if it's hurtful. Go ahead, stab me back. I'll feel better if you do."

"She said you were using me."

I thought Nils and I were into the same casual, flingy sort of thing from the beginning, but once again, I was wrong. "I'm sorry, Nils, really. I'm not up to anything sustainable."

The pissy look is tinged with disgust. "Was that supposed to be funny?"

I guess he wouldn't accept that I was trying to be clever. Or that I'm smearing myself with all the blame so he can walk out smelling almost as sweet and looking almost as innocent as he smelled and looked on the day he walked into the classroom for my lecture six years ago.

"Let's face it," I say, "you're angry because I called it off first, but you would have dumped me sooner or later, and in no time you're going to start seeing some young woman with a better body and a more open mind and you'll fall in love and wonder what you and I were ever about, so why don't we shake hands and move on?" And such are my interpersonal skills that after this stellar speech, I extend my hand in friendship, in the belief he might return the gesture.

"You know what?" he says — and he stands up and, oh shit, here comes his dramatic exit, but at least he doesn't yell or make a scene. He speaks at normal volume and says, "Go fuck yourself."

For a solid minute after he's gone, I examine the floor at my feet (it's carpeted, and it's dirty), then I walk out to my car, where I do not begin to cry, because I'm not destroyed; what I am is tired, tired and worn out and used up and sick of Nils and myself. The classical music station comes on when I turn the key in the ignition — Handel, it sounds like, but I need something messier and sadder, something bluesy and soaked in alcohol, drugs, and shame.

The CD Jesse burned for me weeks ago is still in the car, tucked away in the storage compartment where it has sat since he gave it to me — another reason to beat myself up. I slip it into the CD player and push the select button until I find a song that captures the right degree of despair. A Bonnie Raitt song called "Guilty" fits the bill. I set off through the down-town streets and drive past carousing young people who are unmindful of middle age looming, followed closely by old age, infirmity, and death. I wallow in the song's slow rhythm and tinkly piano and plaintive slide guitar licks and rueful lyrics three times through, and then I switch to Joni Mitchell's song "Blue."

I drove past my turnoff ten minutes ago and now begin to trace out a big rectangle — across the city, down to the lake, along the lakeshore, and north again, back to my neck of the 'hoods. "Blue" is too much of a downer to play again, even in my present state of mind. I push the select button past James Taylor's "You've Got a Friend" (who, Sylvia?) and some more hopeful Bonnie Raitt songs (not now) and come to the last track, which is not like the rest, but is an old R & B tune called "I'll Always Love My Mama." The horn intro rings out, I remember Jesse asking me if I'd listened to the last song on the CD, and now — now I cry.

~ CHAPTER TEN ~

I'm having lunch with Danny (his suggestion, to catch up on gossip) at his favourite French restaurant. I've ordered steak and frites, an appropriately fattening selection to make when a breakup with one's lover has given one reason to think one's naked body will never be seen again by a single soul other than the self and the occasional jaded, seen-it-all health care professional.

Danny opens the conversation with an entertaining in-depth description of his gig on the decorating television show, which was quite successful, by his account, and has given him ideas about extending his career into television. "When I get my own show, I'll be sure to feature you and your work, by the way," he says, "so you can start sucking up to me now."

"Forget it. I look awful on TV. The lighting makes the lines on my face deepen until I look like a hideous marionette."

Danny glances up from his salad niçoise. "You can get those lines done, you know, filled in, plumped up."

"No, thanks. I'd rather avoid television so no one can call me Howdy Doody."

He doesn't reply right away. I say, "You know who Howdy Doody is, right?"

"A puppet on a TV show back in the dark ages?"

"Just checking."

"What about you? How's that big project going for Stewart McBigshot? Any idea who he has in mind to do the interior design?"

"I'm handing over the final drawings this week. And I'd suggest you for the design work but Stewart hasn't been too receptive to my ideas so far. He's a bit of a mule."

"You haven't used your feminine wiles to get your way?"

"I despise wiles, always have. And no one would go for them if I had any, anyway." Except possibly Nils, who clearly needs to have his vision and lack of preconceived notions checked out. "And anyway, relationships suck, and sex follows the law of diminishing returns, and romance is overrated."

Danny puts down his fork. "Oh my god. Have you been seeing someone?"

"I did date a guy for a while, but it's over. As of ten days ago."

"Spill all immediately. Who was he?"

I remind him about Nils at Leo's party and he says, "That young drunk guy with the sexy smile? Score!" I tell him about the square dancing, and he says, "That sounds pretty gay. Are you sure he's a hundred percent straight?"

I summarize the sex and the semi-dating, and the breakup caused by my lack of patience and mounting irritability.

"He was boring, is that what you're saying?"

"I don't know anymore — was he boring, or do I just have no tolerance left for anyone or anything? He *was* awfully earnest. He had a tendency to drone on about saving the world through green architecture."

"That does sound wearisome."

"Thank you."

"Though I saw a magazine spread recently on a green house in Seattle, and it was quite beautiful and serene, the way it was designed, in and out. Quite striking."

"It wasn't a Japanese influence thing, was it? Temple chic and all that?"

"No, no, it was more a celebration of the earth and the trees and the rocks and the water in the area. It was all about being true to the indigenous setting."

"The indigenous setting?"

"I'll get off that topic before you decapitate me with your glare. But seriously? I don't think you should write off all romantic relationships because of one boring guy."

Sylvia had a similar reaction when I told her Nils and I were over. "Oh, no," she said. "Already? And I thought he might turn out to be the one. You're not going to become a hermit again, are you?"

"Actually," I say to Danny, "the thought of being forever single is quite soothing. Like looking out at the lake on a calm day." I mean this — I feel relieved and eased by having one less person to care about and for, though I do regret that, by dumping Nils, I may have pushed him a psyche-hardening step further down the road to my life stage of cynicism and detachment.

I also wonder if anyone will ever again touch me the way he did. Correction: I don't wonder — I'm sure no one will. Unless I try to brave the relationship fray again, which I won't, for at least four more years. Make that eight. Or sixteen. Yeah, maybe I'll have sex again when I'm sixty-six. There's something to look forward to.

Alice calls me that afternoon from Boston to thank me for checking in on Vera's house and to tell me I can stop soon because Vera's due home from the rehab center in a few days, with a walker, two canes, and a part-time caregiver.

"How's she doing?"

"Physically, she's recovering on schedule, but her mood isn't that great — she's been down lately."

"Really? Indomitable Vera?"

"She puts on a brave face most of the time, but she's different since she fell. It's like she turned a corner and walked into the land of old age."

"Maybe she'll cheer up when she goes to the condo."

"You'd think so, but moving seems to be part of the problem. She talked to me about it for half an hour last night on the phone, about how it's so sad that she can't sell the house to someone who will promise to keep it standing."

Poor Vera. Alone and old and sad and powerless and — fuck that. As soon as I hang up the phone, I grab Vera's key and go across the street.

The house has not changed since I was in with the real estate agent — it's as depressing and depressed as ever. The worn fabric on the living room furniture is faded, the drapes drab, the paint colours dull, and a thin layer of dust has settled on every surface.

I go into the kitchen, forage under the sink, find a cloth and some furniture polish, return to the front hall, spray and wipe the newel post on the staircase.

What if — let me go off on a flight of fancy here — Vera could get her wish, and the eventual buyer didn't tear the house completely down? It's possible — not likely, but possible — that someone might gut back to the frame and leave the perimeter walls standing, rebuild from the studs out. It wouldn't be the usual or expected thing to do with an undistinguished house like this, but I've seen it happen, seen a shell and facade remain, post-demolition, to be used as starting points for a new and improved design.

Throw away everything inside the house — the tired railroad room layout, the location of the stairs, the chipped banister I'm dusting, the height of the ceilings, even — and new storeys and new rooms could be configured, within the existing modest footprint, that would permit better light and flow, better functionality of space. Provided the right architect was on the job, that is. Someone who speaks modern languages but who was raised on and appreciates the classics — someone like that, with a fresh eye and an open mind, might be able to create something fine here.

Not me, I couldn't do it, I'm too set in many of my ways. I wouldn't be up to the job, not alone, anyway. But an architect armed with passion and enthusiasm and a willingness to defy convention and go against expectation could take this house on and transform it into a compelling, interesting sort of hybrid house, the sum of its new and old parts.

I know just the person for the job, too: Nils. Also known as Nils who hates me. Allow me to be the big person I may not have, so far, shown myself capable of being, and admit that Nils, Mr. Salvage and Sustainability, has just the right kind of mindset to do Vera's house over, brave-new-world style. Even though his last words to me were that I should go fuck myself. Which I would probably be doing (fucking myself, and royally) if I approached him and his collective about taking on this house, this project, and working with me on it.

It's a stupid idea, the sort of idea a naïf stricken with intemperate youthful enthusiasms would have. Or what if it isn't so stupid, and I pretend for one more imaginary, unrealistic minute that Nils and I could overcome our recent differences and move beyond our recent sweaty, panting, orgasmic, awkward, affectionate, irritating, infuriating — I said, forget about it, not relive it — past, and work together. If we could get past all that, who would be the client in this scenario? Who would put up the money? Not Vera — she has a condo to carry. Not Nils or me, either. He has no savings, and I already have a mortgage to pay.

I've moved into the dining room and am dusting Vera's dining room table now. It's a huge thing, too big for the room, an unwieldy, unfashionable antique with a curvilinear shape to the top and carved animal legs holding it up. I attack it with large sweeping motions of the cloth. Okay, then. What's missing from this fantasy about saving Vera's house is a mysterious benefactor, a generous patron. Like Stewart, only sympathetic. And human. Too bad I don't know anyone like that who would want to invest his or her hard-earned cash on an untried, inexperienced group of young architects supervised by a cantankerous middle-aged weird loner, all to satisfy the whims of a sentimental old woman.

I stand back from the table and admire its shiny surface, whereupon the sun does not break through the wintry clouds and send an illuminating shaft of light into the room, nor does a cartoon light bulb switch on over my head. Instead, I sneeze, violently (all that dust), look around for a tissue, and while doing so, realize two things: one, that I do know a potential investor — Joe. And two, that I seem to have come up with a semi-feasible plan.

I must temporarily set aside my scheme for block domination, because the next day is a busy one, the day of Jesse's casual semiformal. (When I made the bright suggestion that, for accuracy's sake, the party should be renamed the informal, Jesse looked at me with pity in his eyes.) This is also the date, as it happens, that I promised, months ago, to have a drink with English Mary, the archeologist who can't possibly still want to see me, can she? Because I don't want to see her, not anymore, if I ever did, but I can't think of a way to get out of it that wouldn't be graceless and obvious, and since I thought I might attempt to be more gracious, when possible, from now on (in order to be less comparable to animals), I appear to still be going, later, without bells on.

Before that, though, in the afternoon, I go to Stewart's mansion to do a final check on my drawings, to visit another empty house. I pick up assorted flyers and plastic-wrapped advertorial magazines from the porch, unlock the front door with my key, remove more junk mail from the built-in mailbox inside. I reflexively call out a hello, but the house is empty. Also cold and unheated. I keep my coat on, pull the copies out of my satchel, and begin a slow tour of the main floor, stopping to consult the drawings in each room.

The ambience here is different from Vera's; there is peace to be found in this house, as it stands, tall and proud, and waits, in its broken-down splendour, for its next occupants. The sound of my footsteps on the wood floors in the unfurnished rooms is loud, but I am lulled by the quiet stillness, not spooked. As I stroll around, my breathing slows, and my heart and soul slowly warm up.

I work through every room on every floor and find no discrepancies, no anomalies. Well done, Emily. I stop in the main-floor hall and stretch both arms up against the wall, exhale, hold, stretch. And again.

I'm about to leave when I notice that a triangular door built into the wall panelling, a door that accesses a storage cupboard under the main staircase, is ajar, not latched shut. I push it closed with my knee, but it won't close, is caught on something, so I lean down and open it. Inside, on the top shelf of the otherwise bare cupboard, is a still life composed of a plastic bag containing a fist-sized clump of what looks like marijuana, a packet of rolling papers, a pack of cigarettes, a disposable lighter, and two six-packs of beer. I stare at this stash for some seconds without touching anything while I try to recall who has a key to the house and might therefore be the owner of these party supplies. Stewart, of course, would have a key, and his assistant or secretary or whoever probably, and maybe his real estate agent — no, wrong. Stewart had the locks changed when he took possession, and he didn't give me my key until after that. So, Stewart and his staff; Joe and his staff — like the man who helped me when I did the measurements, he could have a key; and me. Me alone, because I have no employees to share keys with, only a teenage son who doesn't smoke or drink because he's an athlete. Was an athlete.

I edge the bag of weed further inside the cupboard and push the door shut. There's no reason to suspect Jesse; the culprit could be anyone. Jesse wouldn't likely remember where this house is anyway, on what street. Though my drawings have been lying around lately, the address marked on every page. No, I'm being overly suspicious. If Jesse wants to drink and smoke he can do that at his friends' houses — there's always one whose parents go out or away a lot. The number of times I've been out in the last few months, Jesse could have been getting hammered in our own living room.

I have no idea how careful Stewart and Joe have been with their keys, no idea if this paraphernalia might not belong to Stewart himself. So I'll stop worrying, and I'll absolutely not mention anything about this to Jesse, in an accusing or other tone. But my already lined brow furrows deeper all the way home.

After school, Jesse does some television-watching and computer-chatting, eats a quick dinner of ordered-in gluten-free pizza, showers and changes his clothes, and tells me to chill when I ask him to make sure he has all of his cell phone, wallet, dance ticket, and emergency money. At six-thirty, I drive him to Sylvia's house, from where he and Ben have reluctantly agreed to be driven to the semi-formal, though they don't understand why they can't take the subway and walk the six blocks from the nearest station through the prime violence district, a mode of travel vetoed by Sylvia, Ed, and me in accordance with our parental pact. Because I have my cocktail appointment with Mary to endure, Ed is doing the drop-off drive, and I am on pickup duty, at midnight, which is the party's official end time, weren't the organizers clever to have set one.

So Jesse is safely at Sylvia's when I stroll into the designated bar to meet Mary for drinks, the consumption of which, and pursuant conversation, I am determined to make last no more than one hour. After that, I can go home and worry about Jesse, and about whether the weed and beer at Stewart's house might be his.

The bar is sparsely populated by people other than Mary, though she sent me a confirmation email only this morning, so she's sure to show up. I have never in my life gone into a bar alone and had a drink, and when I've climbed aboard a stool and ordered my juice combo, I wonder for a second if the bartender or some of the male customers might think I am here to be picked up. But I go unnoticed by all comers and players. Including Mary, whose first imperious glance around the bar on her arrival scans by me without recognition. Have I changed so much?

I know her right away, though she is apple-cheeked no more, has thinned out in the face, and did she always have that long neck? Maybe it only looks long because her posture is so upright — chin up, she holds her rather massive bust, robed in a well-cut blazer, pitched forward, very ship's prow, cutting through the waves. Below the jacket and skirt that may be hiding a thick middle are well-shaped, thin-calved legs and shoes that are stylish but not outrageously so. Yikes. I straighten my own shoulders, give a weak wave, and call her name.

She leads with her chin, but the bust reaches me before she does. "Emily," she says in a plummy accent and proffers a hand, ringed in gold and diamonds. No biker-style silver jewellery here

— the look is lady of the manor. She smiles, revealing a few attractive lines, and says, "Lovely to see you again, after all these years."

I shake her hand, offer her a bar stool and a drink. She orders a gin and tonic, points to the rosy mixture in my tall glass and says, "What's that? A Singapore Sling?"

Am I being paranoid, or with only her second sentence is she already sticking the knife in? "No, it's called an I'm Not An Alcoholic. You should try one."

She pauses, not sure if I'm having her on, but visibly decides she doesn't give a shit and resumes talking. How am I, and what have I been up to, and isn't Toronto's architecture funny and modern and bland? Most of her archeological conferences take place in Europe, so it's unusual for her to visit a country where the oldest buildings date back to the (laughably recent) nineteenth century and people get excited about Victoriana.

I wasn't being oversensitive — her every sentence has an edge. I don't remember her being so biting in 1975 — I'd thought her sickeningly sweet, then — but that was so long ago, any number of personality-changing crises could have happened to make her like this, any number of disappointments and defeats and dashed dreams. Unless increased anger comes with age for everyone.

I give her short, unembroidered answers about my work, my life, and my single motherhood — I will not be goaded into saying anything that could be construed as remotely boastful. Down that path lies certain death.

She says, "So are you a merry divorcee like the women on American television programs, out on the town every night, attending art show openings, dating young men, wining and dining your rich clients?"

It takes me a few seconds to understand she means "merry" as in "merry widow" rather than marry or Mary. Also that she's not accusing me of whining. "No, I'm a sombre divorcee. I stay home a lot and read sombre books, wearing sombre clothes, in my sombre house."

"That's a shame. If I were single" — my eyes involuntarily go to the row of diamonds on her left hand — "I'd become a whole new woman."

As opposed to this old one sitting across from her.

"Tell me about your job," I say. "Thirty years ago, I would never have typed you as a serious student of archeology, let alone as a once and future district head."

She reminds me her undergraduate degree was from Oxford and describes her work (it's important and so is she). Next I ask her where she lives, country or city, and whether she has animals, since I always pictured her in a big old country house with dogs. Slobbering ones.

She cops to what she refers to as a country cottage, five-bedroom, that she makes clear was bought with her family's money, not her husband's, and is located in a charming village outside of York, a short commute to her office. And yes, she owns dogs of some purebred sort that sound yappy. "I also have three children," she says, "all boys, all grown up now." Naturally, one is a barrister, the second is in banking, and the third is midway through his own studies at Oxford.

I gather I'm supposed to cede her points for those resumés, but I'm bored of this game we're playing for I know not what prize or reason. Can we cut the crap now? "You must be proud of your sons. I'm pretty sure mine will end up on the dole."

She says, "Ah well, the world is so much different now than when we were young."

What did I miss? I didn't detect a put-down in that comment. It must still be coming.

She calls for another drink, takes a gulp from it as soon as it arrives, and says, "Doesn't it seem like yesterday that we were in North Cave?"

"Yes and no." The old black and white snapshot of the North Cave digging crew — all four of us — comes to mind, and the long-haired, thin, scowling girl in that picture no longer exists.

"You know who remembers everything about those days?" she says. "Tom Denby. He was full of stories at that diggers' reunion he organized in October."

Maybe the sparring is over and I can unclench my teeth and my brain now. "How *was* that reunion?"

"Quite pleasant, and quite illuminating as well. Tom told me a fascinating story about North Cave." She does not seem drunk, though if I'd drunk as much gin as she has in the last fifteen minutes, I'd be on the floor, with little plus signs drawn in for my eyes and bubbles floating around my head. She says, "Do you remember our last evening in North Cave, when we drove to that pub over in the next village, and Clive and I got drunk and spent the night together in his van?"

"Uh-huh." My body heats up and my arm twinges, but she can't know about me finding the armlet; she was sleeping off her one-nighter when I found it. And if she'd known, she would have said something then. Or before now.

"Well, Tom had the most fantastic story to tell me about the morning after. According to Tom, and he might have been slightly drunk himself when he related this anecdote in the pub, but he stuck by his version when I questioned him the next morning at breakfast, and — Damn, where was I?"

Fucking me up is where. "According to Tom."

"Right. According to Tom, he woke up early, and heard movement outside his tent, and looked out through some sort of ventilation holes in the tent wall, and saw you crouch down on the ground, pick up something, look at it for a while, and then pocket it."

How dare Tom spy on me when I was stealing? And what

should I do now? Deny all, claim forgetfulness, act defensive? "And what was it that I picked up, according to Tom?"

Her eyes shine like those of a torturer pleased that her thumb-twisting methods are working. "Do you remember any of this? Do you know what he's talking about?"

"I'm not sure." Lame, I know, but it's been a long day, week, month, quarter.

"He said it looked like an artifact of some kind, a bronze object."

"What is he, Superman? How could he see that through ventilation holes in his tent, from across the field?"

Again with the glittering eyes. "So you admit you stole an artifact from Her Majesty's government?"

"What does Her Majesty have to do with this? Hey. Did you rehearse that line? It sounded rehearsed."

She dims her eyes. Good. They were getting a little psychotic-looking. "Look here," she says, "I know you took an artifact — Tom searched through your bag when we were packing up that day, and he found it, wrapped in a bandana."

Bloody hell.

"He didn't know what to do about it, so he put it back and never told anyone until the reunion."

"Look here, yourself — we all did stupid things when we were young that we're not proud of. Like you — sleeping with a married man."

"You mean Clive?" She stops to consider my accusation. "Maybe you're right. Maybe that was a mistake."

"Was he at the reunion, by the way?"

"Never mind him. About the arm ring — I'll give you the benefit of the doubt and assume you thought it wasn't a significant object. What's more important is this: do you still have it?"

"Why?"

"Because it may be valuable, after all."

"Oh, come on."

She puts her hands on her hips, a gesture which pushes her bust alarmingly close to me. "Will you stop being so stubborn and listen to what I have to say?"

I'm not being stubborn. But neither am I an uptight, suit-wearing, posture freak. "I'm listening."

A few years ago, she says, the field that we surveyed in North Cave, along with several acres around it, was dug up in order to build a new school for the area, and when the entire site was excavated, more hut circles were found, as well as a grave pit that contained some human remains, household implements, pottery, and jewellery, including a bronze armlet (she calls it a ring) marked with a row of identical symbols — a circle within a square. The symbol in a repeating pattern has not been seen before on any known artifacts of the period, so the find is of some small interest, as would be a matching piece from the same location, should it exist.

"There's no engraving on my armlet," I say.

To her credit, she does not yell, "Aha! You do have the missing relic! I knew it all along," and slap on the handcuffs. She says, "I brought a picture of the engraved ring to show you." She pulls from her bag an envelope, and from the envelope a museum-style colour photo print. It shows an armlet on a pale blue background, a metric tape measure placed below it to indicate scale.

I look at the photo in the light of a tiny halogen lamp positioned above the bar, but I can't discern much from it beyond that the object is round and ring-like and heavy-look-ing and about the same dimensions as mine. I cannot, for instance, make out any symbols indicative of round pegs in square holes, as representative of my lot in life and fitting to the situation as they would be.

"So, at this point," she says, "I don't give a damn about how you got your ring, but I want to see it. May I?"

~ ★ ~

We set a time for me to show Mary the armlet the next morning in her hotel coffee shop. (No need for her to come over and yawn at the sight of my boring Victorian house.) The big confrontation over with, I pay for my drink and not hers, leave, and rehash the conversation all the way home, hold it up to the streetlight bulbs and examine it from various angles, come up with pithier rejoinders than those I made.

Lost in these thoughts, Jesse does not swim into my mental view until I arrive at home, which looks lonely and unoccupied, only one lamp lit, in the living room, the lamp I turned on before I left. Of course. It's now eight-thirty and Jesse is at the semi-formal. Ed will have dropped off the boys, so I can call Sylvia and ask how that went.

I go in, sit at my desk, press the speed dial number for Sylvia, lift the lid of the lacquer box. It's empty, though I could have sworn the armlet was there this morning when I took the key to Stewart's house out, the key still in my purse since my walk-through this afternoon.

Ed answers the phone, a circumstance I normally avoid by restricting my calls to Sylvia to his office hours. "Oh, hi, Ed. It's Emily. Is Sylvia around?"

"She went out to rent us a video but she should be back in about ten minutes. Should I ask her to call you?"

Where could the armlet be? Did I really see it this morning? "I was just wondering how the drop off of the boys went."

He laughs, his usual hearty bark. "It went fine. Jesse and Ben saw someone they knew a block away from the club door, so I dropped them there. They're expecting you to be waiting outside at midnight."

This is not the most satisfactory report, but I accept it, say thanks and goodbye, hang up, and start looking for the armlet in earnest.

By ten-thirty, I have searched every nook, cranny, shelf, and drawer in my office, moved my desk out from the wall, crawled around on the floor, and not found the armlet. Where can it be? I have phoned Jesse on his cell to ask him if he might know, but his phone rang on without being answered. Twice. Three times.

I'm hungry, having eaten nothing since lunch except for a few olives in the bar. So I take a break from the search and make a piece of toast with the caraway rye bread (extra seeds) I keep in the freezer for occasions like this. Toast slathered with butter and sprinkled with salt is a comforting food to eat when I'm under stress. The crunching and chewing actions soothe my nerves (or inflame them further) and then there's the therapeutic teeth-picking and cleaning required afterwards to extricate the seeds that settle into the pockets in my gums.

The phone rings at ten after eleven, when I'm mentally retracing all armlet-related steps of the last month or two and counting the minutes until I have to leave to pick up the kids. The number on the call display is that of Sylvia's cell phone — does Ben have it, or is she calling me from it?

I say hello, and a young male voice says, "Emily? It's Ben." He's shouting over some very loud music.

"Ben, what's happening? Is everything okay?"

"What?"

"What's going on?"

"Can you come pick us up, like, soon?"

"Okay. Where's Jesse?"

"What? I can't hear you."

I cup the phone receiver with my hand and yell. "Where's Jesse?"

"He's in the washroom. He's not feeling too good. You'd better come now."

I'm already standing up. "Okay, I'm coming."

"Call me when you're outside the club." He clicks off.

Who me, panic? I'm out the door with coat, purse, gloves, and shoes on in less than a minute, clear-eyed, pumped, arm burning. I drive quickly down to the entertainment district, navigate the proper turns down one-way streets past various groups of drunk and disorderly young people, pull up to the curb across the street from the club entrance nine minutes after I hung up the phone, dial Ben's number before I come to a stop. His phone rings ten times and goes over to answering. Come on, Ben. I dial again, same result. I try Jesse's phone next, but it's turned off. I try Ben one more time, yell "fuck" inside the empty car, and get out.

I passed lineups of twenty or thirty people at several haunts on my drive through the area but there's no line at this club, only a burly bouncer in a down jacket. He steps in front of me when I approach the closed doors, through which music booms. "Sorry, ma'am," he says. "No admission. Private party tonight."

"This is where the Westdale semi-formal is on, right? I'm here to pick up my son. He's inside, sick."

"Admission was closed as of nine o'clock. All anyone can do now is come out."

I lock eyes with him. His bigness makes his age difficult to guess, but I'd say he's in his early twenties, a kid.

"Look," I say. I want to call him Tiny. I also want to grab him by the scruff of his jacket and pull him down to my height. "My son is sick inside and I'm going in to get him. So let me in. Now." I give my best menacing parental stare, which Jesse doesn't find in any way troubling, but Tiny seems to recognize battle-a-tiger strength when he sees it. He opens the door. "You still have to get by the guy inside."

I run up a dark staircase and into a group of four very drunk girls (so much for the school's zero tolerance policy) who are taking up the attention, time, and space of the guy inside. He glances at me but keeps on dealing with the girls and lets me slip by, most likely because he recognized in that glance how far over the legal drinking age I am.

The music — a rock type of song I don't recognize, not something Jesse would ever listen to — is deafening, and the spotlights that rake the darkened room are intermittently blinding. I spot another adult in the crowd, a waiter, and run over, ask him where the men's washroom is.

I find Ben outside the washroom, where the music is slightly less loud. He is standing with another boy, laughing and talking, way too relaxed, but he blanches when he sees me and comes over, points to the phone in his hand, gestures a question — why didn't I call?

"You didn't answer your phone. Where's Jesse?"

"In the washroom."

"What's he doing in there?"

"Last time I checked he was puking."

"And you left him alone? I'm going in."

His eyes widen. "No, don't. I'll go and get him out. You wait here."

I lean against the wall, arms crossed, steaming in my coat, breath raspy, ears aching. The boy Ben was talking to takes one look at me and lopes off.

One day when Jesse was in grade one, I came to pick him up after school and was waiting for him in the hallway among the cubbies and coat hooks when the class emerged. Jesse's teacher, a young woman who liked the obedient little girls but had less time for the rambunctious boys, told me Jesse had been crying in the classroom for the last fifteen minutes, she didn't know why, he wouldn't explain. This was unlike Jesse, who at age six was actively developing his tendency to laugh at the antics of the class clowns.

The children filed out, and I went in to find Jesse sitting behind a bookcase, sobbing and refusing to talk. He got up when he saw me and allowed me to lead him out by the hand, still crying, his face hidden in my side. It wasn't until we got home that I took off his pants and found that he'd had diarrhea all over them after not making it to the bathroom on time. He must have eaten some food with gluten in it at recess, a snack offered by another child. Or not — maybe the diarrhea had a non-gluten-related cause. But I cursed myself that I hadn't been there to save him the mortification, that he'd had no way to cope, to hide his shame. Still do curse myself.

Ben emerges, says, "He won't come out of the stall."

"Why is he sick? What did he have?"

Ben won't meet my eye, but I'm fierce. "Tell me!"

"He might have had a few beers."

He might have had a few beers. After I've told him, how many times, in all seriousness, that if he ever tries alcohol, he should drink vodka or wine or brandy, and not gluten-full beer.

He must have soiled his pants again. I run into the women's washroom — a cesspool filled with primping girls — and in a dark corner, I slide off my shoes, step out of my jeans, slip the shoes back on, close my coat, which I'm lucky is knee length, and go back out, my jeans bundled under my arm. Without a word or look to Ben, who hovers about, I charge into the men's, ignore the three boys peeing with their backs to me, and call Jesse's name.

He moans mine in disbelief from a locked stall and I push open the door of the one adjacent, lock it quickly behind me, climb up on the toilet seat, look over top.

"Jesse. Are you okay?"

"What are you doing here?"

His pants are down at his ankles. I can smell vomit and shit.
"Do you think you're done, or is there still more to come?"
"I don't know. Go away."

"If you think you've finished, put on these pants and let's go
home." I drop the jeans onto his head.

He groans but he takes the jeans. "Whose are these?"

"Never mind. Pull out your shirttails, hand me your pants and
let's get out of here." I know my jeans will fit him — he weighs
thirty pounds more than me, but the weight is concentrated in his
upper body, he's skinny in the hips. And the oversized shirt he's
wearing hangs down almost to his knees anyway. No one will
notice, especially if we move fast.

"You're crazy. You're a fucking crazy mother," he says, and
someone outside the stalls calls out, "He's got that right."

I whisper, "Give me your pants." I want to climb over the
barrier and get into the stall with him, but I'm not that crazy.

"This is so gross," he mutters and hands me his pants,
which I roll up into a ball and stuff under my coat, a nice bulge
to complement my bare legs and shoes with white ankle socks.

"I'll be outside on the street in the car. Come. Now." I pass
Ben on the way out and tell him to get his parents to pick him
up. He agrees, happy to get out of my orbit and Jesse's. I call his
house myself on the way to the car and tell a startled-sounding
Sylvia that I've had to pick up Jesse early because he was sick,
I'll explain everything later, but could she or Ed please pick up
Ben? She asks no questions, says of course they'll come down
and she hopes Jesse is okay. I hope so, too.

He takes his time coming out, jaywalks slowly across the
street, risking death in his dark coat on the dark night, and gets
into the car.

"What took you so long?"

"I had to get my coat from the coat check and there was a
big lineup. Where are my pants? I didn't shit in them, you know.

I puked on them. The diarrhea and the puke were coming out at the same time and I had to make a choice."

"The pants are in the trunk, in a plastic bag." I pull out of the parking spot into traffic. "Do you still feel queasy?"

"I don't know. A bit. I can't believe you came right into the men's washroom. You're such a nutbag."

"You're welcome."

"You shouldn't have come."

"Ben called me and told me to."

"Ben's an idiot. You don't have to rescue me when I fuck things up. You've got to stop doing that."

I'm stung by these words, partly because he may be right. "Shouldn't I be the one giving the shit here?"

He puts a hand over his face. "Sure. Go ahead. Give me shit. No, wait. Pull over. Now!"

I wrench the car over, he opens his door, hangs his head out, retches, groans, spits on the street, closes the door, says, "False alarm."

When we're moving again, I say, "I need to hear everything that happened tonight. From the beginning."

He doesn't respond.

"Jesse?"

"Almost fifteen years ago, I was born. My weird parents were still married then — "

"You're making jokes now?"

"Real funny ones."

"Where did you get the beer from?"

"Some guy."

"I don't care who, but I want to know how. You got it from a friend, from an older kid, or what?"

"If I tell you, you're going to try and bust everyone, so forget it."

"Did I bust Spencer the dope dealer when I had the chance?"

Silence.

"Where did the beer come from?"

"*Fuck!*" Then, after a pause, "There's this guy, this man, named Jimmy, that you call when you want to buy beer. You tell him what brand you want and how many, and he brings it to your house and you pay him for it."

"How much?"

He names a figure for a case of twelve that is twice the retail price.

"How did you find out about this Jimmy? Where did you get his number?"

He shrugs. "Everyone knows about Jimmy."

"So you met him near the club after Ed dropped you off?"

No, another friend bought beer from Jimmy the night before and hid the beer from his parents, and they all met somewhere to drink them, between the time I dropped Jesse at Sylvia's house and Ed drove them downtown.

"How'd you do that? Where did you tell Sylvia and Ed you were going?"

"We took their dog for a walk."

"And you went and drank in the park?"

"No, not in the park."

"Where, then?" But I know where — in Stewart's house. I question Jesse further, pull Stewart's house key on the twisty telephone cord from my purse, ask him how he got in without it, and hear that he took the key from the box on my desk two weeks ago and had it copied at the local hardware store one night when I was at my yoga class.

I've forgotten about the missing armlet during the washroom crisis, but his mention of the box makes me remember, makes me put away until later my guilt over leaving him alone at night to sneak around making keys while I was out fucking Nils. "Where's the armlet from the box, by the way? Do you know?"

"Maybe."

"Where is it? I need it, badly."

"Then have it," he says, reaches into his coat pocket, pulls it out, and drops it on my thigh, which hurts me. The damn thing is heavy.

I'm turning onto our street. I put the armlet in my pocket, ask the next of the hundred questions I still need to have answered. "Why did you have it with you?"

"Leave me alone."

"No. Why did you have it?"

He angrily mumbles something I can't hear.

"What?"

He yells, "Why do you fucking well have to know fucking everything about me? For good luck, okay?"

We are in front of the house. I turn off the engine. "Keep your voice down, it's late. The neighbours will hear."

"I don't give a fuck about the fucking neighbours," he says, opens the door, gets out of the car, slams the door shut. And, regretting the day I gave birth, I get out too, remove the bag containing Jesse's dirty pants from the trunk, and go inside.

Jesse drops his clothes (including my jeans) on the floor in a trail from front door to bathroom and steps into the shower. I throw everything into the laundry basket, take it down to the basement, and start a washer load, shower or not. After ten minutes of pacing the ground floor and craving a cigarette, I go back upstairs to find Jesse, lying on his bed, a bath towel around his waist. The computer is on, and one of his songs is playing, but softer than usual.

"The music at the semi sucked," he says. "The DJ was terrible."

"Like that matters."

"It matters to me."

I sit down in his desk chair. "How's your nausea level?"

"Better if it's not referred to."

"Oh, Jesse."

"Oh, what?"

"Using Stewart's house was so wrong of you — it was trespassing for sure, and almost breaking and entering. You could have been arrested."

"You're right. My bad. I won't do it again. Now get out of my room."

"Did you also smoke weed tonight? There was a bag of weed in the cupboard at Stewart's house."

His head comes up a few inches off the mattress. "You found it?"

"I was over there checking my drawings, and the door to the cupboard under the stairs was open. Did you smoke any?"

"None of your business."

"You *should* have smoked if you wanted to get high, rather than drinking beer that you know you're allergic to. I don't understand why you would do that, I really don't."

He has flung his arm over his face and hidden it from my view. I'm about to give up and leave the room when he says, "Didn't you ever do anything stupid when you were a kid? Didn't you ever do something you knew you shouldn't do to see what would happen? Or because you just felt like it?"

Me to Mary in the bar, three hours ago: We all did stupid things when we were young, things we're not proud of.

I say, "I'm surprised you didn't follow the beer with a chaser of whole wheat bread and a big bowl of barley soup."

He sits up, says, "Way to make me need to take another shit," and runs out of the room.

I open the closed door of the bathroom a crack once he's in there and roll in a barf bucket, but I don't go in and hold his head. I wait in my bedroom until he's done, and when he comes out, I ask if he's brushed his teeth, he says yes, and he goes to bed alone.

He'll shut off his own light tonight and get up again to use the toilet if he needs to. I'll sit at my desk downstairs for a while and stare at the armlet, and look back at my past and forward to my future. Then I'll go to bed and wake through the night at two-hour intervals, beset by nightmares about Jesse in peril, nightmares in which I cannot save him from injury or heartbreak, in which I arrive too late, after the damage is done, and fail to catch him as he passes through the rye.

~ CHAPTER ELEVEN ~

I'm wasted when I wake up at six-thirty, and I consider trying to sleep for a few more hours and going to see Mary with my hair slept-on and my face haggard, but I can't drop the armlet and run; I need to wait and hear the outcome of her examination, see if I'll be allowed by the self-appointed representative of Her Majesty's Government to keep my little souvenir or be forced to donate it for further study. And she's brought out the competitive instinct in me: I can't let her see me looking the way I know I must. So while Jesse sleeps off his night before, I get up and go through the tedious normalizing process that makes me presentable.

Once out, my first stop is Stewart's house. I empty the under-stairs cupboard, place all the remaining items in a green garbage bag — I'm momentarily tempted to keep the weed for my own occa-sional use but think better of the idea — and deposit the sealed bag in a park garbage bin at an undisclosed location. Done and gone.

I'm irked upon entering the hotel coffee shop to see that Mary is not breakfasting alone. A man faces her at a table for four, his back to me. A colleague, perhaps, or maybe her husband, either one irrelevant chaff. I head over to interrupt, eager to get this meeting out of the way. Mary sees me coming, and when I approach the table, says, "Good morning, Emily. Please join us. You remember my husband, Clive, don't you?"

Clive? The man, who has long grey hair that curls over his shirt collar, stands up, and I look into the still-roguish, now laugh-lined eyes of my former crush. I sit down beside him, across from Mary. "You two are married? When did that happen?"

Mary: "Twenty-nine years ago."

Clive: "We have three sons. Our eldest is twenty-eight."

So Clive must have ditched his wife very soon after North Cave, impregnated Mary, and married her. Or impregnated her first, then ditched the wife.

"And to think the whole romance started in North Cave," I say, "when I thought you two were a throwaway one-night stand."

Clive says to Mary, "I remember her now!" And to me, "I was having trouble placing you — there were so many volunteers over the years — but it's all coming back. You were the saucy Oriental girl. You look the same, except your hair's shorter. Wasn't it very long then, down to your bottom?"

"For pity's sake, Clive," Mary says, "don't flirt with her. You're embarrassing yourself."

Clive twinkles at me. "Mary wants me to act my age. But you know what they say, once a flirt — "

" — later, an old perv." Mary smiles briefly to suggest she was joking, which I know she wasn't, though Clive chooses to pretend she was. "Weren't you going back to the room to read before this morning's seminar, darling?" she says. "Emily and I could use a few minutes on our own. I'll meet you up there shortly."

He says nice to have seen you again and moves off. He's not shambling yet, but he's getting there.

A waitress offers me coffee and a menu, I refuse both, and I ask Mary how old Clive is.

"Fifty-eight. Nine years older than me, but some days the age gap between us feels a lot larger."

I'm enjoying this view of the country cottage prison that Mary has built for herself. "Yet you've stayed married all this time."

"We have three sons, don't forget."

"Didn't you say last night that the youngest is at university?"

"Yes."

"Which would make you and Clive empty nesters. How's that going?"

She shifts uncomfortably in her chair, as if regretting that she got personal with a shop clerk. "Did you bring the bronze ring?"

"Yes, I did." I withdraw from my purse a sealed plastic bag containing the armlet and hand it over.

She moves her coffee things to one side, clears her side of the table, and lays the armlet down on a clean napkin. From her bag, she withdraws reading glasses and a magnifying glass — I was hoping for those jewellers' glasses with the protruding lenses attached, but no — and bends over the object, gives it a thorough going-over.

After a solid three minutes of silent examination, during which I wish I'd ordered a coffee after all, she puts down the magnifying glass and the armlet with a sigh. "This isn't like the other one."

"It isn't?" I'm disappointed; I'd wanted my stolen goods to be special stolen goods.

"As you said, there are no markings on it, and the work is much coarser than the other specimen, the diameter larger. This was probably a part of a bridle or a yoke for oxen or cattle. Not human jewellery."

"It's animal jewellery?"

She starts packing up and hands me the rebagged armlet. "You may as well keep it — it's not of any value, being so long out of context."

"So that's it, then?"

"That's it." She smiles like I would upon coming face to face with a former client from whom I parted on bad terms — she's feigning politeness but can't wait to get away. "Thank you for bringing it to me."

I stand. "You're welcome. And goodbye, I guess."

"Goodbye." She signals to the waitress for the bill.

"Good luck with your conference and life and Clive and all that."

"Same to you."

I've outlived my usefulness as far as she's concerned, but a weak, staticky connection I think I feel between us causes me to say, "You know, being alone, at our age, and being single — it's not such a bad thing. You might like it if you tried it."

She throws some money on the table, stands up, says, "I don't know what you're talking about," and turns on her heel, walks away.

Jesse's lying on the living room couch in his boxers and T-shirt, watching music videos, when I get home. "You're up early," I say. "Did you have breakfast?"

"An apple and some cereal. Where were you?"

"Showing the armlet to an British archeologist who wanted to see it in case it turned out to be valuable."

"What? Who?"

He reduces the volume on the television, I pass him the armlet from my purse, and I tell him an edited version of the story. "The conclusion is that it's worthless."

He holds it, weighs it in his palm. "It didn't stop me from getting sick last night on the beer, that's for sure."

"You know, Jesse, if Sylvia were your mother, she'd find some moral in the story of the armlet that's relevant to last night's fiasco. She'd say something like that it's time to learn the difference between reality and fantasy. Time to leave behind a child's belief in talismanic objects, because there is no magic in maturity, only responsibility."

He tears his attention away from the rappers gesticulating on the screen. "Sorry, I wasn't listening. What did you say?"

"I was trying to give you a taste of a Sylvia-style lecture, but it sounded like a load of crap, even to me, so forget it. Besides, I'm not convinced the armlet is completely powerless — it brought me to you last night at the club, didn't it?"

"That would be proof it's an instrument of black magic."

I yawn. I'd like to go upstairs now, crawl back into bed, and sleep until noon. Maybe I will. "Let's negotiate a peace treaty."

"The kind that exploits native peoples?"

"The kind where we exchange promises to do things differently."

"Let me guess: I'm supposed to promise not to act like a teenager anymore, and you'll promise to act in the same parental way as always."

On the TV screen, a line of dancers executes a series of back-crunching moves that looks like it might be good therapy for my shoulder. "What would you like me to promise?"

"To stop acting like I'm a little kid who needs to be taken care of all the time."

"Okay, I'll try."

"No, you won't."

"Yes, I will."

"I'll believe it when I see it, but here's my promise: I'll never drink beer again."

"What about wine and hard liquor and weed?"

"I promise never to drink beer again — take it or leave it."

"I'll take it."

"This song is good, listen." He turns up the volume on the TV and a song plays that is more tuneful than many he likes. The lyrics do not seem to refer to blow jobs or killings, and the breasts and asses of the young women in the video are covered with clothing. He sings along — he's such a bad singer — and when the song ends, says, "Did you like it?"

"It's not bad."

"Not bad? Are you kidding? It's sick."

"Not as sick as the song you put on my CD — 'I'll Always Love My Mama.'"

"Stop right there. You can't say sick like that, Em, it doesn't work for you. You can only say sick when you're talking about, like, illness. Okay?"

"Okay."

"But I will always love my mama."

He's probably saying this for form's sake, but I'll take it, too. "And I love you, honey."

He has the grace to wait two beats before saying, "Can I have lunch now?"

Monday afternoon finds me at Stewart's office with Joe, presenting the working drawings. I make no mention of the cupboard, the stash, or the extra key at the meeting, taking a page from Jesse's need-to-know philosophy book, and I'm much more a lamb than a terrier when I go over the drawings without rancour, digs, or sighs about lost opportunities for clever improvements. I play it so meek that on our way out of Stewart's building — Joe and I are going for coffee, as prearranged by me on the phone, he knows not why — Joe says, "Are you okay, Emily? You were so quiet in there."

I also successfully covered up my son's trespassing and annexation of another's property for the purpose of partying, so I can breathe more freely now, as well as talk. "I'm a little tired after dealing with my son's teenage antics this weekend."

"How old is he?"

"He turns fifteen in a few weeks."

"Were they normal antics or something serious?"

Two and a half days after the fact, Jesse's deeds don't seem so dastardly. "Normal, I guess."

"Yeah, my eldest gave Susan and me some sleepless nights in his time, but before we knew it, he was off and gone to university, out of our lives."

And here I thought Joe's family was close and friction-free and ate dinner once a week in a big, happy, extended group. "Do you miss your son now that he's grown up?"

"I miss him, and his brother, and now my youngest is in her last year of high school, and I already miss her. You want my advice? Make sure you have a full, satisfying life of your own while your son is still around. Otherwise, it won't be easy to let him go when the time comes."

We've ducked out of the cold and into a nearby coffee shop and are standing in line, waiting to order. I say, "About that full and satisfying life idea, you're probably wondering why I asked you to have coffee today."

"I thought maybe you were going to tell me you'd had enough of Stewart and wanted to get off the job now and not do any supervision."

"Good guess, but no. I'll stick it out until the work's completed. What I want to talk to you about is a new project, a proposal for a joint venture that you might consider undertaking with me. If you're still interested in doing something other than the same old shit."

His smile is encouraging. "Tell me more, Emily."

~ ★ ~

Joe is interested in my throughway route, interested in forming a project-specific partnership for the purpose of buying and rebuilding (not restoring) Vera's house for later resale. He gives his okay five minutes into my spiel, though we stay in the coffee shop for an hour discussing terms and paperwork and making task lists.

At the top of mine is a pitch to Vera, who is home alone when I call that afternoon and ask if I can drop by. "It would be nice to see you," she says, "but can you ring the bell when you arrive and let yourself in with your key? The walker is tricky in tight spaces like the vestibule."

I enter to find her sitting on an easy chair in her living room, looking the part of an invalid, with a throw wrapped around her legs, a book, her reading glasses, and a pill container on a table to her left, a sleek green metal walker positioned to her right. The wan smile and weak hello she produces only underline Alice's description of her as suddenly older.

"If you'd like some tea, you'll have to make it yourself," she says, "I'm too pooped to get up."

"I don't want anything, but can I make you a cup?"

"No, thank you. If I drink some, I'll just have to go to the bathroom, and that's an ordeal in itself." She shakes her head. "I'm sorry. I don't want to be one of those old bores who talks about nothing but their health problems. How are you, dear? And how's Jesse?"

"We're good, thanks. What about you? Are you enjoying being home?"

"The house isn't as easy to get around in as the rehab centre, but my mobility is supposed to be improving daily. To tell the truth, I thought I'd be further along by now, but they say it's a long process and I should be patient and keep doing the damned exercises. The girl that comes in helps me with those. She comes mornings and evenings and takes the afternoons off. What time is it now?"

I'm sure the part-time caregiver is a woman, not a girl, but never mind. "Just after one."

"She'll be back at five, to give me supper, run me through my paces, and put me to bed. That's my day. Thrilling, isn't it?"

I smile, pause, hear a clock ticking somewhere, possibly in my mind, and say, "I wanted to talk to you about selling the house, but maybe this isn't a good time."

She tries to straighten up in her chair, grimaces with pain, but injects a little backbone into her voice anyway. "If you came to say I should give up on trying to preserve the house, you can save your breath. I've already given up. I'll put the house up for sale without any stipulations after the Christmas holidays — I should be walking well enough by then to manage everything that needs to be done."

"Actually, I was going to propose that my business partner and I buy the house from you privately."

"What business partner?"

"His name is Joe Cordeiro. He's a builder I sometimes work with."

"And he wants to build a new house on the site?"

"Not exactly. Let me explain." I lay out my proposal in broad strokes. Twice, because she doesn't understand it the first time.

"I see," she says, when I'm done. Her body is slumped once more in her chair, and she's staring into the middle distance.

"What do you think?"

She doesn't answer.

"Vera?"

A little snappishly, "What?"

"What do you think of my proposal to buy the house?"

Her eyes refocus. "I think it's an interesting compromise in a life that's become nothing but compromises."

Oh. "You probably want to think about it some more, mull over the idea."

"I will. But so far, I like it."

Oh again. "Good. I'll call you about it, shall I? Maybe tomorrow."

"Yes, call me. I'll discuss it with Alice, but I don't really need to hear what she thinks. It's still my house, isn't it? My decision."

"And we'd offer a fair price."

"Of course you would."

"Okay, then. I guess I'll be going now."

"Wait. Before you go, I have a question."

"Yes?" The treacly pace of this conversation is making me crazy, but I can last a few more minutes.

"This thing that you want to do with the house — who are you doing it for?'

I don't understand the question, so I stupidly repeat it. "Who am I doing it for?"

"I hope you're not doing it for me, is all. I hope you're doing it for yourself, because you want to, or because you think it would be rewarding. Are you?"

I visualize awkwardness and tension with Nils and his compadres, heated meetings, me trying to funnel their exuberance into productivity, all of us progressing over time to a kind of intergenerational camaraderie, a mutual respect. I see the house gutted, dumpsters filled, the new frame going up, Joe and I conferring on the street with the plans in hand, the labourers sitting on Vera's porch eating their lunches and smoking their cigarettes, tradesmen arriving to ply their trades, the usual arguments and disputes breaking out with me as arbiter, decision-maker, project leader, the person who made something good and new and different happen, a house to be proud of. And throughout, I see Vera's garden, protected from the destruction of construction, tended, and blooming.

Cue the epiphany music. "Yes, I am doing it for myself."

"And so you should." She shifts in her chair, adjusts the throw over her legs. "So you should."

Three school days left before Jesse begins his two-week Christmas break, and, as usual, he's dawdling. "How about we not be late for once?" I call to him from the front hall.

"Come up here for a minute."

We can make it to school in ten minutes if I drive like a maniac, and the bell will ring in fifteen. I swear, take off my coat, and start upstairs. "Come up where? Why?"

"The bathroom."

Oh, no. "Are you okay?"

"Come see."

"See what?"

He's fully clothed and standing up straight, his back to the wall. He's balancing a ruler on his head and holding a pencil in his hand. "Measure me?" he says. "I think I've grown."

I have to stand on a footstool — the child's one we've had since Jesse was a toddler — to be able to hold the ruler level and make a mark on the wall at his height. The mark shows he *has* grown, a full half-inch since June. He's now six feet, exactly.

"I knew I hadn't stopped growing yet," he says, and my heart seizes up because he still cares about his height, still wants to be tall, to be a contender.

On the way to school, he says, "So this kid on the basketball team, Akeem? He's a pretty good player, and he works out with this trainer guy named Dwayne, and Dwayne's running a day camp for serious ballers over the Christmas break at a community centre downtown, and he told Akeem he'd seen me play last year and I was good, and he suggested I come to this camp, and maybe he'll take me on his rep team for the spring, so can I?"

It takes all my self-restraint not to say, "What?" in an incredulous tone. Also not to ask since when is he back to being a serious baller. "When in the break?"

"Four days before Christmas and four days after."

"What about going to New York to see Henry?"

It's 8:59, my speedy driving has brought us to the school, and Jesse has already undone his seatbelt, is getting ready to bolt. "I could go to New York for a weekend in January instead. And then I could be with you on Christmas Day and I'd even go to Christmas dinner at your gay friends' house, and anyway, think about it, we'll talk later."

He jumps out of the car, but not before I've told him to get all the information on the camp, a brochure, a phone number, the cost, everything, and he's said yeah, sure, and grinned because he knows that I'm considering this crazy, last-minute notion and that if I'm considering it I'll probably say yes, and he may not want me to treat him like a little kid, but he wouldn't mind if I turned myself inside out rearranging all of our schedules so that afterwards he can say, "Thanks, Em, you're a doll."

I wouldn't mind, either, if it'll make him happy.

I go straight from school to meet Sylvia for our weekly walk, and when I lob the camp idea at her, she says that if it checks out, I must let Jesse go and get Henry to pay for the charges to change the flights and for the camp, too, because if Henry hadn't fucked off and gone to New York four years ago, Jesse wouldn't have had to quit the basketball team, drink beer and vomit all over himself, and now need the rehabilitation and healing that some physical training will provide.

"So you think Jesse shouldn't give up basketball, he should keep trying to be good at it? When he could still be relegated to the bench again next year?"

"Isn't there some story about a famous basketball player being cut from his high school team before he went on to achieve true greatness?"

"Yeah, but that was Michael Jordan."

"Everyone needs a purpose, a goal to work toward."

"What are ours?"

"To age gracefully."

"I don't know about that. I think I'd rather hold on to whichever attitudes and behaviours of youth and age make sense to me, and fuck the rest."

"Fine, I'll age gracefully on my own. But what am I going to do about Ed? Would you believe that I caught him wandering around the house yesterday in a T-shirt, underwear, and socks? Like the slob character in a blue-collar sitcom. He couldn't find his sweatpants, he said. Do you think that maybe if he helped out with the laundry once in a while, he'd know where the clothes go? Sometimes I don't know if I can stay married another day or month, Emily, let alone a year. I really don't."

The basketball camp is bigger than I expected — there are about fifty kids warming up when we arrive on the first day. Jesse wants to come and go for the duration on his own, by public transit, but I insisted on driving him down this morning so that I could check out the set-up, meet this Dwayne person, and fill out permission forms and hand over a cheque for the camp fee.

After we complete the paperwork at a registration desk in the hallway, Jesse and I stand in the doorway of the gym and check out the talent. Any minute now, he'll ask me to leave. "Do you know anyone here?" I say.

He mutters, "A couple of people. And that's Dwayne coming toward us."

Dwayne is tall, maybe six-four, black, has a shaved head and wide shoulders, and is an imposing presence. He gives Jesse a black handshake and me a white one, makes sincere eye contact with me, welcomes us, says he's glad to see Jesse. "If you're ready to work hard, you'll have a good time here."

Jesse nods, serious for once. "I'm ready."

"Then why don't you go join the group at the far basket, with Akeem?" He points to a group of boys changing and stretching.

Jesse doesn't look at me or say goodbye. He picks up his bag and walks across and down the sidelines of the court, and I read his body language — his shoulders are set at an oddly jaunty angle and he's swinging his free arm a bit too widely — as speaking of both apprehension and bravery.

I swallow and say to Dwayne, "He's a good kid."

This is the kind of comment Jesse can't stand, but Dwayne's answering smile is warm. "I know."

"And he really wants to be a good player."

"That's what I want him for him, too." Dwayne turns away to greet another arrival, and the contrast between his positive, empathetic attitude and Mr. Dawson's smug, power-tripping one is so marked that I have to thump my chest twice to restart my breathing on my way out.

In the days that follow, Jesse transports himself to and from camp, and I spend the hours he is absent doing paperwork and groundwork on the Vera's house project, including working up the nerve to contact Nils.

On Christmas Eve, I pass the shortened camp day time cooking and wrapping some small gifts for Jesse. (Nothing big — as a combination birthday/Christmas gift, Henry and I have already split the cost of some new software and peripherals that will allow Jesse to record and mix music on his computer.)

Jesse is home by three, in time to shower and change before he and I head out to attend the Christmas Eve open house held annually by Henry's dowager queen of a mother, Ellen, at her well-appointed midtown home. Jesse has avoided this event for the last four years by being in New York. Today, with no excuse not to go, he has asked me to be his escort, and I have agreed, on the condition that we both pretend to be well-mannered people for one hour and ten minutes, then meet at the grandfather clock in the ground-floor centre hall and make our escape.

We walk through Ellen's unlocked front door into a full-scale scene of WASP-style family merriment. The hall is decorated with pine boughs, red velvet ribbon bows, and suspended strings of Christmas cards. Middle-aged and older men and women dressed in holiday wear — including tartan waistcoats and sweaters with Christmas motifs — stand within this preserved-in-amber setting, talk politely, and drink.

Ellen is holding court by the lit fireplace in the living room. She must be close to eighty now, but she's still straight-backed and trim-figured, still holds her head high, and her upswept white hair is still thick and wavy. She's like a taller, older version of English Mary, with about the same tolerance for me and my ways.

I hand her a hostess gift — a jar of rose petal jelly from Fortnum & Mason, just her kind of precious British thing — and Jesse thanks her for the Christmas cheque she sent in the mail. She grand-damely accepts both gift and thanks, and makes the usual happy exclamation that Jesse's grown, and the usual regretful observation that he continues to take after me. (He actually has Henry's curly hair and lean build, but what she means is that his features look, to her biased eye, noticeably Asian.)

"Your boy cousins are around here somewhere," she says to Jesse, "probably in front of the television watching a sporting event, those rascals. Go find them and tell them to be sociable." She's referring to a passel of five boisterous young men, the fruit of one of Henry's sisters. I have long referred to them as the Private School Fucks, though a few of them must be in university now. Jesse likes them and assures me they refrain from what I'm convinced is their usual bullying when they're with him.

We head toward the nearest TV, in a ground-floor den, where Jesse's appearance in the doorway is greeted by several male voices yelling Jesse's name so that the second syllable rhymes with "hey" and the name as a whole sounds as moronic as they do. This is where I retreat and hope that Jesse remembers the time of our grandfather clock assignation, which is in sixty-five minutes.

It's only four-thirty in the afternoon, but getting a drink will help me pass some time. I find the bar and allow a hired bartender to laboriously prepare for me a special cocktail in honour of the holiday, a foamy red concoction of Chambord, cranberry juice, and vodka, crowned with a green paper Christmas tree on a stick in place of a paper umbrella. I ask for it without vodka and take a sip. It's sweet and has a gloved kind of punch. I like it.

I stand in front of the buffet table for a minute or two, eye the standard-issue cheese balls, water crackers, and super-market pâté, ponder what kind of sensibility provides a paid bartender and custom-mixed specialty drinks for a party but gives so little thought to the food, then semi-circulate with the few relatives I recognize who will meet my eye. These include an age-spotted uncle with a gold tooth and an ascot who tells me an interminable war story about London and the Blitz; Henry's sister, mother of the Private School Fucks, who asks me which of the university programs in commerce her sons attend I'm considering for Jesse (the thought of Jesse studying business is so absurd I start to laugh but choke it down and tell her that we haven't thought that far ahead); and another former sister-in-law, Henry's brother's wife, who has an unseemly interest in the houses of my richer clients.

I endure these stiff, uncomfortable conversations, I sit for twenty minutes in a stiff, uncomfortable Louis XIV–style chair in a corner of the living room and half-listen to nearby conversations about ski chalets and golf trips, and despite my recent resolutions to be more open-minded about people and ideas new, young, or old, I'm seized by the familiar grip of boredom, restlessness, and alienation I so often experience at parties.

Sixty-five minutes to the dot after I left Jesse, I'm standing next to the grandfather clock. At the seventy-two minute mark, I risk showing my face in the den. A basketball game is on TV, and Jesse sits on a leather couch, watching it, surrounded by his cousins, all of whom sport striped rep ties over their Oxford cloth button-down shirts.

"Hi guys," I say.

They nod and declaratively utter my first name, their all-purpose shorthand salutation.

"Jesse, we should go."

"After this game."

The game clock in a corner of the TV screen tells me we're only in the second quarter. "I need to leave now."

"Go ahead. I'll get home on my own later."

He what? How? To save (his) face, I say, "Why don't you come see me to the door, honey? Bye, all."

They nod and say Emily again, and one waves.

Jesse emerges, says the game should be over by seven, what's my problem, and did I have to call him honey?

"What happened to us leaving early?"

"The cousins are funny, and the game's close, and it's not like anything's happening at home, anyway."

"You mean you're enjoying yourself? You like it here?"

His reply to both questions is yes. Because he's not me. Maybe if I start repeating this fact to myself five times daily, I'll remember it.

Further questioning reveals that he has no money or bus tickets on him, nor does he have his phone, and he isn't sure how to get home from here on transit, but he'll find out, don't worry, or someone will give him a ride. I press my cell phone and some money on him, settle for a promise of a call when he's ready to leave, locate and thank Ellen, and get out.

Were my vital signs to be graphed on a monitor right now, the fine red line of maternal worry would appear just underneath my heart rate, pushing it up a notch, but the effect is not so debilitating that I no longer look forward to going home, putting on my lounge wear, and settling in for my own Christmas Eve traditions, traditions invented and handed down from my mother. Half an hour from now, I'll be curled up in an armchair with a bowl of dark, rich, Irish stew (simmered for several hours earlier today) ladled over a mound of buttery colcannon, and I'll watch fifties Christmas movie musicals on television.

Afterwards, though, I'll pull out my notes and files again and put some serious time into the Vera's house project, into my life beyond Jesse.

The basketball camp has focused on skills and drills, but the last day features games and awards in the afternoon, parents welcome. "You don't have to come," Jesse says, the morning of. "Most parents won't. And the games are just for fun anyway; they don't count for anything."

Does he say this because he thinks he won't do well, won't stand out? Or because he really doesn't care?

I say I'll see how my day goes, and I send him on his way, my independent son trudging off to the streetcar stop with his sports bag on his shoulder, his lunch packed inside, his music playing in his headphones. Inside the house, I settle in to do some work at my desk, and in a spare moment, I open the lacquer box on my desk and make a silent wish, on a worthless piece of ancient cow jewellery, that Jesse might receive some small recognition this afternoon at camp. A little something to boost his self-esteem and restore some of his basketball confidence. Please.

Six hours later, I enter the gym, where a game has just started. I pick out Jesse's hard-to-miss white face and body, one of only two non-black players on the floor. While I watch, he brings up the ball, beats his man, drives to the basket, and dishes to a wing man who makes a tidy three-point shot. That went well, I'm pretty sure.

The game is close, but Jesse's team wins, and he gets good minutes, makes a contribution, receives friendly low fives from his teammates when he comes off the floor. On the bench, with his teammates, he laughs and talks and looks like he fits in, like he belongs.

I thank the Bronze Age gods for granting my wish and promise never to doubt the power of the armlet again. I need no more, but I get more, when Jesse is awarded a prize for "Best Hustle" on his team. And when Dwayne stops me in the after-camp milling about and pulls me aside for a moment and says, "You might think I say this to everyone, but I don't: Jesse is something special. His skills are improving, but most of all, he has great spirit and drive. I'd like to work with him further over the winter and have him come out for the rep team I run in the spring. I'll be in touch."

For a second, I hesitate and question whether Dwayne could be snowing me, but he seems sincere. So I rush to thank him before it's too late and say Jesse will be so pleased to hear that, and the camp was good, thanks some more, and then he's gone, moved off to tend to other campers and other parents.

On the way home, I ask Jesse how he enjoyed the camp.

"Did you see that great pass I made in the second quarter, to Akeem?"

"You played very well. And Dwayne said you were special and he wants to work with you and have you on his rep team."

"Yeah, he told me that, too."

"So are you happy now?"

"Yeah, I guess. Kind of."

Me, too.

He says, "What about New Year's Eve, though?"

New Year's Eve is tomorrow. "What about it?"

"My crew want to do something. Are you going out, by any chance, so I can have people over?"

"Absolutely not. I'm not going out and you can't have people over."

"What, you mean I can't milk today's success into tomorrow night and have a party?"

"No way."

"Easy there, Em. I was just asking. There's no harm in asking, is there?"

I believe that there *can* be harm in asking, but risky ventures call for risky measures, so in early January, I square my shoulders (the frozen one with some difficulty, still), cross my fingers, bite my tongue, and send Nils a carefully composed email suggesting we meet about a potential work thing. We being me, him, and his collective.

Two days after I sent the email, I receive a one-line reply: *Is this some kind of sick joke?*

Gee, that went well. I come back with: *No. Can we meet?*

His response is to call me, on my work phone, from his office, and say, "Are you for real?"

The sound of his voice does not send any sort of sensation down my spine or any other body part, I'm relieved to report, though I find his hostility nervous-making. "Yes, I am for real. And how are you?"

"Fine. Good. Whatever."

"Would you like me to tell you about the project now?"

"You contacting me about work is such a random move that I'm having some trouble wrapping my head around it. But sure, go ahead. Give me a rundown."

I talk, he listens, he makes no more rude remarks, he asks a few sensible questions, and when I've delivered not much more than a top-line summary, he says, "The job sounds interesting, sure, but what about us? Am I supposed to pretend we weren't sleeping together a month ago?"

"If that's what you want."

"What do *you* want?"

I want him to get over feeling hurt. I want our dealings to be tension-free. And I'd rather not hear about his next girlfriend, whenever she comes along. "I'd like us to be friendly colleagues with our relationship baggage left far behind. Do you think that's possible?"

"I don't know. Maybe. But just so you know? I'm seeing someone new."

"Good for you." And for me, because I'm unaffected by the news that he's moved on. Regret, sadness, jealousy — none of these emotions are hitting me right now, and won't be, as long as the person he's seeing is not Melissa.

"I'm seeing Melissa."

"Well, isn't that great." They won't last any longer than he and I did, not that it's any of my business. And if they do? Still none of my business. "So when can I meet the collective?"

~ ★ ~

I go see Dr. Joan that same month, a cold, bitter January.

"No wonder my shoulder's frozen," I say to her. "It's fucking freezing outside."

She doesn't smile. She frowns and writes something down in my file. Maybe "bad attitude." She says, "Has there been any improvement in the last four months?"

"Yes, there has. A small amount, but some." I reach both arms straight above my head, like a referee signalling a three-point shot in basketball, only my right arm extends slightly lower than my left. "See?"

She purses her lips. What's she going to do with me? "I could give you another cortisone shot. Is that what you want?"

"No. Never again. Do you know how painful those shots are? That shit is toxic."

She makes another note in my file. Probably something like "lost cause." Though if she wrote that, she'd be wrong.

"So, what then?" she says. "You'll keep stretching, and continue to work on increasing your flexibility, and just hope to improve?"

I thought I'd try that, yeah.

I meet the collective in my living room, on a weekday evening, proof of my commitment to the project since I'm breaking my own rule of not entertaining people at home. Jesse is in his room and has promised, or rather, begged, not to come downstairs during the meeting, which I hope will be short but won't be.

Of the five collective members present, I know three: Nils, Raj, and Autumn. The other two appear inoffensive so far, but give them time and I'm sure they'll find ways to irritate me. And inspire me.

Once we're all seated and I've offered drinks, both alcoholic and non, along with some delicious savoury shortbreads, Autumn